PRAISE FOR SORAYA M. LANE

'With stunning imagery, historical detail, and a clever plot, *The London Girls* is a book not to be missed. I couldn't put it down!'

—Andie Newton

'Soraya M. Lane brings history to life in ways that take readers into the heart of some of the most frightening, challenging, and inspiring WWII experiences. Unputdownable!'

—Patricia Sands

'*Under a Sky of Memories* is a thrilling novel full of suspense, intrigue, and romance . . . Highly recommended for fans of World War II fiction.'

—Historical Novel Society

'I became so easily immersed in Soraya's poignant, vibrant, visual story, *The Secrets We Left Behind* . . . I loved this novel!'

—Carol Mason

'*The London Girls* is one of those stories that grabs you by the heart and doesn't let go until long after you've turned the last page.'

—Barbara Davis

The
BERLIN
SISTERS

OTHER TITLES BY SORAYA M. LANE:

The Secret Midwife
The London Girls
Under a Sky of Memories
The Secrets We Left Behind
The Last Correspondent
The Girls of Pearl Harbor
The Spitfire Girls
Hearts of Resistance
Wives of War
Voyage of the Heart

The
BERLIN
SISTERS

SORAYA M. LANE

LAKE UNION
PUBLISHING

Published by Lake Union Publishing, Seattle

www.apub.com

Amazon, the Amazon logo, and Lake Union Publishing are trademarks of Amazon.com, Inc., or its affiliates.

ISBN-13: 9781662504099
eISBN: 9781662504082

Cover design by The Brewster Project
Cover image: © Matt Gibson © SeagullNady © InfinitySetup / Shutterstock; © Joanna Czogala / Arcangel

Printed in the United States of America

For my family

Chapter One

The Ministry of Propaganda & Enlightenment

Berlin, Germany

23 December 1943

Ava's fingers moved quickly over the keys of her typewriter, her back straight as she sat at her desk. When she finished, she took the paper and set it beside her, carefully reviewing it to ensure she hadn't made any mistakes. Although she was one of five women in the room, no one spoke; the only sounds were the constant clack of fingers touching keys and the shuffle of papers, and it would be that way until lunchtime when they all took a short break.

Satisfied with her work, she moved on to her next assignment, although a noise made her pause. It was the sound of a child giggling, which could only mean one thing.

'They're here again,' said Lina, the secretary seated closest to her. 'Don't you just love it when they come to visit?'

Soon all five of them had stopped typing, their eyes glued to the door as first a beautifully groomed Airedale dog trotted in, followed immediately by six immaculately dressed children, their faces beaming with smiles. Their mother was only a few steps behind, wearing a tailored, emerald-green dress, her hair swept elegantly from her face; as meticulously presented as her husband always was, in perfectly cut cloth with never a wrinkle to be seen.

There was nothing quite like a visit from the Goebbels family, and it was almost certain to put her boss Joseph in a good mood. He loved when his children came to see him for lunch – every visit boosted the morale of the entire office – and this time Magda had brought all of them, instead of just the youngest two.

'Frau Goebbels, it's such a pleasure to see you,' Lina said, standing. 'I shall go and tell Dr Goebbels you are here.' As his personal secretary, she was permitted to knock on his door.

'No need, Helga will surprise him. She's been looking forward to seeing her papa all morning.'

Ava smiled at Heidrun, who was standing tucked against her mother's leg, the youngest of the brood. She gave the little girl a wave as the child smiled and fiddled with the large bow in her hair, her smile melting Ava's heart. They were the most gorgeous children, and Goebbels' wife was always as friendly and kind to the secretaries as he was himself. Magda was the epitome of the perfect German wife and mother, and they were always rather star-struck when she came to visit.

'How is your workload today, ladies?' Frau Goebbels asked. 'I trust my husband is treating you well?'

A chorus of pleasantries erupted, and as Ava was nodding the dog made his way over to her, tugging along one of the children, who was holding his leash. Tell, as he was called, had once been nervous of being approached in the office, but he'd soon become used to the secretaries who worked in close proximity to his master. But just as Ava extended her hand to pat him, Joseph Goebbels walked out from his office, his limp noticeable, commanding everyone's attention despite his small stature, smiling broadly as his children

2

lined up in front of him. His son shook his hand, and his five daughters all curtseyed, as Ava and the other secretaries sighed and smiled at how well behaved they all were, watching as he bent down to speak to the two smallest girls first.

It was at that moment that Ava's father appeared, his smile wide as he nodded to his daughter and entered the office, tall and handsome in his uniform. He was everything to look at that Goebbels was not, with thick blond hair and sparkling blue eyes, his shoulders and chest broad, his stride effortless. She watched as he called out hello to Joseph and exchanged pleasantries with Magda, before moving slowly towards Ava. She stood with the other secretaries, laughing as the children showered their father with affection, telling him most animatedly all about their exciting day, but even with such a distraction Ava didn't miss the way her father leaned against one of the desks as he passed, appearing to look for something. She turned her head slightly, careful not to make it obvious that she was watching him, as he reached for a piece of paper.

She stared in disbelief as he casually took the paper from the top of the pile Lina had been working on only moments earlier, folding it before sliding it inside his jacket pocket. Ava quickly looked away, glancing back at the other secretaries, but she could see that they were all focused on the children, enraptured by the little performance taking place before them. No one else had seen what he'd done, only her, and he was such a regular visitor to the office – not to mention a personal friend to Joseph Goebbels – that no one would have thought twice about him being there in the first place. And they certainly wouldn't have dared to accuse him of any wrongdoing. Besides, it wasn't unusual for him to collect documents, but to conceal it in his jacket like that? She swallowed, nervously, knowing instinctively that he'd done something wrong.

'Ava,' her father said as he came to stand beside her, kissing her cheek, and certainly not giving away whether or not he'd noticed her watching. 'Lovely to see you, as always.'

'Father,' she whispered, her pulse racing as she brushed a kiss to his smooth cheek in return. *Does he know that I saw him? What did he take? Why would he do something like that?*

Her papa was one of Goebbels' closest lieutenants, which was why she'd recently been able to secure such a high-paying job at the ministry. She may have been one of the most proficient typists at her previous job, but she was no fool; there was only one reason a nineteen-year-old girl would be appointed one of Goebbels' five secretaries, a position that was not only highly coveted but highly paid, and that was due to her family connections. There were women all over Berlin with years of experience behind them who would have done anything to fill her position, and yet she was certain she'd been the only one interviewed for the job when it had become available.

'Mama said you've been feeling unwell,' she said, keeping her voice low as she stood close to her father. 'How are you today?'

'Nothing more than a cold,' he murmured. 'I actually wanted to see if you'd like to travel home with me tomorrow? It's been too long since I spent some time with my family.'

'For Christmas?' she asked, her voice a whisper. It was no secret that Adolf Hitler was not a fan of traditional Christmas celebrations, not the type her family had once openly celebrated, and certainly not if they were to celebrate it as a Christian holiday. But nothing could stop her from looking forward to her favourite time of year.

'Yes,' he said, with a wink that she hoped no one else noticed. 'I've organised two days' leave. We will travel when you finish work tomorrow evening.'

Ava nodded as Magda gathered up the children across the room, like little lambs being herded, their visit already over. She watched two of the girls stand hand in hand, and it reminded her of her sister, Hanna, and what they'd been like as children. It seemed that Dr Goebbels wasn't joining his family for lunch, after all, nor going home with them as he often did. The children lined up, their little shoulders straight like miniature soldiers as they all lifted one hand.

'*Heil Hitler*!' they said in unison.

'*Heil Hitler*!' Goebbels replied, not even glancing in their direction as the five secretaries all immediately responded in kind, as did Ava's father, saluting their Führer and looking at his portrait on the wall as they did so.

Ava called out goodbye and waved back to the children as they turned at the door, before returning to her desk with the other secretaries, her father smiling to her and then crossing the room to speak briefly to Goebbels. She imagined he was headed straight back to his office in the same building as she watched him go.

'Aren't they just so precious,' said Greta, one of the other secretaries. 'What I wouldn't give for a large family like that. Eight would be the perfect number, if you ask me.'

'Eight?' Lina repeated. 'You only want eight so you can show off your gold Mother's Cross award and have tea with the Führer as your reward!'

'That's precisely the reason,' Greta said with a grin, looking as if she might swoon as she began to fan at her face, her colour rising. 'Imagine that – tea and cakes with the Führer himself!'

Their conversation ended prematurely when Goebbels walked out of his office, going directly to Lina's desk. Ava kept her head down and returned to her typing, but it was impossible not to hear the conversation, given her proximity. Within minutes, everyone

5

seated in the room could hear what was being said to poor Lina. They'd only met when Ava had begun work at the ministry, but she'd fast become a close friend, and Ava hated hearing her being questioned for something she hadn't done.

'You cannot simply lose a piece of paper that I gave to you only this morning! Where is it?'

Ava kept her gaze averted, but her stomach was beginning to do cartwheels as Lina made noises beside her that sounded very much as if she were crying. She'd always been very softly spoken and kind, certainly not someone who could handle being interrogated.

'I am going to ask you one final time,' Goebbels said, in a rare show of anger. Usually he was most affable to his secretaries, and he certainly never raised his voice to them. In fact, most of them were very fond of him, including Ava. 'Where is it!' His hand slammed against the desk and made Ava jump, at the same time as Lina sobbed loudly. Ava's heart wrenched for her.

'It was here when your family arrived,' she cried. 'I haven't left your office, I haven't, I can't—'

'Enough,' he snapped, turning on his heel. 'Find it before the end of the day, or I shall have you questioned for treason.'

Ava felt as if she might be sick, listening to her friend crying beside her. She shook her head when Lina asked if she'd seen the piece of paper, not about to mention what she'd seen her father do, even as she watched Lina drop to her knees and search the floor, asking the other women around them as she looked for it. Ava knew full well that her duty was to her country, that she was obliged to report what she'd seen; she'd been trained to do so since she was a girl. But if she said something, what would happen to her father? What if he'd taken something that he shouldn't have? It didn't matter what she was supposed to do, she kept her mouth shut, even though it meant putting poor Lina in a terrible position.

'Fräulein Müller,' Goebbels called, his voice still sharp.

Ava immediately stood, brushing her hands down her skirt to banish any creases, before walking quickly to the office door. She smiled at Goebbels, hoping he couldn't see how nervous she was or detect that she was keeping something important from him.

'Please take these,' he said, not bothering to look up as he extended paperwork to her.

Ava hurried forward and took the papers, but as her fingers closed around them, his didn't let go.

'You are to seal these court documents, and I'm relying on you to place them in the safe without looking at them,' he said, his eyes meetings hers. 'Do you understand? It is of great importance that they're secured without anyone seeing the contents.'

'Yes, Dr Goebbels,' she said, as he slowly released the papers. 'I understand.'

'And then you are to type this, and return it directly to me,' he said, turning his attention away from her. 'No one else is to see the contents of this letter.'

'Of course.'

'Fräulein Müller, I want you to think very carefully about how you answer this next question,' he said, sitting back slightly in his chair, his eyes narrowing. 'You have sat beside Fräulein Becker since you began work in my office. Have you found her to set a good example for you when it comes to her typing and commitment to her job? Is she a dedicated party supporter?'

Ava's uniform immediately seemed to cling to her as she began to sweat. She could even feel perspiration across her upper lip, and she had to hold the papers tightly to stop her hands from trembling.

'Yes. Lina, I mean Fräulein Becker, has always been most conscientious and dedicated to her work,' Ava said, keeping her voice even. 'I haven't seen anything that would lead me to believe she's anything other than a committed party supporter, as we all are. All of your secretaries are dedicated to our country and to our Führer.'

'Thank you, Ava,' he said with a small smile, taking her by surprise when he used her first name, as if he were trying to reinforce that they were family friends, not just colleagues. 'If you notice anything to the contrary though, you will come to me, yes? I know I can trust you.'

Ava nodded again, dropping her gaze before turning to leave with the papers clasped to her chest. She had no intention of looking at them, had always followed orders without a second thought, but when she placed them down on her desk, she couldn't help but notice the name on the front. *Sophie Scholl.* They were the court documents for the Scholl case, and Ava remembered her well from what she'd read in the papers – the university student who'd been found guilty of high treason for producing propaganda, encouraging others to revolt against Hitler and the party.

She stared at them, knowing that she'd been trusted not to look, and having never disobeyed instructions at work before. But something about seeing her father take something earlier, a feeling beginning to bubble up in her stomach, made her want to look, made her want to disobey an order for the very first time in her life. Lina was still on her hands and knees, going through a pile of discarded papers from earlier in the day, and when Ava glanced around the office, she could see that the other secretaries were all busy with their heads down.

She battled with her curiosity for a few more moments before quickly brushing the front page aside, intending only to glance at the contents. It was when she saw the photo pinned to the pages inside that she realised what type of file she was in possession of, what a court file on such a matter would contain. And why she had been ordered not to look inside.

Her eyes skimmed the first few lines and her stomach lurched for the second time that day.

Guillotine.

Beheaded.

Traitor.

Murder.

The words seemed to leap off the page at her.

Ava knew she shouldn't sympathise, not with a young woman with such radical ideology, but she'd have been lying if she said it didn't affect her, that she didn't question why such an intelligent young woman would risk her life to distribute a leaflet about resistance. And had such brutality been truly necessary? Ava swallowed. Perhaps she simply didn't have a strong enough stomach.

Her heart suddenly began to pound. *Is this what Father was looking for?* Maybe she would never know why her father had taken the paper she'd seen him steal, but as she bundled the documents into a file and took them to the safe, she knew that she would never breathe a word of what she'd seen to anyone. She couldn't.

She also knew that she'd never, ever forget the image she'd just seen either, of a pretty university student with her head in a guillotine, awaiting death simply for telling others what she thought, for disobeying the Nazi regime.

If that was the punishment for thinking the wrong thing, what could happen to her father if his theft was discovered? A high-ranking officer who was trusted by Hitler himself? From the time she'd joined the Jungmädelbund as a twelve-year-old, she had known her duty; the summer camps, ice creams and camaraderie might have been fun, but even as a girl she'd understood that the Young Girls' League served a purpose. They were all to obey and follow the lessons of the Nazi Party, even if that meant turning on one's own parents, even if it meant turning in a sister or a close friend for suspected treason. Even if it meant renouncing someone because they were a Jew.

Ava locked the safe and walked quickly from the room, her hands trembling properly now, not stopping until she was doubled over the toilet in the restroom down the hall, purging her stomach of everything she'd consumed that day as her entire body shook.

And when she returned to the office, her nausea only increased. Because Lina was standing beside her desk, her eyes red and puffy from crying as two SS men searched her handbag and pulled out her desk drawers, emptying the contents on to the floor. Ava put her head down and walked quickly back to her seat, not certain what to do but deciding that the best thing was to resume her work and pretend as if nothing was out of the ordinary. But she couldn't help the tears that pricked her eyes as Lina was escorted from the office, as the rest of them continued to type, all too scared to look up or say goodbye. As if their friend and colleague hadn't just been taken right in front of them. *For something that she hadn't done.*

When Ava looked around the room, no one met her gaze, and with shaky hands she began to work on the document Goebbels had given her. She'd been worried about her father, but what would they do to Lina? Surely they would realise that she'd had nothing to do with the missing paper, that she was nothing like the Sophie Scholl girl?

'She deserved it,' Greta muttered.

'What a traitor,' said one of the others.

Tears pricked Ava's eyes. She'd thought these women were her friends, that they'd been Lina's friends too, but instead of believing in her, they seemed to have no qualms about what had happened right before their eyes. Lina was no traitor, but to prove her innocence Ava would have to renounce her father, which meant that there was nothing she could do to save her colleague from whatever punishment she now faced.

Which perhaps made her no better than the righteous women seated on either side of her.

A man cleared his throat in front of her then, and Ava looked up, surprised to see someone standing there. She'd been so lost in thought, she hadn't even noticed.

Ava blinked at Herr Frowein, one of Goebbels' personal advisors, who was watching her. 'Dr Goebbels has requested that you commence transcribing his diary each afternoon, now that Fräulein Becker is no longer employed by the ministry. You are to be his private secretary until further notice.'

She gulped. 'Of course, it would be my honour.' It *was* an honour, of course it was an honour. Two hours earlier, she would have been delighted with the promotion. She was being silly fretting about Lina; surely she would simply be questioned before resuming her work at the ministry.

A shiver ran down Ava's spine.

If it's such an honour, why do I suddenly feel sick to my stomach at the thought?

Chapter Two

THE MÜLLER ESTATE, BOGENSEE, GERMANY

CHRISTMAS EVE, 1943

Ava stepped out of the car when her father came around to open the door of the shiny, dark green Mercedes. They'd travelled most of the way in silence, other than exchanging the odd pleasantry or when he'd been speaking to his chauffeur. Now, her father was leaning into the car to tell his driver that he was to return to his family for the night, which surprised her. Usually his chauffeur would wait in case her father needed him, but she supposed it was Christmas, and he wanted to give him the evening off work to celebrate the holiday.

She stood outside for a moment and stared at the house, feeling a familiar flutter in her stomach at being back. Her parents referred to it as the country house, but to Ava and her sister Hanna it had always simply been home. She loved that it was far enough away from the city that it felt like a holiday location, but close enough that they could still return if needed, and the house itself was magnificent, set in a forest that had proved perfect for endless hours of make-believe when she was a child. It was the type of place in which she wanted to raise her own family, a big family that would fill every room with happiness and laughter.

'It's good to be here, isn't it?' her father said, striding past her and carrying a bag in each hand. 'I wish I spent more time here instead of being stuck in the city.'

'Yes, Papa,' she said as she hurried after him. 'It's very good to be home.'

She'd held her tongue for the entire journey from Berlin, which had taken well over an hour, unable to think of anything other than the incident on the day previous. She'd been beside herself, wanting to ask him about Lina, but to do that, she would have to admit what she'd seen. Now they were home, though, her mind turned to other things, such as the delicious smell of baking wafting down the hallway, and seeing her mama again after weeks apart.

Ava barely acknowledged their maid, Zelda, as she hurried through to the kitchen, seeing her mother and sister with their blonde heads bent, both with rolling pins in hand. She darted towards them, not wanting to miss a moment of them all being together, and wishing to be part of whatever they were talking about. Before taking the job at the ministry, she'd come home often, but now there never seemed enough hours in the day.

'Mama!' she cried, opening her arms as her mother, Liselotte, immediately stopped what she was doing. 'I'm home!'

Ava kissed her cheek and hugged her, despite her mother's protest that she was covered in flour and would get it all over her.

'Hanna,' Ava said then, grinning at her sister and turning her full attention to her.

'Just in time to help us with the second batch of cookies,' Hanna said, beckoning her over and holding up her hands, as if to explain why she couldn't embrace her. 'We've been hoping you'd arrive in time to help.'

'Let me wash my hands and join you,' Ava said, feeling like a child again, her excitement over Christmas baking impossible to disguise. 'What shapes are we making?'

She scrubbed her hands quickly with soap, before turning around, realising that both her mother and Hanna were silent.

'Little Christmas trees or—'

'Swastikas,' Hanna said, clearing her throat. 'We're making hundreds of little swastika cookies.'

'Oh,' Ava said, laughing to disguise her embarrassment. 'Of course we are. How silly of me.' It wasn't so long ago they'd made gingerbread men and little trees.

'Our Führer would not have us bake silly little Christmas baubles when we can make something as mighty as the swastika,' her mother said, with an overly bright smile. 'Come, you can work on this batch with your sister while I go and greet your father. I haven't seen him for days.'

Left alone in the kitchen with Hanna, Ava stood beside her and dropped her head to her sister's shoulder. There was so much she was brimming to tell her, so much she wished she could speak freely about, but instead she found herself holding her tongue and not saying a word. Had her sister ever had doubts about the work she did, or the way they were expected to behave? Would she keep a secret for their father if she suspected him of wrongdoing? Ava was almost certain that she knew the answer, but still, she wasn't certain enough to mention what she'd seen yet, even though she wanted to. Her stomach was still twisted in knots thinking about Lina, wondering what might have happened to her. She'd even visited her apartment before work, but no one had come to the door when she'd knocked.

'How is work?' Ava eventually asked, pushing thoughts of Lina out of her mind. 'Have you been busy at the hospital this week?'

'Work is fine,' Hanna said, as she placed some carefully cut dough on to an oven tray. 'It's been such a hard winter already, so it's been difficult. And we have a steady stream of patients after each bombing which is always heartbreaking, especially knowing many of them no longer have a house to go home to. The hardest times are when I'm sent out in the ambulance to provide triage care.'

Ava nodded. She knew how fortunate they were to have such a big, warm house that was still standing, when so many Germans were struggling simply to heat one room to keep their children warm – if they had a house at all. She'd overheard one of the secretaries at work saying that she'd recently visited a friend's family and taken cigarettes as a gift, only to be promptly reprimanded for being so thoughtless when what they desperately needed was bread. Which made Ava doubly uncomfortable, as her family still seemed to have a plentiful supply of coffee, meats and even sugar – she'd barely gone without at all.

'Have you had any interesting patients lately? Any stories you can share with me?' She sighed. 'I need something to take my mind off my own work.'

'Is it so bad working in the office?' Hanna asked, her eyebrows drawn together as she seemed to study her sister. 'Other than worrying about daytime bombing raids?'

'No, it's not so bad, just stressful at times,' Ava said, hoping she could fool her sister with her tight smile. 'Your work always seems far more interesting, that's all. Although I can't imagine what it must be like seeing children injured or so unwell, that's not something I'd cope terribly well with.'

Hanna was silent for a moment, and Ava glanced at her and saw a strange look cross her face. They made eye contact briefly, before Hanna smiled and picked up the tray to slide it into the oven.

'Well, I've had some lovely children on my ward lately, and they're always the nicest to treat, even when it's hard,' Hanna said. 'Although I do often end up staying late to play cards with them or read stories. It's so hard to wave goodbye when you know how much they miss being at home with their families.' She cleared her throat. 'Now, tell me what's causing you so much stress. I imagine Joseph Goebbels is rather demanding?'

Ava smiled much in the same way she'd seen her sister smile – almost too brightly, with too much conviction, as if she were trying to convince herself that she was happy.

'Dr Goebbels is actually very pleasant to work for, and the other secretaries are very friendly to me,' she replied. 'He's requested that I work as his personal secretary when I return, typing his dictation and so forth, and I can't say that I mind.'

'That's quite the honour then, working so closely with a man such as he?'

Ava quickly nodded, turning her attention back to the cookies, wanting to distract both her own mind and her sister from this particular line of discussion, or what she really wanted to say.

I don't know what to think, Hanna. I'm so confused about what's happening in the office, and I can't stop thinking about what I've seen. The young woman who was once seated next to me, my friend, has disappeared, and no one has heard from her or seen her since she was taken. I also came across a file about a woman named Sophie Scholl, on the same day that I caught Father taking papers from my office, and every time I think about it I feel sick to my stomach. Do you know why he would do such a thing, why he'd risk his own life to take something that didn't belong to him?

They were all things she was desperate to tell her sister; she wanted to pour her heart out to Hanna as they had when they were girls sharing a room, whispering in the darkness after lights-out. Back then they'd whispered about boys mostly, as well as the other girls in their Bund Deutscher Mädel group. Ava had particularly liked curling up beside Hanna to hear all about her League of German Girls summer camp, before she'd been old enough to attend herself.

But of course she didn't say a word of what she wanted to, for how could she know where her sister's allegiance was, or to what lengths she would go to prove her dedication to the party? They were not simply sisters any more, just as no one was simply a friend. Everyone was ready and waiting to catch the other out, to turn them in, to show their loyalty, no matter what. She'd heard that some families were turning on others to settle old scores, lying to authorities and revelling in whatever punishment was served. Despite everything she believed in, Ava had wondered for some time if that was truly how they were expected to behave. And she questioned why the authorities seemed more inclined to believe the accusers instead of the presumed perpetrators.

'Shall we make icing to use around the edges?' Hanna asked, her voice soft as she moved closer to Ava, their shoulders touching. 'That was always my favourite part when we were girls, but if we don't hurry up here we'll never get them finished.'

They stood like that, neither moving, leaning into one another as if there were something they both wanted to say to each other and couldn't. But neither said a word, simply breathing quietly, as Hanna moved her smallest finger and let it hover beside Ava's, their skin only just touching. They lived together in Berlin, but their work kept them apart, like ships in the night, and Ava missed her sister dearly.

'There's my girls. Please tell me one of those cookies is ready?'

They both turned as their father came into the room, unbuttoning his jacket and placing it neatly over the back of a chair, before striding towards them and embracing Hanna and pressing a kiss to the top of Ava's head. He swiped a cookie straight from the tray, barely even seeming to notice that it was a swastika he was biting into this year. Or perhaps he had and didn't care.

'Merry Christmas, girls,' he said, smiling at them as tiny crumbs caught in his neatly trimmed moustache.

'Take that cookie from him at once!'

Ava jumped as her mother barked her instruction from the hallway, before marching in and snatching the half-eaten biscuit from her poor papa, her face showing her fury and his showing his guilt.

'This first batch of biscuits are for Zelda and her family, and any leftovers are not to be eaten until after dinner,' she grumbled. 'Girls, we have to keep a close eye on this one, do you hear me? A very, very close eye.'

Ava swallowed, turning her attention back to the icing they were making in the bowl before her. If only her dear mama knew the truth to her words. But she forgot all about her worries when Hanna slipped him another cookie when their mother wasn't looking; she could barely suppress her giggles as her father grinned in delight and made a face as if it were the most delicious thing he'd ever eaten.

An hour later, Ava left her father and sister in the sitting room and went to help her mother in the kitchen. Mama was putting cookies into a basket for their maid, and when she saw Ava appear beside her, she nodded towards the small Christmas tree they'd put up in the corner of the room. She'd been humming 'Silent Night' when Ava walked in, and although Ava had learned the new Nazi verses along with all the other girls at BDM, she found it impossible not to sing the original version in her mind that her family had always sung at Christmas time.

'There's a present there for Zelda and two for her children,' her mother said. 'Would you mind getting them for me?'

Her mother had always been generous, giving gifts to those who worked for them and always asking if there was anyone in their family who needed help. Her father's driver was treated with just as much thought, and Ava was certain that when he returned to work, her mama would have a gift packed for him, too.

She went to retrieve them, her bottom lip catching between her teeth as she fought against what she wanted to say. They had been told that Germans were being looked after, that everyone had enough food, but she knew that wasn't true – she'd heard the other women at work whisper about all the shortages. She looked up at the swastika on the top of the tree, not even remembering when they'd stopped using the beautiful gold star. She found herself wondering whether it had been thrown out, or whether her mama had wrapped it in tissue and stored it in the attic in case they were ever permitted to use the beautiful ornament again.

'You're very quiet today, Ava,' her mother said. 'Is everything all right?'

Ava nodded. 'Everything is fine, I'm only tired.'

'Your father says you've been working very long hours at the ministry. That you've made quite the impression on his colleagues?'

Ava nodded again, cutting a piece of ribbon for her mother to use on the basket and passing it to her. 'I've enjoyed the change. It's nice to be working where I'm needed, and I like being kept busy. Everyone has been very welcoming to me.'

'You'll be hoping Heinrich is home on leave soon? You must miss him terribly.'

At the mention of Heinrich, Ava's stomach fluttered and she glanced up, knowing that her mother had caught her smile. 'I do miss him.' She could see him in her mind, his blond hair brushed to the side as he'd stood so handsomely in his uniform before he left, as she'd blown him a kiss from the train station platform.

'Just imagine, a wedding as soon as the war is over. You'll make the most beautiful bride.'

Ava knew she was blushing, her cheeks flushed at the thought of her upcoming nuptials. She'd known Heinrich since before the war, friends through their families, but it wasn't until he was home on leave and her father had brought him home for a weekend that she'd seen him as something more. Two years had passed since they'd last seen each other, and since then he'd risen in the ranks within the Waffen-SS, reporting directly to her papa before he'd been posted away from Berlin, which was why her father had decided to bring him back to their country house. A few months of courtship had quickly blossomed into an engagement, and they'd written to one another ever since. Ava was smitten with the handsome young man that she would marry just as soon as Germany won the war.

'Were you nervous when you married Papa?' Ava asked.

Her mother laughed. 'I was *terrified*. Absolutely terrified.'

Ava looked up. 'Of what?'

'That he'd be a monster. That he'd be cruel to me or want ten children.'

They both laughed, because the worries her mother was describing couldn't have been further from how she'd describe the man who was her father. Ava had friends with overly strict or even cruel fathers, but hers had always treated his daughters and wife with kindness, even though she knew he could be very firm and demanding when it came to his job. She'd overheard as much in the office.

Her mother touched her arm, her fingers light and warm on Ava's skin.

'When I was a child, we were all terrified of my father,' she said. 'He used to thrash us with the carpet beater for the smallest of missteps, and my mother would be next in line if she tried to stop

20

him. I was always so worried that I would end up with a husband who was as cruel, or who took his frustrations out on his family behind closed doors.' She paused. 'I'm afraid there are still many men who rule their family with fear in the very same way that my father did all those years ago.'

Ava blinked back at her, wondering how such a kind, warm woman could have been treated in such a way as a girl. She could see now that her father's gentleness was one of the reasons her mother loved him so, for he had a very warm manner when he was alone with his family, despite the way he could command the men beneath him. Even though he rarely talked about it, she knew from her mother and family friends that he'd been a fearless soldier in the Great War.

'The man we marry has the right to rule his home in any way he sees fit, so if a woman were to have any doubts before her wedding, during her engagement would be the time to speak,' her mother said. 'Afterwards, there is little anyone can do to help. Do you understand what I'm saying?'

Ava blinked away unexpected tears, not used to her mother speaking to her so directly, especially not on such matters. But her words didn't come as a surprise – every young woman in Germany knew the husband was master of his house and family. Just as she knew what was expected of her once she became a wife – to produce as many children for the Reich as she was able to.

'Yes, Mama, I understand.' Heinrich had been nothing but lovely to her, but they'd spent so little time together. He'd lost his temper terribly when someone had dared to question the relocation of the Jews in front of him one day when they were together, but he'd quickly recovered and apologised to her for his outburst, which had reassured her that it was surely out of character for him to behave in such a way.

'Mama, Zelda is ready to leave now.'

Hanna's warm voice pulled her from her thoughts, and Ava stood back as her mother took the basket and the gifts, presenting them to Zelda as she stood in their kitchen, her coat already around her shoulders.

'Merry Christmas,' Ava heard her mama say. 'Now remember you're to take tomorrow and the next day off work, fully paid of course. I'd like you to enjoy some time with your family, to thank you for your dedication to ours this year, and I hope you enjoy the treats we've put together for you.'

'Thank you, Frau Müller,' Zelda said. 'But I cannot possibly—'

'There are to be no *buts*,' her mother said firmly. 'Herr Müller has said it's an order, so you must obey. You wouldn't like to make him cross, would you?'

Zelda took a step back, nodding as she held the gift basket close to her body. 'Thank you.' She peered at the things inside, as tears began to appear in her eyes. 'This is too much, this—' Zelda tried to push the basket back.

Ava could see that alongside the presents there was a piece of meat wrapped in brown paper in the basket, some sugar, the biscuits, and even some coffee and a loaf of bread.

'You will only offend me if you don't take it. Now go,' her mother said. 'I know your family will be happy to have you home.'

'Thank you,' Zelda whispered again, as she clutched the basket closer. 'Thank you, Frau Müller.'

'*Heil Hitler*,' her mother said, softly, in a way that was so different to the way the men in Ava's office sounded when they said it.

'*Heil Hitler*,' Zelda said, at the same time as Ava whispered the words in reply.

She turned to watch her go, through the window, seeing Zelda brace herself against the bitterly cold wind. Her father took her by surprise when he came up behind her.

'Ava,' he said, his boots heavy against the timber floor.

'Yes, Papa,' she replied, turning to see him standing beside her mother.

'I would like you to take a walk with me.'

'Outside?' She glanced back out the window, not particularly wishing to spend even a minute out there. Since when did they go outside in such conditions, and in the almost-dark?

'The cold shall do us good,' he said with a wink. 'It'll make us appreciate coming back into our warm home all the more.'

Her father might be kind, but he was also firm, and she knew better than to refuse a request.

'Let me get my coat,' she said, as her mama exchanged a glance with her father that was impossible not to notice.

Chapter Three

The evening air was so cold that Ava could see her breath puff in front of her in little clouds of white. Her father walked slowly beside her, their boots clomping against the hard-packed ground, silence stretching between them as they moved further away from the house. Everything appeared barren at this time of year, as if the cold wind had stripped the surrounding area of its beauty, with the exception of the pine trees in the nearby forest. Their bare trunks stretched tall and naked but, unlike the oaks, they retained their leaves year-round.

'Ava,' her father said, finally stopping and turning to her. 'I believe you have something you wish to ask me.'

She took a deep breath, not sure if her face was burning from the chill in the air, or her embarrassment at being asked what had so clearly been stretching like a void between them. She opened her mouth, not saying anything for a moment as she stared back at her father. Did he truly want her to ask, or was he going to berate her for the words waiting on her lips?

'May I speak freely?' she finally asked.

He gestured to their surroundings. 'We can say anything here. It's one of the few places we don't have to mind our words, so please, ask me. It's why I brought you out here.'

She wondered then if that was why her father often walked after dinner with her mother, because out in the countryside, meandering through the forest, was the one place they could talk to one another without fear of someone overhearing. She'd heard rumours of listening devices being placed, but surely not in the home of someone with her father's standing in the SS?

'What will happen if you're caught?' she asked, wrapping her arms around herself. 'I know you took that missing paper. I saw it with my own eyes.'

'I won't be caught.'

'But *should* you be caught? For what you did?' She regretted the words the moment they passed her lips, but he'd wanted the truth from her, for her to speak her mind, and that was what she wanted to know. The conflict building inside of her was very real, and she was struggling to reconcile what she'd seen with what she knew of her father and how he usually conducted himself. She was thinking about Lina and what had been contained in the Scholl file. 'I'm keeping your secret to keep you safe, Papa. My friend is in terrible trouble because of what you did.'

'Whether I should be caught or not depends on which side you are on,' he said.

Her father began to walk, and she scurried to keep up with his longer stride. She worried that he was lost in anger, but when he abruptly stopped again and searched her eyes, there was no anger there that she could detect. But what had he meant when he talked of sides?

'Ava, can I trust you?' he asked. 'Can I trust you to keep what I did between us? Can I trust that this conversation will remain private?'

Ava knew what he was asking her: he wanted to know whether her allegiance was to the party, or to her family. If it had been anyone else, she wouldn't have trusted them, would have thought the question a trick, but her papa was speaking plainly. He was asking her to be truthful with him, and she wished he knew her well enough not to ask at all. Because no matter her confusion over what she'd seen and what he was saying to her, her allegiance was not something that needed to be questioned. Not when it came to her family.

She glanced back at the house, her stomach in knots, before reaching for his hands and holding them in hers, looking earnestly into his eyes.

'Of course you can trust me, Papa,' she said, blinking away tears, hating that he'd even thought to doubt her intentions. 'Of course you can. I would never betray you.'

'Is there anything else you'd like to ask me, then?'

Ava went to open her mouth, but closed it, shaking her head instead. She wanted to ask him about Lina, but she knew she was being silly worrying so much about her. She'd done nothing wrong, so of course nothing terrible was going to happen to her, not over a misunderstanding.

The one thing she did wish she was brave enough to ask was why – the question was burning on the tip of her tongue. Why had he taken that paper? But for every part of her that did want to know, there was another that simply didn't want the truth and all that came with it; because if she knew why, then she might find that she didn't agree with what he'd done. And then she'd be in quite the predicament.

Ava hadn't been lying, she did trust her father – he'd never given her reason not to trust him implicitly – and when he extended his arm to her she curled her hand around it and held on to him, dropping her head to his shoulder. In truth, her only concern was whether or not her father could get into trouble, and if he said there would be no repercussions, then she would be satisfied with that. She had to be. She had to believe that whatever he'd done was for the right reasons.

They walked slowly back to the house arm in arm, and even though she knew no more than she had the day before, she felt lighter for having spoken to him about it. She also believed that Lina's innocence would be quickly proven. Perhaps Lina would even have her job reinstated once they'd questioned her and realised their error.

'Mama will be wondering what's taking so long,' Ava said, smiling to herself as they neared the house.

'I'm certain she'll be putting dinner on the table as we speak,' her father replied, opening the door and holding it for her to walk through.

The smell of roast goose wafted to them the moment they set foot inside, and Ava and her father quickly washed their hands before joining her mother and sister. It had been weeks since she'd had her mother's cooking, and her mouth was salivating by the time she reached the table.

'Mama, this looks wonderful,' Ava said as she sat down beside her sister and eyed the feast. There was roast goose with stuffing, and potato dumplings and vegetables. It felt like such a treat after the much more basic food they'd been eating at the Berlin apartment for the past few weeks. Even though they had more than most, their father having access to food that she knew had been in very short supply for others since the last Christmas, they were still more often than not making one-pot meals.

Her father poured himself a glass of wine, and as Ava surveyed the room, she could have almost imagined they weren't at war, that it was just a regular Christmas at home with her family. She wondered what it would be like once the fighting was over, whether she'd have another holiday like this here, or whether she would be in her own marital home, or even the home of her husband's family. She also guiltily wondered what other families were eating right now, especially those in the city with only their ration cards to shop with. Her father seemed to follow Hitler's word to the letter, but he certainly hadn't shown any interest in the vegetarianism that had been suggested by their great leader, taking great pride in being able to hunt for hares or trade with the local farmers when he was home. She for one hoped that Heinrich wouldn't want to go without meat when they were married – vegetable dishes weren't her specialty, and she always found herself hungry if her plate was filled with only plants.

'I would like to suggest a moment of silence before we eat,' her mother said, her soft voice catching as she slowly sat down in her chair after serving them all. 'To remember the family who are not with us tonight. They are gone, but forever in our hearts, and never, ever to be forgotten.'

Ava reached for Hanna's hand, squeezing tightly as silent, fat tears slid down her sister's cheeks; as her own eyes filled with tears, too. She forgot all about her husband-to-be as she remembered her little nephew Hugo who wasn't with them, and her brother-in-law Michael who should have been seated across from her, knowing that her sister would never be able to celebrate holidays as fully as the rest of them ever again.

They all sat, silent, remembering, the pain surely as fresh for Hanna in that moment as it had been when it happened, until Papa finally lifted his wine glass and addressed them all, his own eyes glinting as he looked at each of them in turn.

'Let them never be forgotten.'

It was only after Ava had lifted her knife and fork that she realised they'd forgotten to turn to their Führer's portrait on the wall and say their mandatory *Heil Hitler*. It was very unlike her father to misstep in such a way, but given her sister was still in mourning, and the moment's silence they'd just shared, she decided not to mention it.

Chapter Four

Ava walked around her childhood bedroom, touching framed photographs and looking at all the books on her shelf, the mementos she'd collected over the years. If the war hadn't happened, she'd likely have spent a lot more time at home, but instead she was usually at the Berlin apartment, which was many times removed from their country house. It was modern and warm, with three bedrooms, and positioned conveniently close to everything in the city, but it still never felt like home, no matter how many nights she slept there. Some days she loved walking out on to the cobbled streets and being able to meet her friends or have coffee with them, but other times she craved the solitude of Bogensee, often wishing she was there. And over the past year there had been the matter of the air raids, which were getting closer and closer, and more intense in their ferocity and volume.

She knew that parts of the countryside were being hit relentlessly too, but she felt so much safer with space around her than the close confines in the city. Not to mention that their bomb shelter in the garden here was much more desirable than the nights she had to go down to the basement of their apartment block, or hide in a public shelter if she was on her way home when the warning siren sounded.

Ava had walked to her dresser and sat down, deciding to brush out her hair and change into her nightgown in preparation for bed, when she heard a thump, and then another. She smiled to herself and rose, quick to discard her hairbrush. Over dinner they'd talked about old photo albums and memories of their little vacations by the water many years ago, and she guessed that Hanna must have decided to poke around and look in the attic before bed. Ava had missed her terribly over the past few years, as they had more often than not lived separate lives due to the long hours they both worked – Hanna even more so than her – and so she decided that bed could wait. She could catch up on sleep later, especially if it meant spending some one-on-one time with her sister, and she was also eager to see the photographs if Hanna managed to find them. She was also conscious that Hanna might be finding it hard to sleep; Ava imagined the memories she was wrestling with wouldn't be conducive to slumber, which made her want to be with her sister all the more.

Ava walked to the very end of the hallway and saw that the narrow staircase had been pulled down from the ceiling. She'd been right, Hanna was definitely up there. They'd left their parents sitting in front of the fire, so she knew she wouldn't be disturbing her mother or father – they'd seemed content in each other's company, reminiscing about Christmases past as they threatened that they would haunt their daughters forever if they sold the country house when they were gone. Ava and Hanna had both smiled to each other across the room – they were both united on the decision that the house would stay in their family for generations.

She climbed the stairs, careful with each footfall, although there was some light coming from a lamp flickering upstairs that helped to guide her way. As children they'd sometimes snuck up in the dark, each trying to pretend they were so brave when in fact they were almost paralysed with terror at night.

'Hanna, what have you found!' Ava called out, her eyes trained on her feet so she wouldn't misstep. 'I heard—'

Ava froze. Her words died in her throat, gurgling away as if she were choking on them. Four strangers were sat on the floor, cross-legged and blinking back at her, eating from white plates with little blue flowers on them that she recognised from her own kitchen, and what appeared to be a replica of the very same meal that Ava herself had just consumed. The youngest of the two men had a piece of meat on his fork, but it was suspended between the plate and his mouth, a line of grease across his lips as he stared back at her.

'Papa!' Ava screamed, almost falling down the ladder as she stepped back. 'Papa, come quickly!'

The light from the single oil lamp flickered, and Ava found that she couldn't tear her eyes from the four people looking back at her: two men and two women. Who were they? And what were they doing in her attic? What were any strangers doing in her house! As she heard her father's heavy footfalls approaching, one of the women spoke, taking her by surprise. Ava edged back further, careful to avoid the open trapdoor behind her as her eyes darted around for a weapon, anything to protect herself with. She reached out, hoping to connect with an unused lamp to defend herself.

'Ava,' said one of the women, softly. 'It's me. Eliana.'

The younger of the two women slowly stood, leaving her plate of food on the floor. She smiled, nervously, and there was something familiar about her face, as shadows from the lamp flickered across her skin, something—

'*Eliana?*' Ava whispered, her heart racing as she took a tentative step forward, the lamp she'd been reaching for forgotten. Eliana, her old neighbour and school friend? Eliana, the Jew? 'Eliana Goldman?' Ava looked at each face in the attic more intently, her fear rising instead of abating, even as she realised that they were not strangers to her. But they were Jews, and that was possibly even worse.

Ava's stomach twisted as Eliana nodded. She needed them to get out of her house, and she needed them out now!

'Papa!' she screamed again.

'Ava, I'm so sorry you had to discover us here like this.'

'I, I—'

Ava's father appeared beside her then, and when she looked at him, when she saw the way his face seemed to crumple as he looked between her and the family, *she knew*. This wasn't a surprise to him. If it were a surprise, he'd have yelled and strode forward, taking the two men seated in his attic by force, marching them from his home. Instead, he only nodded to the family, before turning his attention back to his daughter, with a look that could only be described as annoyance. And the annoyance wasn't directed at the intruders, but at her.

Her mother came up the ladder then, followed by Hanna, and Ava had an unfamiliar sinking feeling deep in her stomach as they all stood and blinked back at her. She was the only one who hadn't known who was hidden in their home. They'd all been keeping this a secret from her, all of them! They'd sat together and had dinner only hours earlier, sharing memories and laughing, all while keeping what was truly going on in their home a secret from her. Without telling her that they were hiding an entire family right above her!

'Would someone please tell me why the Goldman family are hidden in our attic?' Ava asked, hearing the high lilt of her voice as she finished her sentence, the unmasked panic of her words. 'We will all be hung if they're discovered!'

'Ava,' her papa began, his brow furrowed as he stared at her. 'Please just take a moment to—'

'No!' she cried, not caring how hysterical she sounded, as she looked at her mother, her sister, and then her father again, not knowing how they could all seem so unflustered, how they could all be standing there so calmly while she felt as if she could explode. 'No, I will not take a moment to do anything! They cannot be here! We have to get them out of our house!'

Why was everyone looking at her as if she were the crazy one? As if she were the one in the wrong? As if she were the one making them uncomfortable?

'What is even happening here?' she demanded. 'We have to check all the doors are locked, that the curtains are drawn. If the SS—'

'No one would dare to enter my home without knocking and waiting for me to open the door, most especially any member of the SS,' her father said, coming to stand between Ava and the Goldmans. 'Ours is one of the safest homes in Germany, given my rank, which is precisely why I made the decision to allow this in the first place.'

Ava closed her eyes, her head beginning to throb. *I thought it was Hanna. I thought we were going to spend time together, just the two of us. I thought my sister was in the attic.*

'Papa,' she murmured, as she opened her eyes. 'Papa, you know what happens to those who help the Jews. You must know that it's not worth the risk, not for anyone. I know you think I don't understand, but I understand very clearly what would happen to us. '

'Ava, if you knew the truth, if you understood what was happening, you would know that it is very much worth the risk. And it's because of your blindness that we chose to keep this from you.'

Ava recoiled from her father's words. Her blindness? She swallowed, her mind swirling as everything began to make sense, including her mother giving Zelda time off work. She'd never given her two full days off before.

'Ava,' Hanna said, coming to stand beside her and placing her hand on her arm, at the same time as her mother went to sit with Frau Goldman. 'Please let Eliana tell you her story, of how they ended up here. I would like you to understand how they came to live in our attic, if you'd give them the chance. It's time you listened, so that you can understand the truth.'

Ava looked at the faces all turned to her and recognised hope, sadness and possibly desperation, mixed most likely with despair at the way she'd reacted. But how was she supposed to act, when this went against everything she knew and believed in? Was she *not* supposed to be hysterical at finding Jews in her attic?

Ava brushed tears from her cheeks and looked around the dimly lit room, at the books stacked on a small table, at the piles of clothes and belongings, at the makeshift beds where the Goldmans had been sleeping. It simultaneously broke her heart and filled her with fear; her family had done something so deeply kind for others, but in doing so, they had risked all their lives.

'Ava?' Hanna asked.

She didn't feel as if she had a choice other than to listen, not with her family and the Goldmans all watching her, and so she reluctantly went and sat beside her mother, her knees tucked up to her chin as Eliana finally stopped her pacing and sat down across from her. Ava was struck by how pretty she was, how wide and beautiful her eyes were, but she shouldn't have been surprised – Eliana had always been one of the prettiest girls in the neighbourhood, and for many years they'd been friends, often walking home from school together, or chatting at the park or when their families had dinner together over summer. But Ava would have been lying if she'd said she'd thought about them in the years since. She had dutifully joined the youth groups for girls along with her other eligible German friends, swept up in the excitement of the time, of the new Germany that was being created under Hitler. Never once had she wondered what became of them, or what it must have been like for them to try to survive.

Where had Eliana been when Ava and Hanna had been at summer camp, training with all the other girls who'd been chosen to join the League, dreaming of meeting a dashing soldier and doing their duty to have beautiful, blonde, blue-eyed babies?

Where had Eliana been when Ava had stood on the streets, waving little flags and screaming out *Heil Hitler* with the rest of the crowd? Or when she'd lined up to join the party with her other friends, chatting excitedly with their ten-mark notes in their hands to pay their membership dues.

'Where would you like me to start?' Eliana asked as their eyes finally met.

'Start from the very beginning,' Hanna said, before Ava had a chance to respond.

Eliana looked at Ava once more, and she nodded to her. 'Yes,' Ava said, clearing her throat and deciding that she would hear her out, that if the rest of her family had chosen to help the Goldmans, then they must have good reason to. Perhaps there was something that she didn't understand, that made them different. 'Please, start at the beginning, Eliana. Please, tell me your story.'

She watched as Eliana turned to first her father and then her mother, waiting for them to nod their approval, before she folded her hands in her lap, the soft lilt of Eliana's voice forcing Ava to consider how she'd ever forgotten about such a kind-hearted, gently spoken friend. Her face felt hot and she knew it would be bright red, her embarrassment impossible to hide.

'I knew the world was changing for a long time,' Eliana said. 'I think we all did. But I also don't think any of us could have comprehended what would happen next.'

Ava wondered when the last time was that Eliana had raised her voice beyond a whisper, how long they had actually been hidden in her home. Had they been here last time she'd been to visit?

'Even when I was the last Jewish girl in class at school, even when I was told not to return by a teacher who had once praised me for my academic achievements, when I was told that I couldn't swim in the pool because I had the Jew disease, I still didn't believe . . .'

Ava found herself holding her breath as Eliana looked to her family again, pausing for a long moment before continuing. She remembered that day; she had sat there and listened to Eliana be berated by their teacher, and not once had she imagined what it must have been like for her.

'I still didn't believe that my people would be persecuted and murdered so brazenly, that people who'd once been our friends, who'd once frequented my father's shop, would stand by and not even think to question such violence against their neighbours.'

Eliana's arms went around herself, as if she were suddenly cold, as she spoke of her memories, as everyone watched and listened to her, and it was so quiet Ava could have heard a pin drop.

'You were subjected to violence? Personally?'

Eliana met her gaze, and Ava saw a sadness there that she knew would haunt her forever. 'We were subjected to violence long before your father smuggled us from the city, when crowds of Jews were being rounded up and dragged from the streets, as fathers were murdered for trying to protect their families. That's when I understood that everything I'd heard was true, that no one was going to stop what was happening to our people.'

Ava looked over at her father; her father who'd only hours before been dressed in his perfectly pressed SS uniform, the picture of a dedicated Nazi, a man who was so well respected he was on a first-name basis with the highest-ranked party members. Was the SS truly using such violence against the Jews?

'We lost everything, Ava. Our home, our business, our friends.' Eliana's mother began to cry as she listened to her daughter speak, but Eliana only lifted her chin. 'Everything we once loved and cherished, it's gone. It was all taken from us, as if our lives never existed in the first place.'

Silence wove deeply between each and every one of them as they sat with Eliana's words ringing in their ears. Ava shuddered as she digested what she'd just heard, as she acknowledged how little she truly knew about what had been going on around her. She'd believed the Jews were being relocated, she'd thought it was peaceful. How wrong she'd been.

'Tell Ava about *Kristallnacht*,' Hanna murmured. 'About the night of broken glass, and what it was like for you. Tell her what happened.'

Eliana's gaze was fixed on Hanna. 'You want me to tell her the truth of what happened that night?'

Hanna nodded. 'I think it's time she understood everything, don't you?'

Chapter Five

ELIANA

10 NOVEMBER 1938

BERLIN, GERMANY

There was so much glass. Everywhere Eliana looked, there was glass. Every step she took, glass crunched beneath her shoes. It littered the pavement and the floor inside the shop; it stretched like a glittering blanket in every direction. There was nowhere that it hadn't spread.

Her father had told her what had happened, had tried to prepare them all for the worst, but nothing could have prepared her for seeing the glass shattered from so many windows, the devastation lining the streets, the cries of humans who'd lost everything in one endless, evil night.

Eliana had seen the headlines as she'd passed, the stalls selling papers with big black letters screaming 'Reich Night of Broken Glass'. But even then, she hadn't truly begun to understand the scene that would confront her, hadn't comprehended how quickly their lives had changed.

'It's not just here.' Her mother's hand fell heavily to her shoulder. She was standing so close Eliana could feel her breath against her cheek. 'They're saying our synagogue is gone too, burned to the ground along with all the others.'

Who would burn a place of worship? What evil could permeate the city she loved, to the point that they would burn a synagogue to the ground?

'Why are they doing this to us?' Eliana asked, wiping at her cheeks as tears streamed down them. 'Why do they hate us so? How can anyone be allowed to behave in such a way?'

Of course, she understood some of what was being said about them, the lies that were being told, but still; she couldn't comprehend such hate. She'd been spat on at school – boys had taunted the few remaining Jews, blaming them for their fathers losing their jobs among other things – but even then, she hadn't truly understood.

'Everything of value has been taken,' Eliana's father said, emerging from the mess, a broom in his hand as he tried in vain to brush a path through the thick layer of glass. 'Looters have taken it all. It's all gone.'

Eliana stood by as her mother went to her father, as they embraced each other, not even trying to disguise their tears. She decided to walk past her parents, not wanting to stand on the street, feeling the angry eyes that followed her. Some crowds had gathered, mostly young men who were jeering and laughing, but there were others who seemed sympathetic, their eyes downcast, their expressions sorrowful. But still, they did nothing to help. Eliana didn't want to be seen by any of them – she wanted to help her father find anything of value, help him put his shop back together. But as she searched through what had once been his beautiful store, filled with antiques and rare paintings, she knew that it was unlikely he'd ever be opening again. Almost everything was either gone or damaged beyond repair; there was nothing here for them any longer.

'Eliana?'

She turned when she heard her brother's call, his eyes wide as he stepped over the mess to find her.

'Can you believe it?' she asked. 'Everything is gone, David. Everything is ruined.'

'We need to hide Papa, we need to do something to keep him safe.'

'What do you mean?'

'Georg's father was just taken. They stormed his house, smashed everything to pieces, and then dragged him out,' David told her, grabbing hold of her hand. 'There are men disappearing all over Berlin. No one knows where they are taking them.'

An unfamiliar voice made them both turn, and Eliana kept hold of David's hand as they picked their way back to the door. A policeman was standing there, talking to their parents.

'I'm sorry,' he said, his hat in his hands, holding it to his chest. 'May I see what they've done?'

Her father stepped aside, so she and David did the same. The policeman took a few steps inside, muttering under his breath as he surveyed the damage.

'This is a disgrace,' he said, turning around slowly in their once-beautiful store. 'An absolute disgrace.'

'What will be done about it?' her mother asked. 'What are we supposed to do?'

Eliana saw tears fill the policeman's eyes, knew in that moment that there was nothing he or anyone else was going to do to help them. And if he couldn't help them, then no one could.

'I wish I could help, I wish I could offer assistance, but—'

'You cannot help us?' her father interrupted. 'You mean to say there's nothing that will be done? That this violence will be tolerated?'

'I cannot intervene,' the policeman said, sadly, putting his hat back on his head. 'If I do, I'll lose my job, and I have a family to take care of. They'll only do the same to me as they've done to you.'

Eliana blinked away her own tears as she saw her father's shoulders slump, as she recognised the defeat in his expression. Was this to be their life now?

As the policeman walked away, telling them one last time how sorry he was, a rock landed near Eliana, hitting the fallen glass on the ground. Before she knew what was happening, another rock was thrown, this one hitting her father on the side of his head, causing blood to slide down his skin, staining the collar of his shirt.

'They can't do this to us!' David cried, pushing past Eliana as a group of young men, barely older than her brother, pelted another rock at them before moving on to the store beside theirs as they jeered. 'Someone has to stop them!'

'No!' their father said, grabbing hold of David's arm, his head still bleeding. 'No, we stay quiet. We keep our heads down until it's safe enough to go back to the apartment.'

'Father, we cannot—'

'We will be dead before the end of the day if you retaliate, so we will do nothing,' he said firmly. 'We will find any valuables here, I have some antique jewellery hidden in a safe, and then we will make a plan.'

'A plan?'

'To leave Germany,' her mother said. 'We cannot stay here, it's not safe.'

'Herr Goldman!' came a cry from outside. 'Herr Goldman, are you in there?'

Maria Schwabe, the wife of her father's friend Thomas, was cowering near the front of their store, and Eliana watched as her mother quickly ushered her inside.

'Thomas has been taken,' she cried, her body folded inwards as she clutched a shawl around her shoulders. 'They came into our apartment last night, stormtroopers with guns, and they held a revolver to his head as they smashed everything. Everything!'

'Where is he now?' her father asked. 'Maria, where have they taken him?'

'I don't know,' she cried. 'But they're coming for all the men, they're rounding them all up, and they say they won't stop until they've damaged every last store and every home. Until they've gotten rid of the lot of us.'

Eliana looked to David, who moved closer to her, his hand finding hers again. He'd been right about them needing to keep their father safe, but she had a feeling that she needed to keep him safe, too.

'We could send the children to the orphanage,' her mother said. 'They could seek refuge there, to keep them safe for now.'

'Mother, no!' Eliana cried. 'I won't leave you.'

'Maria, gather your children, we shall take them there at once.'

'I'm not leaving you, either,' David said. 'I'm not a child any more, and I won't have our family separated.'

It was their father who turned to them, looking at each of them, his usually bright eyes dull. 'We shall search for anything of value, and you should do the same in your store, Maria. Hide what you can on your body, and get your children to as well. But we will not leave the children at the orphanage with no protection. If they've razed the synagogue to the ground, then they may do the same to the orphanages, too.'

No one argued with her father as he turned and ambled over the shards of glass and broken timber to the back of the shop, appearing to have aged twenty years overnight. Everything he'd worked so hard for had been destroyed, but Eliana knew that he wouldn't give up without a fight, that he would find every last item of value. Her father was the hardest-working, proudest man she knew; she only hoped that he'd be strong enough to survive what was to come.

A wail from outside sent her mother running to the open door to see what had happened, but Eliana stayed behind, feeling safer inside the store than out, even though she knew the stormtroopers with bats and guns could come back down the street at any moment.

'The orphanages have all been burned to the ground. They're gone!' someone cried. 'Our rabbi was beaten to death as he tried to stop them!'

A shiver ran the length of Eliana's spine and her mother began to cry. David angrily kicked broken glass aside as he followed their father. If even the synagogues and orphanages had been torched, what hope did any of them have to stay safe?

'We shall go home then,' her father said, calling from the back of the store.

'Home?' she whispered to David. 'How can we go home? What if they come for us there? Won't that be the very first place they look?'

Her mother began nodding, as if she couldn't stop, as if it were out of her control. 'We should go home. Yes, we should go home. We will be safe there, we shall lock the doors and hide, wait for all this to be over.'

'But, Mama—'

Her mother's eyes lit up. 'Herr Müller won't let anyone into our apartment block. He wouldn't want his girls to see or hear such a commotion, of that I'm almost certain.'

'I don't think anyone can stop these mobs,' David said. 'You heard the policeman, there's nothing they can do. Not even a man like Herr Müller could put an end to it.'

'They can't tell them to stop what they're doing to us, but Karl Müller likes order, he's very high up in the SS, and he wouldn't allow any type of rioting or troublesome behaviour at his place of residence,' her father said, his shoulders straighter than they had been only moments earlier, his eyes brighter. 'We are the only Jewish family there. If they haven't come for us yet, we might well be safest at home, so long as we're not seen. I think your mother is right.'

'But what if Herr Müller comes for us himself?' Eliana asked. 'What if we can't trust him to protect us? What if he is the one to drag us down the stairs to the mobs to be rid of us?'

'She's right,' David said. 'They are treating us like vermin that needs to be exterminated. Why would Herr Müller not come for us himself when his family are out?'

Her father frowned. 'We've known the Müller family our entire lives. We've lived the floor above them for two decades, before you children were even born. I have to believe that he wouldn't do such a thing, that he's not as depraved as the others.'

Eliana didn't say what she was thinking – that their years of knowing the family might not mean anything now. She'd once been friends with Herr Müller's daughter, Ava. They'd been in the same year at school and they'd often spent time together, especially when they were younger. But she doubted Ava would even notice her if she walked past now, and she certainly wouldn't trust her not to report them. Wasn't that what they trained for at their Bund Deutscher Mädel meetings? To help make Germany pure again by ridding the country of anyone and anything that didn't conform to their ideals of purity?

'It is decided, we shall go home,' her father said, in a voice that told her there was to be no further discussion. 'We will gather everything here, we will try to find some food, and then we shall lock the doors and stay inside until the unrest is over.'

'But what if this is just the beginning, Papa?' David asked. 'What if it doesn't end?'

'It will end, son. It has to end. Eventually everyone will come to their senses. This madness cannot go on forever.'

'But if they don't?' Eliana pressed. 'If they don't come to their senses and we have to live in fear like this? If we are persecuted against forever?'

'Then we shall leave Germany,' her father said, with tears in his eyes. 'We shall find somewhere new to start again, to prosper. We will not live like this.'

She couldn't imagine leaving Berlin, let alone Germany, and starting a new life elsewhere. But deep inside, she didn't believe this was ever going to end, not now.

'Bastards!' A yell from outside, followed by another rock thrown, this one larger and landing squarely inside the store.

'Hurry,' her father said. 'We must gather what we need as quickly as possible. The longer we're here, the more danger we're in.'

Eliana wanted to move, but her feet were stuck as she peered out at what was happening, imagining what it would be like once night fell again, wondering what these mobs of angry men might do to her if they found her alone, if they snatched her away from her family. Her stomach burned, as if something were going around and around deep inside of her, the pain impossible to ignore.

They were chanting now as they marched past, throwing whatever they could get their hands on. Eliana clamped her hand to her mouth to stifle her scream when she saw one man, a Jewish shopkeeper, being dragged from his store by his ankles, beaten with lengths of timber, the men like a crazed mob set on violence.

'Jews! The destroyers of German culture!' they all screamed, over and over again, until his body became lifeless.

'Come away from the window,' David said, his hand on her back as he guided her away, seeming so much older than his years, always so quick to protect her. 'Don't look at them, and block your ears.'

'Filthy pigs!' someone else screamed. 'Pimps and whores!'

She looked into David's eyes and saw his fear reflected back at her. 'How can they do this? Why do they hate us so much? Do they truly believe we're so evil?'

He held her as she cried, her face pressed against his shoulder.

'I don't know,' he whispered in reply. 'All I know is that I want to leave here and never return.'

That afternoon, as they tentatively walked up the stairs to their apartment, Eliana froze when she heard the front door to their building open. She looked to her family, and they all looked back, as terrified as her – they'd been avoiding violence all day, had believed that once they reached their apartment block they might be safe.

But it wasn't the shouts of looters or troopers that reached Eliana's ears, but the chatter and laughter of girls. She knew immediately who it would be – Ava and Hanna Müller were the only schoolgirls in the building besides her, and they soon came running up the stairs. They were wearing their smart uniforms, their blonde hair beautifully braided, their blue eyes bright as they paused a few steps below the Goldman family. *I wore that uniform once. I laughed and giggled with not a care in the world, just like them.* But now she was acutely conscious of her tangled hair, messy from searching through the ruins of their store, her clothes most likely filthy from the dust. They'd had rotten fruit thrown at them as they'd scurried down the street, too, and she hated to think how much of it had stained her coat.

'Herr Goldman,' the oldest of the two girls said. 'Frau Goldman. Good afternoon.'

The younger one, Ava, kept her eyes downcast, as if she shouldn't be looking at them, let alone talking to them. Eliana stayed quiet, as did David, but her parents replied and said good afternoon in reply. She knew David was watching them and she wondered how he felt, seeing them live so normally while their own lives were being stripped away from them. He'd been such a fun-loving brother when they were younger, but over the past years she'd noticed him becoming quieter, no longer as quick to smile as he'd once been.

The girls hurried past, and Eliana knew her face had flushed a deep red with anger. Only months ago, she'd sat beside Ava in class. They hadn't been close friends, but they'd always gotten along well, and they'd often walked home together. But Ava had been one of the girls who'd stayed quiet when her teacher had refused to let Eliana swim in the school pool, lest she contaminate the German water, whispering about Eliana and the other Jews as they passed by. When Eliana had been the last Jewish pupil in their class, Ava had shyly glanced at her when she'd been alone without her friends, but otherwise ignored her along with the rest of the children, and she certainly hadn't spoken up for her when the boys had taunted her and called her a dirty Jew as she'd tried to sit quietly and eat her lunch, tipping her food so that it spilled all over her lap. The silence from her former friend had hurt even more than the taunts, when all she'd needed was one girl, one other human, to stand up for her.

But the worst day of all had been when they were walking home from school, and she'd seen Ava pasting posters on all the lamp posts of happy, smiling little girls, to encourage schoolchildren to join the youth groups. Ava hadn't done anything directly cruel to her, hadn't called her names or pulled her hair like some of the others had, but it was the fact she hadn't spoken up for her or continued to be her friend that hurt the most.

Which was why she very much doubted that Herr Müller would be any different. Why would he risk anything to be kind to them? Her own father might be right that he wouldn't allow any violence or disruption in their apartment block, for the sake of his family living there, but he could easily have them thrown from their apartment entirely. And then what would they do? Or what about when his family went to their beautiful country house? Perhaps he would wait to come for them until then?

But as they passed the Müllers' apartment, Eliana saw that Hanna was standing by the door, and she forgot all about Karl Müller and what he might do. Hanna's cheeks were flushed and she was out of breath, as if she'd been running, and that was when she called out to her.

'Eliana?'

Eliana paused, looking to her mother before taking a few tentative steps towards Hanna.

'Take this,' she said. 'I'm sorry for what is happening.'

Hanna passed her a package wrapped in brown paper, and when they reached their apartment, quick to lock the door behind them, Eliana pulled at the string and unwrapped it. Inside, she found a small piece of meat, an entire loaf of bread, a thick piece of cheese and a small jar of jam.

'We were right to trust them,' her father said. 'At least we have food to last a day or two.'

Eliana nodded. *At least we have food.* They hadn't been successful in finding any on the way home, the lines closed to Jews – and if there was a loaf of stale bread left at the grocer's or bakery, she doubted they would have given it to them, even in exchange for gold.

'This is for tonight and tomorrow,' her mother muttered. 'But what do we do after this?'

Six months after the night of broken glass, Eliana huddled beside her family in the dark in their apartment. Her father comforted her mother, who seemed to do little more than cry most days. And then there was David, who was becoming more restless with each passing week in their permanent state of confinement.

'We should have left, we should have left when we still had the chance,' he muttered, standing up and beginning to pace, as he did most evenings.

'You make it sound as if emigrating is so easy,' her father said.

'It would have been easy last year, or the year before that!' David said. 'Papa, you know we should have gone then, and now look at us. We're prisoners in our home. We will starve here before we manage to leave now!'

'At least we're not prisoners in a camp,' Eliana said, bravely, raising her voice, hating hearing her brother and father argue.

'What do you know of camps?' her father asked.

'I know that all of the women from our synagogue who remained in Berlin have been taken. They were rounded up and taken to a place for women.'

Her mother began to cry again, and Eliana turned away. She couldn't keep comforting her, couldn't even bring herself to look at her mother in so much pain.

'I am going to see Herr Müller,' Eliana announced.

Her father turned and looked at her as if she were mad. 'You are not leaving this apartment.'

'I am,' she said, lifting her chin. Her father wasn't used to defiance from her, but she'd been thinking about this for days, and she wasn't going to let him stop her. 'You were right to trust him, Papa, and we all know where those food packages are coming from.'

'The fact that their daughter is giving us food—'

'She would not be able to keep giving it to us without at least her mother's permission,' David said. 'I agree with Eliana. If we are to find a way to leave Berlin, Herr Müller might be our only chance. If not, how many weeks or months will we last here, before we are discovered? What if the Müllers move away and we have no way to access food?'

Eliana rose, deciding then and there that she was going to take herself downstairs to ask him for help. She knew that she could be arrested, that she could be taken to the camps like the other women or that her family could be killed, but there was only so long they could rely on food parcels. And only so long before their apartment was raided. Jews weren't allowed to own property – everything had to be taken from them – but for some reason, theirs hadn't. Yet.

She walked the flight of stairs and then bravely knocked on the door, standing back to wait. Eliana kept glancing behind her, worried that the Müllers might have a guard now, given Karl Müller's rank – that someone other than him might discover her.

The door opened, and it was Frau Müller who opened it. Her eyes widened, but she never said a word, other than to call for her husband.

Eliana had never had a proper conversation with Herr Müller, other than to say hello at parties when she was younger, or to greet him as they came or went from home, and so when he came to the door in his terrifying SS uniform, she almost wilted before him.

'Herr Müller,' she said, her voice trembling. 'I would like to ask for your help. My family must leave Berlin, for our safety, and we cannot do it without assistance.'

His eyes narrowed, and he stepped forward, looking out of the door and down the hall as if to see if anyone could be watching or listening. But of course the Müllers' house took up the entire floor, and there was no one coming up or down the stairs.

'Please, we need your help. We are still living together as a family, but there are hardly any Jews left, and—'

He stepped back, his eyes meeting hers for the briefest of moments, before he shut the door on her. Eliana's entire body trembled, emotion rising in her throat, tears filling her eyes, as she stood there alone in the hallway. She half expected the door to open again, for Hanna to give her a parcel as she had that day in November, but no one came.

What have I done? Perhaps he didn't even know we are still upstairs? Perhaps he doesn't know his daughter has been helping us?

All Eliana could think was that, somehow, her desire to help her family might have risked their entire existence.

Four days later, there was a knock at the door. They were all sitting in the living room, trying to pass the time by playing cards, so when the noise sounded out, they all froze.

'Should we hide?' Eliana whispered, jumping to her feet and holding out her hand to her mother.

They all looked at one another, and her father quickly nodded, so she and her mother ran to a bedroom, hiding among coats and dresses in the wardrobe, their backs pressed to the wall just as another knock rapped against the timber.

'Would they knock if they were coming for us?' Eliana whispered. 'Wouldn't they just kick the door down?' They had pushed a large piece of furniture across the door, to try to stop any intruders, but they all knew that would only hold an angry mob for so long. Their plan had always been for her and her mother to hide, for her father and David to confront whoever came through the door, and she hated that they were prepared to sacrifice themselves.

Her mother didn't answer, she only clutched her hand tighter, her breath raspy as they stood in silence.

They were close enough to hear muffled words, and Eliana knew that her father had opened the door to whomever it was. They must have only been hiding for minutes before David came looking for them.

'Who was it?' Eliana asked, pushing past a heavy fur coat to emerge into the room. 'What happened?'

'It was Herr Müller,' he said, his eyes shining with a light that Eliana hadn't seen for months now. 'Eliana, Herr Müller came to see us.'

'Is he asking for us to turn ourselves in to the authorities?' her mother whispered.

'No,' her father said, coming in behind David. 'He's going to help us.'

'But he closed the door on me the other night. He didn't even say a word when I begged for his help.'

Her father looked perplexed, shaking his head as he seemed to think through what had just taken place.

'He wants Eliana to go to their apartment tomorrow afternoon. His eldest daughter will dress her in her clothes, and they will leave the apartment block together. Herr Müller will be driving his own car tomorrow, and will take Eliana to their country house.'

'In Bogensee?' her mother asked.

'Yes.'

'How long will she be there for?'

'He said they will keep her safe. I didn't ask him questions.'

'What of the rest of you?' Eliana asked, fear rising in her throat as she thought of being safe in the countryside while her family stayed hidden in the apartment, of them being parted.

'He said he will do what he can for all of us, but that it will take time.'

'I can't go,' she said. 'I won't leave you all.'

'Eliana, you have to go,' David said, staring at her from across the room. 'We'll be fine, but if you have a chance to leave, to be safe . . .'

'He's right, you will go,' her father said. 'You must.'

She blinked away her tears and wrapped her arms around her mother, squeezing her eyes shut as she tried her hardest not to cry.

'Father, Karl Müller is rising in the party ranks. Are you certain this isn't a way to lure us out into the open?' said David.

'Son, if he wanted to arrest us, he'd have sent men to storm our apartment. We have no choice but to trust him.'

Eliana knew he was right; there was no one else they could turn to, and if the Müller family could help them, then they had to believe the offer was genuine.

'He said he'll try to get the rest of you out, too?' she asked.

Her father nodded. 'He did.'

Then she would be ready tomorrow. If he managed to get her to safety without any trouble, then she had to believe he'd find a way to return for the rest of them.

'You need to tell them, Papa,' David said, as he sat down on the bed, his head hanging. 'You need to tell them what else he said.'

'Papa?' Eliana asked. 'What did he say?'

Her father was the one with tears shining in his eyes now, and he sat down beside his son, as if his legs could hold him no longer. 'He said that there are terrible things happening to our people, that the violence has escalated. Some Jews have still been managing to emigrate, but he doesn't know if we'll be able to leave. He thinks it's too late.'

'So we are stuck here? We will have to live with this hatred forever?'

'He fears that the Nazi ideology will spread through Europe quickly, that we must flee to America if we can. He doesn't think we'll be safe anywhere that Germany can reach.'

They all sat in silence for a moment, before Eliana stood. 'I shall pack a bag, so I'm ready for tomorrow.'

Her father shook his head. 'He said not to take anything. You are to appear as a friend from school, and you will walk from the building to the waiting car so that no one notices you. You mustn't carry anything that could identify you or make you look suspicious.'

Eliana understood, but as she looked around the room, at all of their beautiful furniture and possessions, she wondered how they were to survive if they couldn't have any reminders of who they were. Of who they'd once been.

'We shall all keep jewellery on our bodies,' her father instructed. 'We will take everything we can, everything of value, so that we have something to sell, even if we have to hide it in our undergarments.'

They were all silent again, the uncertainty of their future hanging heavy. And Eliana couldn't stop wondering if Herr Müller would keep his word and come back for the rest of her family, or if this might be the very last time they would all be together.

'We must be strong,' her father said. 'Others have lost their lives, families have been ripped apart, but we are survivors. We will do whatever it takes to stay alive.'

'David?' Eliana said, looking to her brother, wishing they could both go together, finding the very idea of parting from him even harder than leaving her parents behind.

They'd been through so much – they'd walked to school together and held their heads high despite the jeers; they'd stead-fastly continued their studies when they'd been forced to stay home; they'd whispered their plans for the future late at night, the countries they could move to, far away from Nazis – and now, after all of that, they were to be parted.

When their parents left the room, she went over to him, dropping to the floor beside the bed. He moved to sit beside her, their shoulders touching, knees bumping together.

'He said that there are tens of thousands of men incarcerated,' David whispered, 'and that there is a new camp just for women, called Ravensbrück.'

'What do they do there? Why do they take the women there?'

'I don't know. But he said he doesn't think any of the women will ever come back, that it is a place of horrors.'

Fear tangled like a knot, nestled deep in her belly.

'You must go, Eliana, and then you must fight for us. But you have to make sure he comes back for us, because I can't be here for long without you, and we can't let them take Mama to that camp. I would rather die than know that she was incarcerated there.'

'I will never stop fighting for you, David,' she said, throwing her arms around him and burying her face in his shoulder. 'I will fight for you and for Mama and Papa until my very last breath.'

'And I you,' he said. 'I would rather die than let anything happen to you.'

Chapter Six

Ava

'I walked straight out the front door of our apartment block with Eliana, dressed in your Bund Deutscher Mädel uniform, Ava, and straight to Papa's waiting car,' Hanna said. 'It was the first time I'd ever done anything like it, and it showed me what someone in our position, in our family's position, could do to help others. Dressed in that uniform, no one batted an eye at us.'

'I walked past two German SS officers who smiled at me and nodded their heads,' Eliana said. 'I'd prayed that I'd be invisible, and in the end I was the opposite of that. I was seen as one of them, because they couldn't imagine I was anything other than a carefully vetted pure German in my beautiful uniform.'

Ava couldn't believe it. She was speechless as she looked from Hanna to Eliana, finding it almost impossible to imagine that her sister had commandeered her full blue skirt and white blouse for such an elaborate ruse. She actually felt queasy thinking about it, trying to separate what she'd believed for so long with the truth of what was being told to her, but she still couldn't stop imagining how she'd be thought of if anyone discovered that a Jewish girl had worn her prized BDM uniform. 'What happened next? How did you get the rest of the family out of the city?'

'Mama did a similar trick with Frau Goldman, a few weeks later,' Hanna said. 'She dressed her in her best clothes, and they both carried armfuls of knitted items and blankets, clearly destined for our soldiers at the front. No one would have dared question them.'

'My father and brother weren't so easy to disguise though,' Eliana said. 'It wasn't until we were reunited that I learned your father had marched them from the apartment block with a revolver pointed to Papa's head. It was the only way to move him, but it could so easily have gone wrong.'

Ava gasped, imagining the scene. 'What did *you* do next?' she asked her father. 'Where did you take them from there?' How had he taken them anywhere but to their deaths?

'I told the SS men who were present that I wanted to take care of the Goldmans myself, for daring to live right under my nose, in my apartment block,' Ava's father told her. 'I said awful things about them that were necessary as part of the ruse, and when we got to the park, I told them to run and fired my gun two times, to make it sound as if they'd been executed. But I'm not proud of the things Herr Goldman was witness to hearing, nor the compulsory hit to his head with the butt of my gun for effect.'

'But it worked,' Herr Goldman said. 'We were so frightened, but we had no choice other than to believe in your father. Without him, we would have rotted in our apartment, or been found and beaten to death.'

'They ran and hid when he let them go, in a building Papa had told them was empty,' Hanna said. 'He went back to find them that night and collected them.'

'And brought them here?' Ava asked.

'To an empty house not so far from here,' Hanna replied. 'But it wasn't long before we had to move them, and eventually, our only option was to come here. The crows were circling, and it would have only been so long before they were discovered by someone.'

'But why couldn't they leave Germany? Why could you not find a way to get them passage to America, or somewhere else far away, rather than bring danger into our home?'

'By the time we had them all out of the city, there was no safe way for them to emigrate. If they'd been caught—'

'We'd be dead,' Eliana said. 'Or worse.'

'We should have gone years ago, when so many of our friends left. My cousin sent us letter after letter, telling us to follow him to England, warning us of what was to come, that we would be blamed for everything that was wrong in Germany.' Herr Goldman wiped at his eyes. 'But I didn't believe him. I never believed that this madness would ever be allowed to come to fruition.'

Ava watched as her sister went to Eliana, opening her arms and folding her against her body. They stayed like that for a long moment, and Ava waged a fight within herself as she saw the warm, tender way in which Hanna treated Ava's old friend, eventually turning away so she didn't have to see it.

Besides, Ava didn't want to look back at the Goldmans again, the discomfort of their situation not something she wanted to witness. So instead, she went back down the ladder, taking a moment to catch her breath, to come to terms with everything she'd heard, before slowly walking to her bedroom and sitting down on the bed. She only looked up when Hanna came to the door, her arms wrapped around herself as she stood, barefoot, in her nightdress.

'You knew, all this time,' Ava whispered. 'You knew and you chose not to tell me what was going on in our home?'

Hanna's silence told Ava that she was right.

They'd treated her as if she were a child, not privy to their discussions or decisions, to the secrets they'd chosen to keep. To the effect it could have on her if someone else discovered what they'd done.

'I don't know you the way I used to, Ava,' Hanna eventually said, coming to sit beside her on the bed, her voice low. 'We used to be so close, but I honestly didn't know if you'd agree with our decision, if you'd have the same sympathies as—'

'Agree? Of course I wouldn't have agreed to this! Are you actually mad? If someone came here, if someone discovered—'

Hanna lifted her finger to her lips, shaking her head. 'Keep your voice to a whisper.' She sighed. 'Have you truly never wondered what happened to Dr Goldstein? Or our grocer, Herr Lewinsky? Our schoolteachers? Did you even notice that the people who used to be part of our lives suddenly disappeared as if they'd never existed in the first place?'

Anger rose within Ava, and she felt as though she might be sick right there on the carpet as Hanna spoke to her as if she was somehow the one in the wrong. Heat rose to her face, fuelling her nausea.

'Did you truly never wonder what had happened to the Goldmans?' Hanna whispered. 'After all this time, after their home was abandoned and their shop windows were smashed? After all those years living in the same apartment block as them?'

'No,' Ava answered truthfully, still whispering. 'No, Hanna, I never once thought about what happened to them. But if you'd asked me, I'd have told you that they moved on with all the others.' Guilt crept over her skin and made her shiver as she said the words. They were just like all the other Jewish families, families that she knew she was never to speak of or to think about again.

Why did I never wonder? Why did I never think about where they'd gone or what their fate was? Should I have?

'You didn't listen to your beloved Goebbels scream to the crowd at the Sportpalast and secretly think he was a madman?' Hanna asked. 'Were you truly so gullible when he claimed that Judaism was a contagious infection? Did you actually believe his lies?'

Ava glared back at her sister. 'You're asking if I was the one person in the crowd who disagreed with him?' she whispered. 'As if I'm somehow wrong to believe what everyone else believes! We are not supposed to question our Führer, Hanna, and Goebbels was simply spreading his message. We are *supposed* to follow the rules! You're acting as if I've done something wrong, when all I've ever done is try to be the perfect German girl, just as I was told to be!'

'What happened to my fiercely determined little sister, the one who could beat me at every game and who read so many books she knew more about the world than any of us? Did she truly lose herself so entirely that she never thought about anyone other than herself? Did she not use that knowledge she'd gathered and question what she was being told?'

Ava smarted. 'That girl grew into a woman who knew what was expected of her! Look at Sophie Scholl. If she'd only kept quiet, if she had just kept her head down, she'd still be alive,' she hissed. 'It's not worth the risk! We shall all be arrested for treason if we're discovered!'

If only you'd seen the photos, Hanna. If only you'd seen with your own eyes the things they do to people who don't obey them.

'And if we do nothing, then the blood of thousands, millions even, will be on our hands.'

Silence sat between them until their father came to the door and beckoned for her.

'Ava, would you join me in my study, please?'

She rose, not making eye contact with her sister as she followed her father downstairs. 'After you,' he said, ushering her into his study, a room that she rarely set foot in. One entire wall was adorned with dark-stained oak shelves, filled with endless books, and two leather chairs sat in the middle of the room, facing his desk. Hung behind it was a large, framed photo of him standing with Hitler, shaking hands, and Ava found herself staring at it, as her father busied himself with pouring a drink. He was in comfortable clothes now, and she found he looked so different at home to the man he presented himself as in his perfectly tailored uniform.

She was surprised when he returned with not one but two glasses, with brandy in the bottom of each. Hers was short, and his was a much larger pour, and she watched as he took a sip, indicating that she should do the same. Ava lifted the glass and let the amber liquid touch her lips. The tiniest of sips sent a burning fire down her throat to her stomach, a feeling she wasn't entirely certain she liked, and it took all her willpower to stop from coughing.

Her father crossed the room again and went to his gramophone, taking out a record and filling the room with music as she sat down. She'd heard him listening to records before, but usually it was when her mother joined him for a drink before or after dinner – certainly not with her.

'Ava, I believe it's time we had a frank conversation, in light of your discovery tonight.'

She took another tentative sip of brandy and found it didn't burn quite like the first.

'You raised me to join the party,' she said, fixing her gaze on her father, speaking freely now in a way she'd never done with him before. 'You never once discouraged me from joining the Jungmädelbund or the Bund Deutscher Mädel, or told me to think differently from everyone else. And now I find out that you are a – what? A socialist?' The girls in her old BDM group were still like sisters to her, but she knew that if they overheard this conversation, they'd immediately report her and shun her and her family forever.

'Ava, you know we had no choice in whether we joined the party or the youth groups, or how we appear on the outside, not if we wanted to survive, but we do have a choice in what we do inside our own home.'

She took one more sip of her drink before setting the glass down on the low table between the two leather chairs, holding her father's gaze as she inclined her body slightly towards him.

'I didn't expect to be having this conversation with you tonight, but you're an intelligent young woman, Ava, and it's time for you to understand what our family has been fighting for.'

'Papa,' she whispered, so low she barely heard the words pass through her own lips. 'Are you part of some sort of *resistance*? Are you all doing some sort of covert work?' *Are they hiding other Jews somewhere?*

She wanted to turn away, to not hear or see his reaction, but she couldn't. It was only when she saw him nod that her eyes fell shut, that she tried to block it from her mind. So that was why he'd taken the paper, why he'd risked so much to take something from the office, why he was prepared to have the Goldmans hidden in their attic. Her father was part of something that was punishable by death, something that she now understood her own fiancé would kill her father for with his own pistol.

'You know what they will do if they find out. You know more than anyone what would happen,' she said. Of course he knew – her father was as high up in the party as a man could become, with the exception of a handful of Hitler's closest advisors. 'Have you truly thought this all through?' *The implications will affect all of us. Is it truly worth the risk?*

'Yes. It took me years to act, but in the end I felt I had no choice,' he said, firmly, although she noticed that he looked away as he spoke, staring at something she couldn't see, as he raised his glass and drained the brandy from it. Perhaps he was still wrestling with the weight of his decisions, despite the resolution of his tone. 'Our country is under the control of a madman. It's as if we were all under a dome, as if everyone has been blinded to what is happening, but there is a movement that is working to change that.'

He rose to pour himself another glass, but she didn't miss the way his hand shook as he held the decanter. She wasn't to know whether it was fear, anger or something else entirely, and she didn't dare ask.

'It's like we are all part of a horrible experiment, an experiment that has pitted one group of people against another, one country against the rest of the world. To not act, to not do something when we are in a position to do exactly that, it's not something I can live with any longer. And I'm not acting alone, there are others who share my views.'

'But you have been part of what has happened here,' she whispered, leaning against him as he sat down beside her. 'Papa, you work hand in hand with Dr Goebbels. Does that not mean you have helped to make everyone believe? To perpetuate what you are now renouncing? That you have been even more involved than almost every other German in spreading these, these . . .' She swallowed. '*Lies?*'

When he met her stare, she saw that his eyes were filled with tears, and it was the first time in her life that she'd ever seen him show such obvious emotion. 'I have done what I needed to do to survive, Ava, to keep our family alive and put us in a position of safety. I'm not proud of that, but I also know that if I were faced with the same situation again, I would protect you girls without question.'

Ava leaned forward and picked up her glass, nursing it as she waited for her father to speak again, torn between what she believed was now true, and what she wanted to believe.

'The war is not going to be easily won. Times are changing, the war is changing, and the quick victory we were promised no longer exists.'

She didn't know what to say.

'Ava, you must know that most Germans do not have the luxuries we have. That we are privileged in all we do and receive?'

Ava slowly nodded, understanding what he was trying to tell her.

'Our Führer is asking everyone to follow his vegetarian diet, as if it will make them healthier, but in truth he is preparing our country for the hardships to come, for the hardships many are already facing.' Her father leaned forward. 'The Third Reich is slowly being strangled, our Luftwaffe are suffering heavy casualties, and our men are returning broken from the front lines.'

She watched him, feeling a question coming, knowing that he was going to ask her to do something.

'You are in a very special position, Ava,' he continued. 'You have access to classified information, and that means you could be very valuable. More valuable than you could possibly understand.'

'To a resistance cause?' she whispered. 'Is that what you're trying to get me to do, to pass along information to some sort of underground movement? You want me to act against the wishes of our Führer?'

He grimaced. 'Yes, Ava, that's exactly what I'm asking of you. Now is not the time to be complacent, not if we want to see Germany and all of our people prosper again.'

'This is what I saw you doing the other day? This is why you took that paper?'

'It will be so much easier for you than it has been for me,' he said, without directly answering her question. 'You are right there, you have eyes on so many documents that others could only dream of seeing. And it will only be little things at first, whatever you feel confident in recounting.'

'What happened to her, after they took her?' Anger rose inside of her, pooling in her belly. 'That day, when they came for my colleague, I need to know what happened.'

She watched her father shift uncomfortably in his seat. He knew who she was speaking of, there was little doubt in her mind about that, even if he hadn't known her personally.

'Her name was Lina,' Ava said, lifting her glass and draining it, her eyes smarting as she swallowed. 'They called her a traitor and marched her from the office, right in front of me. Everyone believes she is guilty, and yet she did nothing.' Ava looked away. 'And now you are asking me to do things that could result in my arrest? In *my* being called a traitor?'

He didn't say anything, he just returned her gaze, as steady as an owl as she began to cry.

'What if that had been me, Papa? What if someone had done that to me, and I was taken? Could you have lived with yourself if it were me in her shoes?'

Ava stood up, torn between wanting to please her papa and believing that what he'd done was wrong. But instead of storming from his study, she stayed there as he rose and took a step towards her, kept her chin lifted, not prepared to back down until he gave her an answer.

Her father lifted his hand and placed it against her cheek. 'Ava, you have a choice to make, and no one else can make that decision for you. There are risks, and at times they will be great, but there are times in life that our individual risk is outweighed by a greater good. You are also in the privileged position of being my daughter, which means you will always be the last person anyone suspects of wrongdoing. Our family is greatly respected by the party, by Joseph Goebbels himself.'

She swallowed, fighting the urge to lean into his palm, wanting him to know that none of this sat comfortably with her, that she couldn't simply agree to what he was asking. Ava had bitten down hard on her bottom lip, listening to him, knowing that he was right even though she didn't want to admit it.

'But if you were to guess, about what happened to Lina,' she pressed. 'I want to know what one should expect, in that situation. If one were to be caught doing these things that you're asking of me.'

He cleared his throat. 'Your friend will have been taken for questioning by the SS. I would say that they used force to make her talk, that they would have only given up when they'd exhausted all options available to them.'

'And then?' Her voice was so low it was barely audible. She knew her father's role in the SS, knew that he was likely the one who had ordered Lina's interrogation, as much as she didn't want to admit it.

'There is a small chance she would be able to return to her family, if they believed she was telling the truth. But there is also a chance that her entire family could now be suspected of being traitors. They may have all been deported.'

Ava didn't need to hear any more; she knew from what he wasn't telling her what the alternative would be, what could happen to her friend.

'What you're asking of me, what you want me to do . . .'

He leaned forward and pressed a warm kiss to the top of her head. 'All I ask is that you consider what I've told you tonight,' he said.

'And what of Heinrich,' she said. 'Is he part of this?' Was he also keeping this a secret from her?

Her father's expression darkened then, as if storm clouds had settled between them.

'Ava, you must never mention this to Heinrich,' he said, reminding her immediately of the formidable SS man she saw him being in the office. 'He must never know of what we've done, or what we're planning to do. Even a whisper that made its way to him, the slightest seed of doubt planted in his mind about me, you or our family . . .'

'I understand.' Ava would be too afraid to confide in her fiancé, anyway.

He patted her shoulder, affectionately, his anger disappearing as quickly as it had appeared, and Ava stepped out of his study, walking down the hall and going up to her bedroom. She was surprised to find Hanna lying there waiting for her, and she lifted the covers to let Ava in, cuddling into her for warmth as they'd done as children, Hanna's anger clearly forgotten.

'I don't know if I'm as brave as you or Mama,' Ava whispered. 'I don't know if I can do what Papa has asked of me.'

Hanna hugged her close.

'There is truly no such thing as a peaceful relocation?' Ava whispered into the dark. 'The Jews aren't taken somewhere to live their lives together?'

'No, Ava, there is no such thing.'

She sat up bolt upright then, pushing the covers off her and striding over to the framed portrait of Adolf Hitler that she had on her wall. Ava took it boldly from the hook, turning it around so that he was no longer facing the room, leaning the frame against the wall on the floor.

She knew she would have to rehang it before she left, before their maid Zelda came back into the house, but for now her small act of defiance sent a little thrill through her body. And when she crawled back into bed, as she wrapped her arms around her sister once more, she refused to whisper the words *Heil Hitler* that she'd so faithfully said for the past few years at every opportunity.

At home, those two little words would never pass her lips. Not now, not after everything she'd come to understand. *How could I? When everything I've come to believe in has been proven to be a lie?*

'Hanna, is there anything else you're doing that I should know about?'

Hanna squeezed her hand beneath the covers, and she waited such a long time before speaking that Ava thought she wasn't going to answer. 'I've been smuggling Jewish children out of Berlin in an ambulance,' she whispered.

Ava shut her eyes tight as she digested her sister's words, as she understood the risks Hanna had been taking for others.

'Ava, these children are no different than any other child. The things that are happening to them, the way they're being treated, it's not something I can stand by and accept. Smuggling them out is often the only way to keep them alive, and if I can spare one parent the agony of losing a child? Then I'm willing to do whatever it takes.'

Ava blinked away tears, squeezing her eyes shut, the depth of her sister's confession heavy in her heart. Her brave, fearless sister.

'I'll keep the Goldmans' secret,' Ava whispered, tightening her hold on Hanna's hand. 'I would never betray you and Mama and Papa. *Never.*'

Chapter Seven

Ava's fingers were trembling so much when she returned to the office three days later, that for the first time since she'd taken her position at the ministry, she made three errors in a row in her typing. Taking the paper from the typewriter, she scrunched it into a ball, hiding it on her lap, and took a clean sheet of paper to feed back into the machine. If she didn't manage to shake off her nerves, someone was going to notice.

'That's not like you,' Greta whispered, glancing over at her. 'What's wrong?'

Ava knew her face had turned a dark shade of red, but she also knew that she had to come up with the right answer to disguise her nerves. 'I think I might have caught a cold when I went home.' She did a little cough for effect and gently patted her chest. 'It's not helping my concentration.'

'Well, take your time, you're better to be slow than making mistakes.'

Ava nodded, taking a deep breath and cursing how nervous she was. She knew that no one could read her thoughts, but still she was acting as if at any moment she was going to be caught for treason, despite the fact she hadn't even done anything. The fact she hadn't seen her father to talk to since she'd returned wasn't helping either, because she had no clue whether she was supposed to be doing anything yet. Would he tell her when there was something she should look for, or was she supposed to commit to memory everything that crossed her desk? And her conversation with Hanna kept playing in her mind, the way her sister had looked at her when she'd spoken, the pain in her words twisting through Ava's body as she'd absorbed them. *I couldn't even make eye contact with Eliana Goldman, and yet my sister was out there risking her life for a stranger.*

Her sister had confessed to being responsible for helping countless Jewish children, using her cover as a nurse to smuggle them out of the country, and yet here she was, nervous about simply looking at papers in an office. Until today, she would have likely stepped around a child with a yellow star and called for the authorities, and yet Hanna's compassion had encouraged her to behave in a way that Ava hadn't even considered. Until now.

Her hands began to shake again, and she was just about to rise and take a moment's break when Herr Frowein strode into the room, holding a clutch of pink papers. Ava slowly sank back into her seat, sitting to attention as he stood in front of their desks. She'd never seen pink slips of paper before, and she wondered what he could possibly be holding.

'These,' he said, holding up the papers in one hand, 'are to be referred to as the daily truths. It is of the utmost importance that you prioritise these when they are put on your desk, for immediate distribution once you have typed them.'

Ava found herself nodding along with the other secretaries, glancing down when a few of the papers were put on her desk. She was surprised how many there were, and wondered who had made the notes.

'Your job is to type and expand the numbers, to ensure all Germans understand the truth of what is happening to our soldiers and to our good German women.'

Expand? Her eyes ran over the first few lines on the page at the top of her pile, to better understand what he was talking about.

'Fräulein Müller,' Herr Frowein said, addressing her as he gestured for her to rise. 'Please hold up your paper and tell me how many German women have been raped by Russian soldiers this week.'

She stood. Looking from him to the paper and back again. The report clearly said twenty, and she wasn't certain what he expected of her.

Ava pointed to the number as she spoke. 'Twenty women.'

He shook his head, looking as if he might strike her for reciting to him what was on the paper in front of her. 'Germans must understand the brutality of Russian soldiers and their behaviour, the way they are treating our women,' he barked. 'I ask you again, how many German women were raped, Fräulein Müller?'

'Forty women,' she said this time, raising her voice as it threatened to waver. 'Forty women were raped.'

Herr Frowein nodded. 'Forty women is correct. We do not want to underestimate what is happening, the people must know the truth. They must understand the monsters our people are faced with – why winning this war is so important to us as a nation.'

He moved to Greta beside her, who'd quickly realised what was expected of them all, and as each number on the papers in their hands was read out, Ava wondered what the true figure was. Had it already been inflated before it was noted on the pink paper? And if they were to make such gross exaggerations, then what else that passed her desk wasn't actually the truth? Why had she never thought to question what she typed before?

She found herself thinking of the Goldmans, of the way her father had looked at them, at the way they'd looked back at her, their fear palpable. She'd swallowed every untruth that had been fed to her, as had most of those around her, and yet her own family had seen the truth with their own eyes. Ava knew she'd feel like a fool for some time to come, and that it also wouldn't be easy to stop seeing things the same way she'd seen them for so many years now – to not believe the lies.

I have been one of the cowards, but I am not going to be a coward any longer. That was what she'd told herself that morning, when she'd crept up to the attic before their maid had returned, taking an armful of books, along with a new notebook she'd received for Christmas and her favourite pen for Eliana. She remembered how much she'd liked to write when they'd been at school together, and it was all she could think to give her, other than the cookies they'd made on Christmas Eve. Although it hadn't been lost on her that they were formed in the shape of a swastika, so she wouldn't have been surprised if they'd spat on them rather than eating them. All she'd wanted to do was throw open the window to let air into the stuffy attic space, to let sunlight stream in, even if it was only a small ray of light, but instead she'd left them in the dark, like birds in a gilded cage, and she hadn't been able to stop thinking of them since.

'Fräulein Müller?' Her name, said loudly as if for a second time, made her jump. She saw that Herr Frowein was walking back towards her, his boots thudding with each step.

Ava broke out in a sweat as she slowly looked up at him, waiting for him to ask her to go with him, to say something, anything, that told her he knew what she had agreed to do. Why had he singled her out? Why was he back at her desk again? Had he said something to her that she hadn't heard, because she'd been lost in a daydream?

'I trust you had a pleasant time at home with your family?'

She swallowed. 'Yes, I certainly did. I was very fortunate to spend time with them.' *He knows. The way he is looking at me, it's like he's been trained to sniff out deceit like a Nazi dog.*

'Your father said it was well worth the drive, even if he did only have the one evening with you all in the end. Family is everything to a man.'

She nodded politely, unsure what to say so deciding not to say anything at all. This was why her father was able to help the resistance, why *she* would be able to continue on his work. Because as far as anyone around them could tell, they were the perfect German family, dedicated to the cause. Her nerves began to ease then, as she began to understand why her father could be so calm in his deceit. *My father is highly ranked in the SS, my fiancé is a dedicated SS man, my mother is the model German wife.* No one had any reason to doubt their allegiance, not for a moment. If someone dared to suggest otherwise, it would be more likely that they would be hanged for treason than her father be questioned.

'I have documents from Dr Goebbels for you to type as soon as you've completed your daily truths,' he said. 'I would like you to prepare them and then deliver them directly to my office.'

'Yes, Herr Frowein,' Ava said. 'I shall make them my priority.'

He nodded. 'Please collect them from me personally once you're done here.'

Ava reached for her handbag and took out a handkerchief, pressing it to her forehead and upper lip when he'd gone. Her heart rate had slowed, but she was certain she was still shining, even though her nerves were beginning to abate.

'Ava, you might need to go home. Your colour isn't right today.'

'Thank you for your concern, Greta,' Ava said, straightening her shoulders and placing her hands on the typewriter keys. 'But I am perfectly fine. I shall rest tonight once my work is done. *Heil Hitler!*'

Greta looked hurt, her eyes like saucers, not used to such a rebuke from her usually pleasant and softly spoken colleague.

'*Heil Hitler,*' Greta repeated, before turning her back slightly to Ava.

It wasn't in her nature to be anything other than nice, but right now, she had to wear the mask of the perfect German. Not being caught was all that mattered now – she had a job to do.

Ava had only just finished with her pink slips of paper when her father came to the door of the office. She stood and quietly excused herself.

'Ava,' he said. 'I'm sorry I didn't get to see you yesterday.'

'We missed you,' she said honestly. 'Hopefully we can all have dinner again soon? Mama said she will be joining us at the apartment this week.'

'Your mother has actually just been asked to host a very important dinner party in a few weeks' time,' he said. 'Many important ministers and their wives will be in attendance.'

Ava found it almost impossible to mask her surprise. 'What an honour for her to be hostess. Will Hanna be assisting her, or should I—'

'She would very much like you both to return for it,' he said. 'Also, I have other important news. News that I know will be even more exciting to you than a party.'

She raised her eyebrows. 'News?'

'Heinrich has been granted leave. I personally signed the papers.'

Ava's heart began to hammer in her chest. 'He will be here? In Berlin?' She swallowed. 'Soon?'

'Yes, my dear. Your fiancé will be home within the month. He will have a short period of leave, and then he is to be stationed somewhere closer to home on a special assignment. I'm certain he will tell you more about it when he's here.'

Her father's hand closed over her shoulder, and she shut her eyes momentarily, seeing Heinrich's face swimming before her in her mind. A week ago, even a few days ago, such news would have set her heart racing for an entirely different reason, but now, everything had been turned upside down. Because she knew, in her heart, what someone like Heinrich would do if he found out what was happening. He would tell her to cast her family aside and denounce them as Jew-loving traitors, and she had little doubt that he'd treat her any differently if he thought she had involvement in the situation. Any allegations that Heinrich made would be taken seriously, of that she was certain, but it didn't stop her heart from fluttering at the thought of being in his arms again.

'Thank you for telling me,' she said. 'It gives me time to prepare for his arrival. I'll be certain to make it a wonderful homecoming for him.'

Her father gave her a long look then turned away, leaving her standing in the open doorway. She took a moment to gather herself, before going to Herr Frowein's office and collecting the notes he'd asked her to type.

'These are to be returned to me immediately when you've finished.'

'Of course,' she said, taking her time on the walk back to her desk, her mind a jumble of thoughts as she wrestled with her feelings.

Ava set her typewriter, checked her paper and opened the file beside her. She usually glanced over whatever she was given before typing, to ensure she had a grasp of the work and to check for any errors that she would have to change, and this one was no different. In fact, it seemed even more important to do so, especially given her nerves and that she'd been personally requested to type it.

The Final Solution. The words meant nothing to her until she read on, and then her stomach dropped.

The reports from guards at Auschwitz have already proven the success of the recently completed chambers.

Recommend a tour at your earliest convenience, to see the simplicity of the design.

Approximately four thousand or more Jews can be disposed of each day.

Request for more deliveries of gas to ensure ongoing productivity.

Ava quickly shut the folder, coughing as she tried to disguise her dry-retching, as she realised what she was being asked to transcribe.

'I've told her to go home, but she insists she isn't unwell,' she heard Greta mutter to one of the other secretaries.

'I'm fine,' Ava managed, still coughing as she imagined the Goldmans there, imagined what their fate would have been. Imagined the fate of *all* the Jewish families she'd once known.

Would she have even understood what she'd read a few days ago? A week ago? A year ago? Would she have understood what the word *Auschwitz* meant, and been able to comprehend what was happening there? If she'd had any doubts about her decision, about what she'd agreed to do, or what her family had tried to tell her, she certainly didn't now.

She dabbed at her face, as she'd done only moments earlier, to remove the sheen from it. She was doing a good job of appearing to be unwell. So much for thinking she was ready to mask her deceit – she was going to have to learn not to react, no matter how horrible her work was.

'Ava, I think you should—'

But before Greta had time to finish her sentence, the Goebbels children unexpectedly arrived, and Ava was on her feet with the others to greet them. Magda was as polished and beautiful as ever, but today she only had two of the children with her – the two youngest, who waved to all the secretaries.

'Your husband is still in his meeting, Frau Goebbels,' one of the secretaries said. 'Would you like me to make you a coffee while you wait, or fetch something for the children?'

Magda nodded her thanks, before turning to all the women and beginning to make small talk, at the same time as Hedwig and Heidrun came running over to Ava. She wished she had sweets for them, because they were always so polite, and today, without their older siblings, they seemed even more confident.

'Can you teach us how to use it?' Hedwig said of her type-writer, smiling shyly.

'Can I pretend I'm a secretary?' Heidrun asked.

'Of course!' Ava said brightly, careful to cover the file she'd been working on and deciding to slip it into one of her drawers, in case they were to knock it over. 'Shall I show you how to feed the paper into it?'

'Yes!' they both squealed, earning them a sharp rebuke from their mother.

But Ava didn't mind; she was only too happy to be distracted from her work for a moment. No one would dare reprimand her for taking time to play with the children, and it at least gave her time to think about something her sister had said, gave her a moment to breathe and calm herself down.

What was it she said, about all children being equal? Now that she knew what was truly happening, that their father was a monster due to what he was orchestrating, it didn't mean that the children were monsters. They were yet to grow and understand the world.

They were simply living their childhood, and because of that she couldn't be anything other than kind to them.

And as Heidrun climbed on to her knee and proudly began to tap at the keys, tears pricked Ava's eyes, for she couldn't comprehend how these children could be treated with such reverence, and yet elsewhere children were being killed, seemingly without a second thought.

The children are sent with their mother. We find they go more willingly than when we separate them.

Those were words from the Final Solution file that she'd just read and would never forget, and even thinking them made it almost impossible to breathe, with bile rising inside of her every time she closed her eyes and imagined their screams.

'Leave Ava to do her work now,' Magda said, as if she'd only just noticed that her children were climbing all over her. 'Your papa won't like it if you stop everyone from working.'

'But Mama, it's so fun!' Heidrun said, bouncing on Ava's knee as she tapped on the keys, her little fingers tiny against the machine.

'It's always such a pleasure to see them. I don't mind at all,' Ava said.

Magda Goebbels placed a hand on the desk, smiling warmly at her. 'I'm very much looking forward to visiting your country house soon, Ava. Your mother is always such a wonderful hostess.'

Ava was pleased her father had warned her – if not, she'd have wondered what on earth Magda was talking about. But even the mention of her home made her pulse race.

'I'm certain my mother's already busy preparing what will be served. It's such an honour for her to host you all.'

'Come on, children. It was lovely to see you, Ava. I'll be certain to tell your mother how kind you were to the girls.'

Ava smiled, forcing herself to hold it, to appear as if her entire world wasn't falling apart, as if she wasn't thinking about the fact that so many party members, *high-ranking party members*, would be at her home in just a few weeks' time, only two floors beneath a Jewish family who would be sworn to silence for the entire evening.

Ava's heart thundered in her chest, her resolve strengthening by the minute. She would protect the Goldmans' secret, their very existence, as fiercely as if they were her own family. Now that she knew the truth, she could be a coward no longer.

Even if it meant risking her own life for the cause.

Chapter Eight

Hanna

'Let's pray for another miracle.'

Hanna settled into her seat a week after Christmas, thankful to have Dieter with her to transport the children. They'd formed an unlikely friendship through working together, and although she was most often working at the hospital as a nurse, they'd been paired together more and more to work in the aftermath of the bombings, when a triage nurse was sent out with an ambulance driver. They were often able to work without talking, understanding what the other needed, and although many of her fellow nurses found Dieter to be overly gruff, she had always appreciated his quiet, practical manner. There was no hint of anything romantic between them, just a deep-founded respect for the work they were doing, and he'd come to be like the older brother she'd never had.

They'd also both experienced deep loss attributed to the war, which gave them common ground, and it was the reason they were both risking their lives to help Jewish children – neither of them felt as if they had anything to lose. With anyone else, that might have felt like a reckless attitude, but they were both determined to save as many children as they could, while they still could.

'I'm worried we won't be able to do this much longer,' Hanna said. 'I always pray for the best, but sometimes I wonder—'

'Whether it's even possible for them to make it to safety any more?'

She sighed. 'Yes. It doesn't mean I don't want to keep trying, but sometimes I think about all the people involved, all the pieces that have to fit together for this to work. It just seems more impossible with each passing month.'

'I know. But all we can do is try, which is more than most people are doing.'

'I wish there was a way to do more, to keep the families together instead of having to send children off on their own like this.'

Dieter grunted in reply, and she took that to mean he agreed with her but had no idea how to do so. Other than hiding more Jews in her own home, Hanna was all out of ideas, too.

They travelled in silence for some time as the ambulance bumped along. There were roads close to the hospital that were littered with concrete, timber, and other parts of buildings from the air raid the previous night, and about fifteen minutes out of the city they passed the smouldering remains of a factory that had been targeted by the Allies. As much as she hoped they would succeed in pushing back the German army and winning the war, Hanna also knew that the factory would have been full of young unmarried women and mothers who had to leave their children home alone or with grandparents to earn enough money to pay the rent, many of them casualties of the bombing.

'Has there been any word?' Hanna asked, turning her attention back to Dieter. 'No letters since we last spoke?'

He shook his head. 'I don't know if she's even alive still. Last time I demanded information, I was told I'd be arrested and taken too if I wasn't careful.'

Dieter's wife had been discovered to be half-Jewish, and they'd arrested her on the street and rounded her up with others who'd lived on their block. That had been two years ago, only months before Hanna had met him and so soon after her own tragedy – when the Nazis were intent on expunging from society anyone who had even a drop of Jewish blood.

Hanna looked out of the window then at a large carcass lying on the grass just outside of the city. It took her a moment to realise it was a horse, and although her first thought was how sad it was to see a magnificent animal lying dead, she also hated that the meat had gone to waste when so many families were so desperate for food. It was so much harder for those in the city, who couldn't hunt or grow their own vegetables to supplement their rations.

'Do you know what happened there?' she asked as they slowed down.

There were other things smouldering around the carcass, as if it had all recently been burning.

'They were a gypsy family,' Dieter said, glancing through the window. 'Most of them were moved on long ago, but these ones appeared last week.'

'They were all taken?'

'The story is that a little girl was found talking to them. She was seen patting the horse by a local man, who ran in and *saved* her. He was lauded as a hero for saving her life, as if they were going to kill her.'

Hanna blinked away tears as she thought of what was happening around her. The cruelty, the depravity of her fellow Germans, their willingness to believe such lies, broke her heart.

'They shot the horse, the husband and the grandfather, and they set the rest on fire before herding up the women and children.'

'On a train headed for the camps,' Hanna murmured. 'If they're even still alive.'

The Nazis hated gypsies almost as much as they hated Jews. As a very young girl, she'd been fascinated with the travelling families when they passed by her country house, often going to visit them under the watchful eye of her mother. She'd sometimes take jam or something homemade to them, and eventually her mother would leave and tell her to run along home after playing. The gypsy children were always easy to make friends with, because they were used to meeting new people as they moved around the countryside. But by the time she was a teenager, going near them had been forbidden, for fear that someone might see her.

'Do you think it will ever change?' Hanna asked.

Dieter looked across at her, and she could see from the hollowness of his eyes that he was as pessimistic about the future of their great country as she was.

'There was a time when I did, but I don't know any more,' he said. 'I want to believe that everyone will come to their senses, but it's as if everyone has fallen for a spell that cannot be broken.'

'If my sister can change the way she sees the world, then perhaps there is hope for everyone,' Hanna eventually said.

'You think she'll keep your secrets? You trust her?' he asked.

She nodded. 'I do. She might still be conflicted, but not when it comes to family. She wouldn't do anything to put any of us in danger.'

Hanna leaned back deeper into her seat, watching the world pass by. Some days she wondered if it was all worth it, but then she'd think about all the children they'd already saved, and all the others still needing their help. Which also made her think about how few of her fellow countrymen or women were doing anything to help those in need. She understood – perhaps she would have been afraid if she'd had children of her own to keep safe too – but it still broke her heart thinking of their acceptance of such cruelty, or simply their indifference to what was happening. But seeing the way Ava had changed, it did give her hope that perhaps others would begin to change, too.

The children in her ambulance now faced a long journey; they had to pass through the resistance network in France and make it to Portugal before they'd be truly safe, but Hanna knew they were doing everything they could to give them a chance. She knew little about what happened once she passed them over, but she knew the city they would be billeted to, and she'd secretly recorded copies of their paperwork to ensure that, one day, it would be possible to find them.

There was only so far they could plausibly take the ambulance, and so they were heading for their usual meeting spot, just far enough out of Berlin on a country road that they wouldn't be seen. Another ambulance always met them, and so long as they all stuck to their cover story, even if they were stopped they knew they shouldn't have any problems.

'He's just ahead up there,' Hanna said, sitting up straighter as she looked into the distance. 'Let's get this done as quickly as possible, just like last time.'

They pulled over on to the side of the road, and Hanna's heart began to race as it always did. Not so much from adrenalin as fear of something going wrong; because it wasn't only her life hanging in the balance if it did.

Once they'd stopped, she ran around the back and pulled open the two doors, hauling them back and smiling at the two young children sitting there. Even though they were perfectly healthy, they'd been bundled up as if they were unwell, their little cases of belongings hidden beneath the stretcher beds.

'Hello, my loves,' Hanna said brightly, climbing in and dropping a kiss on one head, and then the other. 'Remember how I told you we must hurry when it's time to put you in the other ambulance?'

Both children nodded, their eyes wide.

'Well, we're ready to do that now. So let's get your things and hurry along.'

Hanna helped the little girl first, taking her hand and reaching for her case. She took her papers out and pinned them to her coat so they wouldn't get lost, before passing her out to Dieter. Then she helped the little boy, lifting him as he trembled, hating how scared he was.

'Come on, we just have to move you to the next ambulance.'

She paused for a moment, feeling his little warm body in her arms, remembering what it had been like to hold her own son, to be a mother, to have a child cradled against her chest. Sometimes the memories caught her at the hardest of times.

'Hanna?'

'Coming,' she said quickly, checking the boy's papers and belongings before passing him out, too.

When she climbed out she followed Dieter to the next ambulance, watching as the children were loaded in and waving to them. Sometimes they had to hide the children, but these two had papers and a good cover story, and they'd decided it was easiest to move them in plain sight. If they acted as if they had nothing to hide, then they would be relaxed if they were questioned, which could be the difference between being successful or not – the SS were experts at detecting fear, and she didn't want to give them any reason to doubt the story the children would give if they were stopped.

'See you next time,' said the other ambulance driver and nurse.

Hanna nodded, standing there on the road as they pulled away, until Dieter touched her shoulder, his hand heavy. She wished she could hold the children for longer, show them how much they were loved, soak up the feeling of having a little one in her arms.

'We need to go, too.'

She turned to follow him, wiping her eyes and wondering how life had become so cruel that two little children were being smuggled into another country in order to stay alive, while their parents were either still in hiding or being sent to a camp where they might or might not live. The more she heard about the camps, the more convinced she became that no one would ever return.

'Let us pray for a night free from bombings,' Dieter said with a sigh. 'The other night I almost stayed in my bed. I was so exhausted I couldn't face dragging myself to the shelter.'

'Would you have been fine?' she asked, understanding how he felt. 'If you'd stayed?'

Dieter looked over at her, taking his eyes from the road for a second. 'That night I would have been, our house was missed. But at the last moment, I thought about Amelia, and I couldn't stop thinking that there was a chance she could come home, that she might just survive whatever hell she's living through right now, and then how angry would she be with me? That I was too lazy to climb out of bed and take myself to safety without her there to hurry me along?'

Hanna started to laugh despite her sadness, appreciating his effort to lighten the mood. It began as a giggle at the way he spoke, as if he were genuinely terrified of his wife hunting him down, so cross at him for his laziness, and suddenly they were both laughing so hard that she could barely catch her breath. Hanna laughed like she hadn't in such a long time, her cheeks aching and her belly tender when she finally stopped.

She reached out to put her hand over Dieter's then, knowing how quickly laughter could turn to tears, how much he was hurting despite his attempt at humour in an effort to cheer her up. He was like family to her, and she knew that if she had the choice of reuniting him with his wife, she'd swap places with her in an instant, to give him back his family.

'She's going to come home, I know she is,' Hanna whispered. 'We have to keep believing in miracles, otherwise what do we have left?'

They rode the rest of the way in silence, Hanna's thoughts turning as they often did in moments of idleness to the day she'd lost everything.

Hanna smiled to herself as she made a cup of coffee, planning on sitting outside in the sun to relax until Michael and Hugo returned home. She knew how fortunate she was to have her husband at home still, as his work as a pharmacist had meant he was exempt from receiving his military orders, but she was still exhausted. Running around after a toddler was never easy, and she'd had a week of working the night shift at the hospital, so a moment to herself was something she'd been craving for days.

Once she had her coffee in hand, Hanna made her way outside, taking a sip as she sat. She closed her eyes and enjoyed the feel of the sunshine on her skin, tempted to take off more clothes to work on her tan. Before having Hugo, she'd gone to the park on her days off and sunbathed with friends, but now she barely had time to even see the sun, let alone lie in it.

Hanna sighed and opened her eyes, taking another sip of her coffee. But her perfect little oasis of calm was ruined by a loud bang, followed by screams for help. She set her cup down and hurried inside to find her shoes, before making her way out of the door. She followed the screams down the road, surprised to see a crowd gathered on the street not far from her house.

Hanna began to run, realising that there must have been an accident of some kind and wanting to help if she could. There were far fewer doctors in the city than there once were, and she knew how long it could take for an ambulance to arrive.

The first thing she noticed as she neared was the shiny black Mercedes that was parked at an odd angle, and then the sight of a short man yelling at another man, who appeared to be the driver. It was Dr Joseph Goebbels – she'd have recognised him anywhere – and another high-ranking Nazi officer who looked vaguely familiar to her, perhaps someone her father was acquainted with.

'Drive me back to the office at once, and watch your speed this time.'

'Yes, sir, but what about the man and child? Should we not wait for an ambulance or to give a statement to—'

'Who cares about the man? He isn't a soldier, so he's of little concern to me, and the child is already dead. Someone else can see to it.'

Hanna was pushing her way through the crowd when she heard him mention a child, and it only strengthened her resolve to help.

'Please let me through, I'm a nurse.'

As she moved past the final person in her way, Hanna stopped, her eyes landing on a little navy shoe that was lying on its side, on the road. She blinked, as a wave of panic ran through her. That was Hugo's shoe, was it not? She'd squished his tiny foot into it only fifteen minutes earlier, had chosen them to match his new woollen coat.

Please, not Hugo. Don't let it be Hugo.

But the moment she saw the child's body, his legs contorted in the most unnatural of angles, she knew. The dead child spoken about so cavalierly was her son. A sob erupted from inside of her as she ran forward, dropping to her knees and falling over the body of her little boy as she listened for a breath, felt for a pulse, tried to frantically locate a heartbeat that would tell her he was still alive, that they'd been wrong.

The child is already dead. The words she'd overheard kept running through her mind as she tried in vain to wake him, before cradling his head, her tears falling on to his too-white skin as she sobbed.

She heard a noise then and was pulled from her grief, looking around and realising that Michael was lying nearby. The moans were coming from him, and as she scrambled over to him on hands and knees, she saw the pool of blood staining the concrete and knew it was coming from his head.

'Michael,' she whispered. 'Stay with me, please. I can't lose you, too. Please don't leave me.'

But as she held his hand, gripping his palm tightly against hers as if she could will him to live, she heard the last of his breath shudder from between his lips. And at the same time, she looked up to see the Mercedes pulling away, its angry beeps from the horn dispersing the crowd.

The man who was their Führer's second-in-command had hit a child; a father and his son. And despite telling them all that German children were the most precious things to their nation, they'd driven off without seeming to care about the life they'd taken.

Hanna crawled back to her son, as two kindly older women bent down beside her and tried to offer her comfort, not stopping her as she carried him back with her, collapsing beside Michael as she tried to pull her husband and son into her arms together.

They were only supposed to be going for ice cream. They were supposed to come home to play in the garden together, to lie in the sun and stare up at the blue sky after he'd had his little treat, before she put him down for a nap.

Instead, Hanna had lost them both, and the man responsible had acted as if he'd hit a worthless animal instead of a beloved father and son. How could they have driven off as if nothing had happened? As if they hadn't taken two precious lives? Her darling husband and son, simply walking hand in hand in the afternoon sunshine, their lives snatched away from her without warning.

Hanna wailed, and it was like nothing she'd ever heard before, her cries more animal than human as someone tried unsuccessfully to pull her away from her family and off the road. All she wanted to do was curl up and die with them, to not suffer the pain of going home without them.

Her beautiful boy and darling husband, the loves of her life, were gone.

Chapter Nine

Three weeks later, Hanna arrived back home to the country house. There was only an hour or so until her mother and father would host their glittering dinner party, and she'd been asked to return home for it to assist her mother. Ava would be here soon, too, having convinced their father that she was ready to be part of their world, of their deception, and Hanna only hoped she was as ready as she thought she was.

'Thank goodness you're here,' her mother said when she found her upstairs in her bedroom, getting dressed. She had a small glass on her dresser, and as Hanna watched, she drained the liquor that was left in it. 'I told your father I don't know how many more of these evenings I can stand.'

'Even as your skin crawls,' Hanna said, coming to stand behind her mother and taking a pin from her to secure her hair at the back, 'just remember that they are the traitors, not us. We have every right to hold our heads high.'

Her hand closed over her mother's shoulder as Liselotte spoke. 'I know, my love, I know.'

'We moved two patients today,' she said, smiling at her mother in the mirror. But even Hanna could see what a sad smile it was, and she certainly wasn't fooling her mother.

'Well, I shall think of that when I'm smiling through my teeth tonight.'

Hanna made sure her mother's up-do was perfect, before bending down to whisper in her ear. 'I need to go upstairs to see Eliana. Could you help me so I can go up there for maybe ten minutes?'

Her mother stood. 'Of course. Why don't you go and choose your dress and I'll set Zelda to a task so that she doesn't come upstairs.'

Hanna went to her room, closing the door and going to her wardrobe, standing on tiptoes to get the shoebox down that she'd placed there. She took it to her bed and sat, opening the lid and looking at all the pieces of paper inside. She knew without counting how many there were – fourteen – but still she lifted each one, saying the name of each child before letting the paper flutter back down into the box. Then she reached into her pocket and took out the names of the two children from today, wondering where they were at that exact moment as she added them to the box.

When she'd started collecting the names, she hadn't known how to record them safely or what to do with her notes, but last night she'd realised what she needed to do. It was as if the wind had changed; she'd had this overwhelming feeling that something was catching up to her, that she needed to have a safe place for the names before it was too late.

'Hanna?'

Her mother called to her from the other side of the door, tapping gently before coming in.

She put the lid back on the box and hurried down the hall with her mother, being as quiet as they could be as they pulled the attic stairs down.

'I'll come back in ten minutes, you don't have long.'

Hanna climbed up, the box under her arm, and as her mother closed the door she blinked a few times for her eyes to adjust. The smell was unusual, a combination of body odour and perfume – of too many people and belongings in the same space – but she refused to wrinkle her nose.

All four of the Goldmans stayed where they were, used to being silent and moving as little as possible during the day, and so Hanna walked carefully over to Eliana and David, whispering hellos as she went. They'd already been informed about the party taking place downstairs, so Hanna didn't mention it again, but she did field some whispered questions from David the moment she sat down.

'We heard bombing last night,' David said. 'What's happening? Where are they targeting?'

'The Luftwaffe have been bombing southern England and this is the retaliation for it,' she said. 'Ava tells me that less than half of the planes made it, though, although I'm sure it will be reported as a great victory for us.'

David and Eliana leaned forward, clearly eager to hear about all the events that had been taking place.

'But it seems that the English have been more successful,' she continued. 'The RAF bombed Magdeburg again overnight, that's what you would have heard, and they were relentless, so it's no wonder you heard it from here.'

'What do we do, if they hit here?' David asked. 'We're like sitting ducks up here in an air raid!'

Hanna waited for a moment as Eliana calmed him, listening while she reminded him to keep his voice low.

'I'm tired of keeping my voice down,' he muttered. 'I want to be out there, I want to be fighting instead of hiding away.'

'I'm sorry,' Hanna said, because there was nothing else she could say. 'I wish I could find a way to get you out of here, but moving Jews anywhere now is almost impossible, you know that. Father is working on false papers for you, but these things take time, not to mention the risk involved.'

'But I could help you, Hanna. I had already begun my medical training, I could help to save the children in your care.' He looked away, and she could hear the emotion clogging his voice. 'Perhaps I would be better off in a camp. At least there I could try to help, I could be useful to someone.'

'I understand, David. At least, I understand as much as anyone can,' she said. 'But if you were caught and taken to a camp? There is every chance you wouldn't even make it past the first night, that you wouldn't get the chance to help anyone. At least this way . . .'

He nodded, and she saw the man he was before, the young man who'd been full of dreams of becoming a doctor, who'd always been the first to open the door to their apartment block if the Goldmans were coming down the stairs at the same time as her and Ava or her mother, always sporting a smile. A man whose dreams were still alive, but hanging on by a thread.

They all fell silent then, and Hanna took the chance to open her shoebox, knowing she only had a few minutes before her mother returned for her.

'Eliana, I'd like to ask you to do something for me,' Hanna said. 'These are the records of all the children I've managed to smuggle out of Berlin, and I would like you to seal each record in a glass jar for me.'

Eliana took the box from her, taking out the papers one by one and passing them to David to look at. Frau and Herr Goldman edged closer too, their eyes on Hanna.

'All these children? They are all safe because of you?' Herr Goldman asked.

'I can only hope they're safe, and no, not because of me. I am only one small part in a much bigger network of people through Berlin, France and Portugal. We have done our best to smuggle them out of Germany.'

'Where will you hide the jars?' Eliana asked. 'Do you want us to keep them up here?'

'I intend on burying them all in the garden this weekend, where no one will ever think to look, then we'll plant vegetables over the top of them so it doesn't appear obvious that we've been digging.'

Eliana smiled. 'That's ingenious. Of course we'll help. It's a beautiful thing you're doing, Hanna.'

Hanna heard a tap from below and she quickly leaned forward to give Eliana a hug. 'You'll find the jars stored somewhere over there, in one of those large boxes,' she said. 'I have to go, but stay quiet as a mouse tonight, won't you?'

'We will,' David said.

Hanna looked at them one last time, as Eliana cleared her throat before speaking.

'Would you allow me to do a jar for my family? To record our names and our family tree?'

Hanna's heart ached for the Goldmans every day, but to hear Eliana say those words, to know that there was a chance they wouldn't make it to the end of the war, if there ever was an end, was like a knife being pressed into her. Seeing Eliana and David up here broke her heart every single time.

'Of course.'

Within seconds the stairs had been lowered, and Hanna hurried down, helping her mother to secure them quickly behind her.

'You reminded them about tonight?'

'Mama, I did, but I don't think it's something they're likely to forget, given who our guests are.'

They stood for a moment, breathing, staring into each other's eyes, both dreading what was to come. The moment the door to their home opened, they would have to move, act, feel, *laugh* as if they had never been happier, as if it were such a privilege to have a group of monsters and their wives in their home as guests.

'We will be all right, Hanna, we always are. We make a good team.'

She leaned into her mother, resting her head on her shoulder. 'I know, Mama. I know.' Only in truth, pretending had never seemed harder, which was most troubling when she was expected to give the performance of her lifetime. But she did have something to be grateful for – no longer having to hide who she was and what she did from her sister.

Less than an hour later, Hanna looked at her reflection and barely recognised herself. Her cheekbones seemed to be more prominent, her mouth wider, but she imagined it was because she'd lost some of the fullness from her face in recent months. She forced a smile, seeing the way it lit up her eyes and transformed her face, and she knew that by the end of the night her cheeks would hurt from having to hold it for so long.

If only my cheeks hurt from laughing, from smiling without abandon with my family. With my friends.

She gave herself one last, long look, before taking a deep breath and squaring her shoulders. *I can do this. I just have to remember what it's all for, what we're protecting, and it will all be worth it.*

Ava came to stand beside her then, her fingers closing around Hanna's as she stared back at her own reflection, and Hanna clasped her hand tighter, feeling the tremble in her touch. Ava was as scared as her, or perhaps even more so, for it was her first night of truly being part of the subterfuge.

'Are you ready?' Hanna whispered.

Ava nodded. 'As ready as I'll ever be.'

Chapter Ten

Hanna walked down the stairs, her eyes downcast as her fingers danced over the handrail. They ached to grip it tightly, but she wouldn't let herself; she had a part to play, after all, and Ava was only a few steps behind her. When she did look up, she saw her mother, poised and elegant, the picture of the perfect wife, her blonde hair swept up off her neck, showing off the beautiful diamond necklace Hanna's father had given her for their twentieth wedding anniversary the year before the war began. Then she saw her father, who was smiling up at her as he stood with a few of his colleagues, all dressed in perfectly starched uniforms, their gazes fixed on her.

She knew what all the men were thinking; they would like her for themselves or for their sons. None of the guests here tonight would even know that she was a widow, not a maid. She was thankful that they would be less interested in leering at Ava, knowing that she was already promised to one of their own.

'Here she is,' her father said, beaming as he came forward and took her arm, kissing her cheek. 'I trust you all remember my eldest daughter, Hanna?'

She smiled and used her free hand to smooth imaginary wrinkles from her dress, as she heard Ava being greeted by her mother and the women surrounding her. But it took everything to keep her smile in place as she saw the full glasses of wine and smelled the lavish array of food being cooked for the party. The table would be set as if for a feast, the bellies of all the men around her full to brimming, when the families she treated at the hospital were so hungry that their ribs were protruding, their ration books doing little to sustain them. So many were having to cope with so little, yet this glittering set of the Nazi elite hadn't been subject to so much as coffee rations.

'Fräulein Müller, what a pleasure to see you again,' one of the men said, extending his hand to her. She politely extended hers in reply, trying not to cringe when he pressed a wet kiss to it, holding on for longer than was necessary, his moustache itching her skin. 'Tell me, is there a lucky husband-to-be waiting in the wings yet? Or could I interest you in meeting my son when he's home on leave?'

She glanced at her father, who only smiled at her. 'I've been so busy with my work at the hospital that I haven't had the opportunity to meet a young man, unfortunately,' she said. 'But I'm very much looking forward to all our victorious men coming home in the near future.'

'Well, between us, we have some very eligible sons who are to be posted closer to home soon,' said one of the other men, nudging her father with his elbow. 'We would be only too pleased to introduce you.'

'Darling, come with me,' her mother said as she appeared, sweeping her into her embrace and flashing her most dazzling smile at the men. If Hanna attracted the men's interest, her mother positively captured them. She seemed to know just how to move, how to use her eyes, to distract a man from almost everything, without doing anything that could be seen as improper. 'No more talk of weddings or husbands, we already have our Ava to be married as soon as the war is over, and dear Hanna here is very busy with her nursing. There is plenty of time for marriage, she's still young, after all.'

There was a grumble between the men, immediately arguing over how unbelievable it was that women were having to fill so many men's jobs. But she'd heard it all before; a woman's place was at home, tending to her husband and producing babies. Sex was supposed to fulfil a purpose only, it was not to be for pleasure, but simply to keep populating their great country with endless children. Only, the old men ogling her tonight certainly seemed to have pleasure in mind. She wished she could scream at them that she wasn't some unmarried maiden but a widow who was still grieving her husband. She doubted they'd even care if they knew; all they saw was a young woman who fulfilled their little list of ideals, which made her perfect breeding stock.

'You look beautiful, as always,' her mother whispered to her, before taking her by the hand to introduce her to the women she'd been talking to. 'Just keep smiling and remember to breathe, that's all you have to do to charm them. Make them think you're pleased to see them.'

'Hanna, I hear you're a nurse,' one of the wives said, taking a sip of her wine. 'Tell us, how bad are the injuries from the bombs?'

'I heard that they are targeting children and factories where they know mothers are working!' said another.

Hanna looked at the wide-eyed women forming a circle around her, and she wondered what they truly knew about the war. They were like pretty birds kept in a cage, with no idea what happened outside in the world. She looked over at Ava, who was smiling politely.

'It is true, many of the injured are women and children,' Hanna said. 'I spend most of my time on the paediatric ward, caring for those children who need us most, and sometimes I'm deployed with an ambulance driver to provide triage care at the scene of a bombing or fire.'

The women all gasped, a collective intake of breath that made the men take notice and look over at them.

'What is being shared that's so dramatic over there?' one of them called out.

'I must apologise, I was shocking these lovely ladies with tales of injuries,' Hanna said sweetly, taking a small step back and looping her hand through Ava's arm when she came closer. 'From the recent air raids.'

Hanna almost lost her breath then, as Goebbels himself appeared. He must have been using the lavatory when she'd come downstairs, because she certainly hadn't seen him. A hot flush came over her body, and her mother took a tight hold of her hand, beckoning Zelda to bring him a glass of wine.

'Tell away, Fräulein Müller,' he said. 'Or do you still go by your married name of Frau Wittelsbach?'

She gulped, but her father came to her rescue, seeing her distress. 'Joseph, I think it's important that everyone, even our womenfolk, understand how barbaric our enemy is, don't you think? I have always encouraged Hanna to share the truth of the horrific injuries she's seeing, and I know our new daily truths will help our womenfolk understand our enemy all the more, wouldn't you say?'

'I agree wholeheartedly,' Goebbels replied with a smile. 'Ivan is a vicious enemy, ape-like in intelligence but brutal in his fight, but the English are cunning. They don't see our vision as clearly as our friends in Poland or Italy, so they are presenting more of a challenge.'

The room was silent when he spoke. Goebbels was second only to Hitler, and a man to be both revered and feared, so no one would dare speak over him.

'What do you think, *Fräulein* Müller?'

Hanna dipped her head slightly, taking a slow breath before meeting his gaze. *It's as if he knows what he took from me, but he can't possibly. There is no way he could know, there is no way he could understand my loss.* But questioning her surname before had made her feel as if he were taunting her.

'I think it was the right thing for many families to move from the city, because you are right about how cunning they are,' she said. 'We've lost too many good Germans to their bombs, and it's imperative we protect the children.' Her voice caught on the last word as Goebbels held her gaze. 'They are our future, after all, which means nothing is more important than them.'

'Well said.' Goebbels nodded and gave her a brief smile, before turning away.

Hanna looked to her father then, expecting him to say something, but when she saw the sweat that had broken out on his brow, the way his hand had moved to his chest, she knew she had to act before one of the men standing near him noticed that something was wrong.

'Papa,' she said, rushing to his side and taking his arm. 'I'm so sorry to interrupt, but I forgot that I—'

'Leave your father, girl,' one of the men said, chuckling to himself as he gestured for her to move out of the way. 'Unless Hitler himself needs your—'

'Sir, I do apologise, but it's regarding the brandy and cigars for the men after dinner,' she whispered demurely, giving him a quick smile. 'I wouldn't want you gentlemen to be disappointed.'

That brought about another round of laughter, but this time not at her expense, thankfully, and she clutched her father's arm tightly as she walked him down the hall and to his office.

When they reached it, she shut the door behind them and helped him to the leather sofa. His face was pale and clammy now, and she loosened his top button and tie. 'You need to see a doctor,' she whispered. 'I don't have enough experience in—'

'No doctor,' he said as he shut his eyes, one hand over his chest. 'You know I can't.'

Hanna felt his pulse, staring down at him with concern, but she froze when she heard the door click behind them, her breath catching in her throat.

'Ava!' she gasped, letting go of her father's wrist. 'You gave me a fright.'

'He's sick, isn't he?' Ava said, blinking away tears. 'I knew something was wrong, I knew that it wasn't just a cold when he was unwell at work last week, and I can see that he is not a well man now.'

Hanna caught her bottom lip in her teeth, meeting Ava's gaze before slowly nodding.

'Am I the last in our family to hear this news, too?'

She was spared from having to answer when their father spoke, but she did put on some music, knowing how paranoid her father was about their conversations.

'It's important that no one knows, that we keep this between these four walls, between the members of our family,' he said, in a voice so low and raspy that it forced Ava to come closer to hear him. 'Any sign of serious illness or incapacity will be seen as weakness, and that's not something I'm prepared to give them, not yet.'

'We've been trying to hide it,' Hanna whispered, 'but he won't see a doctor and I think it's his heart.'

Hanna saw the way Ava's grip on her wine glass tightened, the tears that slipped down her cheeks. 'We shall give him a moment to catch his breath, give the morphine time to work. I was able to take some from the hospital, and a small amount seems to help without impeding his ability to function.'

'He's going back out there?' Ava asked.

'He doesn't exactly have a choice.'

Ava wiped her cheeks and lifted her chin. 'Tell me what I can do to help, then. Should I go back out there or stay here?'

'Go and charm them all, make them forget that Papa is missing,' Hanna said, reaching for her hand. 'We'll join you shortly, I promise. Just give me time to treat the pain and get some colour back into his face.'

'I can do that. I see these men every day in the office. I know exactly how to behave around them.'

Ava bent down and kissed their father's cheek as Hanna retrieved the morphine she had hidden in his desk drawer, and within minutes she'd straightened her father's tie and helped him to his feet, walking arm in arm with him as he rejoined the gathered men.

'I'm going to see if there's anything I can do in the kitchen,' Hanna said, letting go of her father's arm and giving the men what she hoped was her most captivating smile. 'Please excuse me.'

'Karl, what took you so long?' one of the men asked, as he clapped her father on the back.

Hanna held her breath, seeing the pain etched on her father's face as he coughed, his hand rising to his chest, but Ava's quick laughter captured the men's attention, and Hanna had never been so grateful for her sister. She glanced at her father, seeing that Ava's distraction had given him time to right himself. Ava hadn't been lying when she'd said she could handle their guests.

As Hanna walked away, she heard murmurs about her beauty from the women gathered, about what a waste it was that she hadn't had children yet, that she was having to work such long hours. But when she reached the door leading to the kitchen, she turned, not to look at the women talking about her, but at Goebbels. She had a feeling he was watching her, that his eyes had followed her, but when she saw him he had his back to her, speaking to the group of men who seemed enraptured by whatever tale he was telling. *It's my mind playing tricks on me, he doesn't know at all. He doesn't know what he took from me, and there's no way he can know about my father.*

Hanna turned and kept walking, finding Zelda in the kitchen, surrounded by food. It was all she could do not to collapse right there, her legs wobbling from her earlier subterfuge.

'Hanna, are you feeling all right?' Zelda asked, stopping what she was doing.

Hanna nodded. 'So long as you don't tell me to go back out there, I'll be fine. I just need a moment away from it all.' She closed her eyes for a second, gripping the edge of the kitchen counter.

'Hanna—'

'I'm fine, or at least I will be. Let me prepare something for you to take home tonight,' she said, opening her eyes and fixing her smile again, her moment already over. 'This is far too much food for one dinner party, and I dare say that no one out there will be interested in taking leftovers home with them.'

Zelda moved around the kitchen and looked into Hanna's eyes, taking her hand for a moment. They had an unspoken understanding between them, both having loved and lost during the war.

'Take your time, it's nice to have some company in the kitchen.'

'Thank you for understanding,' she said, squeezing Zelda's hand.

They both wiped their eyes and Hanna surveyed the feast once more. 'I shall start putting everything on the table while you finish here. This is a meal fit for a king.' But it wasn't just the food she had to prepare – if she were to sit at the table, she was to be charming and demure, to model what an excellent daughter her father had raised, which was always the best way to elevate one's status within the party. Which also meant she was going to have to pretend to be interested in at least one of the sons who'd been mentioned to her, for she knew it wouldn't take long before the subject of courtship or marriage was brought up again.

Thankfully, the women present were busy talking about their own children over dinner, and Hanna found herself listening intently to Magda Goebbels telling them all about how one of her daughters had recently joined the Jungmädelbund, and how gorgeous she looked in her little uniform. It only made Hanna's smile harder to hold, because it brought back memories of when she was first accepted into her local group, and the humiliating exercise of having to take off her clothes and lie very still while an old male Nazi doctor inspected her. All she remembered being told that day was to stay very still when she tried to squirm, and then eventually she was told that she was a very special girl. At that time, she hadn't known what they were trying to tell her; it was only later that she realised they were referring to her as being the very best of breeding stock. The blonde-haired, blue-eyed, healthy-looking girls were always the ones that left the doctor's room with sweet treats in their pockets as their reward.

Hanna forced her memories from her mind and smiled along with the other women, trying ever so hard to swallow her mouthful of food instead of spitting it out on to the table in disgust.

Once the evening was over, and she'd stood beside her mother and father and bade everyone goodnight, Hanna felt as if she could collapse.

'Great show tonight,' her mother whispered, kicking off her shoes and massaging her feet. 'Please tell me I won't have to host another glittering evening for a few months now though, Karl?'

'That, my love, is a promise I cannot make.'

Hanna watched as her father pressed a kiss to her mother's forehead as he passed. She knew he was struggling – both with his health and his dedication to the cause – and evenings like this were his worst nightmare as much as they were hers.

'You're feeling all right now?' her mother asked him.

'I'm fine. Nothing to worry about, not with Hanna looking after me.'

Her mother sighed, but didn't stop Hanna's father from walking away, heading straight to his office.

'Did you make certain that Zelda had food to take home?' Her mother's attention was on her now.

Hanna nodded. 'I did. She had plenty.'

'Good.' Her mother sighed. 'Ava, could you prepare the leftovers to take upstairs?'

Hanna and her mother walked around the house as Ava went into the kitchen, checking each door and double-checking the drapes were pulled tight, before carefully putting together plates for the Goldmans. They'd become a good team, and Hanna had seen more and more over the past months how similar they were. Her mother was also the only person she could talk to about her loss, about how much she struggled at times, which had brought them even closer.

All three women made their way upstairs, and Hanna set the plates on the ground so she could pull down the attic stairs. Soon the light from one of the oil lamps shone down, and Hanna called up to the family.

'You can come down and stretch your legs now,' she said. 'Everyone has gone.'

Eliana appeared first, helping her mother down after her, followed by David and then his father. They all blinked at her, their eyes adjusting to the light in the house. She'd told them not to make a sound or have so much as a lamp going from the moment the first guest arrived, so she knew it must have been a very long, very dark evening for them up until then.

'We have beef, some roast goose, potatoes, carrots and fresh bread,' Hanna said, surprised when Ava turned and walked away, but deciding to let her go. 'Oh, and some chocolates.'

'This looks amazing,' Eliana said, but Hanna noticed she was looking at Ava's retreating figure.

'I'm only sorry you had to wait so long for it,' Hanna said brightly. 'I can tell you it tastes excellent.'

The family had become much quieter recently, and although Hanna hadn't shared her worries with her own family yet, she was certain her mother would have noticed, too. Hanna also understood – the Goldmans been cooped up like chickens for so long, and she couldn't imagine how they were coming to terms with their new life being so small. Not to mention they were probably worried about Ava having discovered them.

But they had a life, and that was what she had to keep reminding herself when she began to fret about them. It wasn't a full life, but so long as they were safe for now, they might one day have a full life again. She would work on Ava.

'Come on, let's stretch our legs before we have dinner,' David instructed his family. 'We need to move as much as we can so our muscles don't waste away.'

Eliana stepped aside as David and her parents walked past, and Hanna turned to her, sensing she wanted to say something.

'Are we still safe?' Eliana asked.

'Of course. Why would you ask such a thing? You are as safe as you were yesterday, and the week before that.'

Eliana reached for her hands. 'I mean now that Ava knows. Do you trust her?'

'Yes,' Hanna said, holding her hands in return. 'I do trust her. If I did not? I would have moved you somewhere immediately, I would never knowingly put you in harm's way. She's just struggling, that's all, and I imagine most of it is guilt.'

She watched as Eliana went to say something else, opening her mouth, before a loud knocking sounded out downstairs. Hanna froze, turning to her mother. The impatient knock sounded out on the timber again.

'Quickly,' her mother cried, as the Goldmans ran back to the attic stairs again, picking up their plates and sending some of the food flying.

Hanna ran past her mother and down the main stairs to answer the door, knowing that the longer it took them to answer, the worse the situation could be. Had her father fallen asleep? Ava appeared wide-eyed at the top of the stairs, already changed into her night-gown, her hair loose about her shoulders.

'Papa!' Hanna called as she ran down the last two steps. 'Papa, someone is here!'

Her father appeared and strode ahead of her, flinging the door wide as she hovered behind, expecting the worst. But it was one of the officers they had hosted, his cheeks still ruddy from the alcohol he'd consumed.

'Back so soon?' her father said with a laugh. 'If you'd wanted another brandy, all you had to do was ask.'

'My wife left her scarf here,' the man said, walking straight on into the house and clapping her father on the back. 'But another brandy would have been an excellent idea.'

'I shall find it for you, just a moment,' Hanna said quickly, frantically looking around the room for it before he happened to march off to find it himself. Within seconds she spied a pale pink silk scarf and collected it to give him, just as a thud sounded out from upstairs.

She imagined she visibly paled at the noise, her hand trembling as she held out the scarf. 'I must go up and check on Mama,' she said, deciding not to hide her alarm. 'That sounded as if she might have fallen. I certainly hope she didn't have too much to drink tonight.'

That made both men chuckle, and Hanna dashed up the stairs to the sound of them joking about women not being able to hold their drink, hoping her quick thinking had sounded plausible, and not wanting to look back downstairs to make sure she'd fooled their guest. But as she neared the landing at the top of the stairs she paused, watching as Ava bent to collect an errant bread roll that must have rolled there as the Goldmans went back into hiding, tucking it behind her back. And she was only thankful that she hadn't had to explain why a bread roll had fallen to the SS officer standing at the foot of the stairs.

'Sorry to scare you, darling!' her mother called out in a theatrical voice. 'I tripped in the bathroom!'

Her mother's voice was loud enough that it would reach the men downstairs, and Hanna breathed a sigh of relief. They'd had two near misses in one evening; how much longer could their luck possibly hold?

Chapter Eleven

Ava

The following week, Ava didn't immediately look up when she heard someone walk into the office. She was concentrating on the document she had to type, so it wasn't until she heard someone clear his throat, and realised that the other secretaries had stopped tapping and were now silent, that she lifted her gaze.

When she did, her stomach felt as if it were sliding straight to the floor, and she couldn't help but think about the replica she'd been about to start – an identical second letter to pass to her father before she left for the day.

Heinrich was standing near the door, in uniform and holding a small bunch of flowers, and she could tell by the collective sigh in the office that she was immediately the envy of all the other women. He looked so handsome, and exactly as he had when she'd last seen him, with his blond hair neatly parted on one side and brushed back, his blue eyes twinkling as he watched her, his lips moving into a smile as soon as she met his gaze. Even with her recent change of heart about everything that was happening around her, she still managed to forget everything else and jump out of her chair to greet him. Just seeing him was enough to set her heart to racing.

'Heinrich, you're home! I can't believe it.'

He grinned and passed her the flowers, stepping forward to kiss her cheek. Warmth flooded her body when his hand brushed her waist, and she knew her face would be bright red from his open display of affection.

'You look as beautiful as I remembered,' he said. 'What a sight for sore eyes.'

Ava laughed, gazing up at him. 'Thank you. I can't believe you're here, after all those months of writing letters . . .'

She glanced over her shoulder, noticing that no one had returned to their typing, more interested in watching what was unfolding before them than resuming their work.

'I can see you're very busy, but may I come back and walk you home after work? Or perhaps even take you out to dinner tonight?'

Heinrich took her hand and she let him, remembering immediately how much she'd enjoyed his company before he'd left, and the thrill she'd always felt when he touched her. Just having him standing in front of her reminded her exactly why she'd fallen in love with him.

'Of course. I will check with Papa and—'

'I've already been to see him, to ask permission to take you out. Although I did promise that there would be a small group of us, so that there was no need for him to worry about a chaperone.'

Her heart skipped a beat. 'May I ask Hanna to join us too, then?'

'Of course. I'll come back for you at five.'

Ava watched as he took her hand, holding it for a moment before giving her one last smile.

'It's so good to see you again, Ava. I've been thinking about this moment for months, and you're just as pretty as I remembered.'

She smiled back at him. 'It's good to see you again, too, Heinrich. What a lovely surprise it is, having you home.'

Her fears about how she'd feel seeing him again had well and truly disappeared by the time he walked backwards a few steps, winking before turning and leaving, and she clutched the flowers to her chest as she returned to her desk, trying to ignore the excited whispers around her. Her mind knew that they were now on different paths, but her heart wanted to believe that she could change the way he thought. Her father had warned her not to talk to him about her change in sympathies, and she would never disobey him, but surely if he could change, then Heinrich could, too? What was to say that her fiancé wasn't also repulsed by some of the things happening around him?

'If I were you, I'd marry him while he's home on leave,' Greta whispered as she passed her on the way back to her desk, fanning at her face. 'He's one of the most gorgeous men I've ever seen.'

Ava just laughed, placing her flowers on her desk and trying to concentrate on her work, even though she knew it was going to be almost impossible. But when she glanced at the chair Lina used to sit in, her happiness turned to sadness, because it was Lina she would usually have whispered and chatted to, and she still didn't know where her friend had gone.

At five p.m., Ava and Heinrich had walked the short distance from her office to her apartment block, her hand tucked into the crook of his arm. Despite everything, she'd felt special and swelled with pride when Goebbels himself had appeared to speak to Heinrich, commending him on his achievements and welcoming him home. Although she still felt as if her hands were shaking. Only minutes before Heinrich had arrived, she'd slipped the replica document into her father's hand when she'd embraced him, and she couldn't shake the feeling that someone could have seen.

'You haven't mentioned how long you're back for?' Ava asked. 'Is it for a few days?' She intended on soaking up every moment of time she possibly could with him.

'Longer, actually,' he said. 'I believe I'm to be posted close to Berlin.'

'In a new role?'

He winked at her. 'That's top secret for now, but I'll tell you just as soon as I'm given clearance.'

Her stomach flipped, as it had done earlier when she'd first seen him. She supposed it was because she was so torn between excitement about seeing him and terror over the idea that someone she loved might not come around to her new way of thinking – and quite what that might mean for her. But now that he was here, part of her wondered if he even knew about the atrocities with the Jews, about what was happening in the camps.

'I'll only be a short time getting ready,' she said when they reached her building. 'I'm certain Papa wouldn't mind you coming up to wait?'

Heinrich flashed her a smile. 'If you're certain.'

She nodded and they both went upstairs, the lights indicating that Hanna was already home and preparing dinner in the kitchen.

'Your mother's not here with you?' he asked.

'No, she's stayed at the country house,' Ava said, glancing at him over her shoulder. 'Papa likes to know she's safe there, far away from the bombings.'

'It must be hard for him, not having her to return to at the end of each day.'

'Hanna!' Ava said excitedly when she saw her sister, happy not to have to continue discussing her mother's whereabouts. 'We have a guest.'

'Heinrich?' Ava saw the almost frightened look that passed over Hanna's face, but she was so quick to correct herself and smile that Ava knew Heinrich wouldn't have noticed. 'How lovely to see you. You're well? No injuries?'

'No injuries,' he replied. 'But I'm in need of a night out, with the very best of company of course. Would you like to join us?'

'I would very much like to join you both,' Hanna replied. 'I shall quickly finish preparing dinner for Papa, in case he comes home early, and then I'll get changed.'

Heinrich sat on the armchair that was her father's, although Ava chose not to ask him to move, and she went to get him a drink of water before hurrying into her bedroom. It took only minutes for Hanna to join her, and her sister closed the door behind her when she entered.

'You knew he was coming home today?' Hanna whispered. 'Why didn't you say something?'

Ava frowned. 'No, I did not. Father just told me that he'd be back later this month, and he surprised me at the office. But I asked him immediately if you could join us as soon as he suggested dinner.'

Hanna's expression changed. 'Do you have any knowledge of what he's been doing, Ava? Has he ever spoken with you about his work?' She sighed. 'I should have discussed this with you sooner.'

Ava shook her head. 'He's been away at the front, that's all I know.'

Hanna pulled her to the bed and sat with her, holding her hands, still whispering. 'Ava, there's a reason he's a favourite among the SS elite. I've heard he's going to be posted to Ravensbrück, the women's concentration camp north of Berlin.'

Ava knew she must have visibly paled because Hanna placed a hand on her cheek, as if to warm her.

'From what I've heard, he has a particular' – Hanna glanced behind her, as if to check he wasn't there, that they weren't being listened to – 'set of *skills*.'

'Skills?'

'We can talk about this later, but just be careful. Your being with him, it means we have every chance of not being discovered, but you have to know that he's ruthless when it comes to following orders. There's a reason he's the protégé of Heinrich Himmler.'

Ava swallowed, feeling sick to her stomach at even having to go back out there again. 'He's always been so kind to me, so sweet. Even when I saw him today, I just know in my heart that he isn't the man you're describing, that—'

'Ava, listen to me. I know this is a lot, but just promise me that you'll be careful. You can't give anything away, no matter how attentive and sweet he is to you. Do you promise? You cannot tell him anything.'

Ava only nodded, and Hanna watched her closely, as if trying to decide whether she believed her or not.

'Say it,' Hanna said. 'I need to hear you say it to me. Promise me that you'll be careful.'

'I promise,' Ava replied, seeing how much it meant to her sister that she did so.

'Let us get ready then,' Hanna said, rising at the same time as she raised her voice, as if she wanted Heinrich to hear them. 'We shall have a glorious night in the company of some dashing young SS men.'

Ava wondered how her sister could put on such a good show, how she could fix her smile and prepare to go out with Heinrich and his friends after telling Ava such horrible things about him. But now it all made sense – the way her father had looked at her when she'd mentioned Heinrich that night in his office, the way he'd warned her about him coming home on leave. Her father had publicly declared that he couldn't want for a better son-in-law and had even thrown them a party before Heinrich had left, but now she was realising that he was likely her father's worst nightmare for a son-in-law.

She dabbed at her eyes and then sat in front of her mirror, knowing that she needed to make herself look nice for him, even though all she wanted was to curl up on her bed in a ball and try to figure it all out in her mind. Now that she'd passed confidential information to her father, she was officially a traitor to her country.

Heinrich couldn't have been more attentive as they sat with his friends that night, which was only making Ava feel more anxious, torn between the man she was seeing and the man her sister had described. She kept looking over at Hanna, who was holding court with two of the other young men and telling them about some particularly gruesome injuries that she'd had to deal with recently. Ava knew it wasn't Hanna's work tales that were fascinating them – her sister had always drawn the eyes of men, young and old – but she admired the way she was able to play such a cat-and-mouse game with them. Hanna might despise the SS men, but she certainly wasn't letting them know that. It seemed that she could fool anyone.

Heinrich turned to Ava then, his hand brushing against her back as he rested his arm over her chair. Everyone else was engaged in conversation, and she suddenly found herself the sole object of his attention, his eyes dancing over hers.

'I'm sorry we didn't get to have a night together alone,' he said, smiling as he searched her eyes. 'I would have preferred dinner for two.'

'It's fine. I'm certain everyone has missed you, so it's good we can have a fun night together with your friends. I'm just thankful you came straight to see me.' She looked shyly up at him as he moved closer. 'I have missed you so much, Heinrich. It's so lovely to have you home safe.'

'Ava, I've been dreaming of you every day since I left,' he said, reaching up to brush a loose strand of hair from her face. 'Of course I came to see you first.'

Ava's eyes ran over his face at his sweet words, leaning into his touch, as she found doubts bubbling up inside of her again, wondering if he could truly be as awful as Hanna had insisted he was.

'I was thinking, now that I'm going to be based closer to Berlin and away from the fighting, that we could consider bringing our wedding forward.'

Ava's heart began to pound and her mouth went dry. 'Our wedding?' She tried to calm her breathing, wondering how on earth she'd carry on her covert work with her father if she was married to Heinrich. 'I thought we were going to wait. I haven't even—'

'I know how busy you've been with work, and all the added responsibility at the ministry must have taken its toll. It's unconscionable, women like you having to work so hard instead of being at home, but I don't want to put off our wedding any longer, not now that I'm back.'

She smiled, hoping she appeared sincere. 'I'm honoured to do my duty. It's important work, although I do dream of the day that I can stay home and raise my children.' She saw a look cross his face and leaned forward to touch his arm, immediately realising her mistake. '*Our* children.'

'Of course, and I've heard wonderful things about you. All of your superiors speak very highly of you, and they're very happy about our upcoming nuptials.' He grinned, not seeming concerned by her misstep. 'I suspect we are to be one of the golden couples of the SS family once we're married.'

Ava swallowed, glancing away and hoping she seemed modest rather than terrified. Her feelings were jumbled; she was no longer sure how she felt about anything. 'Well, that would certainly be an honour. But I don't think we'd be thought of very fondly if I had to

118

step aside from my work at the ministry, just when they need me the most.' Not to mention she would be useless to her father and sister if she was no longer in the office.

'That's why Dr Goebbels and your father weren't particularly enthusiastic about my finding a cottage for us near the village of Ravensbrück. It seems he thinks you're rather irreplaceable, despite all the women who would be perfectly capable of the secretarial work you do.'

She felt her heart begin to thud again, not even caring about his obvious insult. 'Ravensbrück?' *Does that mean Hanna was right about him?* 'That seems an awfully long way from Berlin.'

He nodded, a big smile spreading across his face. 'Ravensbrück is where I shall be based for some time, although I'm not permitted to talk about my new role just yet.' His smile widened even further. 'It's why we're all here tonight though, to celebrate. We've all received new postings away from the front line, at the camps.'

The camps. She forced her chin up, to look straight back at him, hoping to see a flicker of something cross his face, to believe that he wasn't involved with the atrocities taking place there. That the man she'd chosen to marry was who she'd believed he was. 'Those camps sound like wretched places, Heinrich. I don't particularly like the idea of you being there. Is there nowhere else you could be posted?'

Heinrich only laughed at her. 'You'll soon get used to the idea, and I've already been able to put my new role to good use. Your family are to be given labourers from Ravensbrück to work at your country estate. It was supposed to be a surprise when they arrived next month.'

'Labourers?' She exhaled the word, finding it almost impossible to expel.

'They're women, Jehovah's Witnesses actually, but they've all been taught how to put in a good day's work, and they'll keep the place looking immaculate. I don't know why your father didn't request them himself months ago.'

Heinrich didn't seem to notice that she'd failed to reply, that she was struggling not to gape back at him; he was so busy regaling her with his importance, his chest puffed out.

'I spent time with my uncle and aunt, Rudolf and Hedwig Höss, before making my way home, and she's very happy in their cottage near Auschwitz,' he continued, before leaning in and whispering to her, his words very much for her ears only. 'Would you believe that Rudolf had a chair made for her from human bones? And they had collector's copies of *Mein Kampf* tucked away in the attic, bound with human skin. The experiments they are doing in the camps are truly extraordinary, Ava. Absolutely extraordinary.'

Ava failed to hide her disgust at his whispered comments, her recently consumed dinner rising dangerously high in her throat. She'd been wrong. She'd wanted so desperately to believe in him, but he was as much of a monster as the rest of them. What a fool she'd been, swept up in the idea of him, not seeing him for the man he was.

'Heinrich, that is truly awful. How could you tell me such things!'

Everyone around them fell silent, and she looked up and into the eyes of her sister, who carefully shook her head, as if in warning. Ava gathered herself, trying to stop her face from showing her horror.

'My beautiful fiancée, she is more delicate than I remembered,' Heinrich said with a laugh, although she saw the way that his fingers tightened around his water glass as he spoke. 'It appears I have forgotten myself, after so long in the company of men.'

When everyone resumed their conversations, she felt him turn away from her slightly and knew that she needed to do something to bring him back to her, to defuse his anger. She'd unintentionally belittled him, and she knew he would expect her to grovel.

'Heinrich, I'm so sorry, I simply thought that such matters were to be kept from the wives. I don't believe my father shares such things with my mother, that's all.' She paused. 'You took me by surprise.'

He lifted his drink and took a slow sip, before turning back to her. 'Maybe not, but Hedwig is privy to much of what her husband does, she is his confidante, and I want you to be mine, Ava. I need you to believe in the Final Solution, as I do. It is of the utmost importance that we purge this country of the filth that was allowed to exist here for so long.'

She blinked, taking little sips of air, drawing on all her strength as he spouted his words of hatred. 'Of course, my love,' she said, carefully. 'I understand what you're asking of me. It might just take time for me to become fully used to my new role, and your expectations of me. Perhaps you're right and I am more delicate than I realised.'

His smile returned and he leaned forward to kiss her cheek, taking her by surprise. It was as if he'd had a complete personality change all over again. Clearly he liked her best when she was demure and apologetic.

'Tomorrow, I've been invited to lunch at the Reich Chancellery with the Führer himself,' he whispered. 'When I said we were to be the new golden couple of the SS family, I meant it. Everyone is going to love us, Ava. Imagine the guests we'll have at our wedding.'

Ava squeezed his hand and beamed at him, doing her best to appear excited, at the same time as her sister stood and announced that it was time to go home, which resulted in groans from the men at the table.

'I shall see you soon, Ava,' Heinrich said, rising and gently stroking her arm.

'It's so wonderful to have you home, Heinrich,' she said, forcing herself to stand on tiptoe and whisper a kiss to his cheek, lingering just long enough to ensure that he felt wanted, her hand pressed to his shoulder. 'Goodnight, my love.'

'Please, let me walk you home,' he began.

'We shall be perfectly all right on our own,' Hanna said for them both. 'You enjoy your night off with your friends, Heinrich. I dare say you deserve it after all those months serving our country.'

As they left, arm in arm, Ava dropped her head to her sister's shoulder, trying to hold back her tears and failing. They streamed down her cheeks as she gripped Hanna's arm.

'You were right,' Ava whispered, walking as quickly as she could to put as much distance as possible between them and Heinrich. 'He's a monster. An evil, heartless monster.'

'He is a monster who could become very dangerous to us, sister. You must be very careful with this one.'

Ava didn't need to be told. She'd seen the danger reflected in his gaze, how quick he'd been to anger when she hadn't behaved as he'd wanted, and she was starting to realise that she wasn't in love with him any more; she was *terrified* of him. Of him and all the other men like him, who were nothing more than wolves in sheep's clothing.

Ava washed her face, splashing water on her skin and then doing the same to her arms and neck – anywhere that Heinrich might have touched her. Once, she'd basked in his attention and craved his touch, but now it only made her feel dirty, as if she needed to erase any evidence of where he'd connected with her.

There had been no air raid sirens that night so far, and Ava prayed that they would have a peaceful night, because she was exhausted. The last thing she felt able to do would be to drag herself out of bed to go down to the cellar.

Once she was ready for bed, she walked past her sister's room, pausing at the open door and listening to see if she was asleep. But instead of heavy breathing, there was Hanna calling out to her.

'Do you want to come in here for a bit?'

Ava smiled. Lying there with her sister sounded much more appealing than crawling into her cold bed alone. So she went in, tucking in beside her as they both pressed together for warmth.

It was just the two of them in the apartment tonight – she presumed their father was working late – and it was nice to have time alone with Hanna again. She wondered if perhaps her sister had been avoiding her and using work as an excuse for the past months, whereas now that Ava had been brought into the fold, they were spending more time together, as close as they'd been before the war.

'I miss having someone in bed with me at night,' Hanna said, her voice barely a murmur. 'Sometimes I'd have Michael on one side, and Hugo on the other. It's one of the things I miss most, having his chubby little hands patting my face to wake me up in the morning, his little body snuggled tight to me.'

'I wish you'd told me,' Ava whispered back. 'I would have come in here every night and slept beside you.'

They were silent for a long moment before Hanna spoke again. 'How did you feel, having to be with Heinrich tonight? You truly understand who he is now, don't you?'

'It was as if my skin was crawling with bugs,' she replied. 'I don't know how you can smile and act so normal around them. I thought I was going to be sick.'

Hanna sighed. 'I've had longer to practise than you, that's all. And it helps to imagine men like him being arrested and crammed into cattle cars, just as they have done to those they hate. It's something I think about when I'm smiling sweetly at them.'

'Do you think that could ever happen? That they would ever be punished for all the things they've done? What they've been part of?' Only hours earlier she'd been torn in her feelings towards him, but now she could quite clearly see him for the brute he'd become.

Hanna turned to her, and Ava could just make out her eyes in the dark. 'I don't know. But the one thing I do know is that he and his friends must never suspect a thing. We must tread more carefully than ever, now that he's back.'

They lay there a little longer, and Ava tried to stop thinking about Heinrich, about what he might do to her if he ever found out what she and her family were involved in. She moved her hand slightly so that her little finger was touching Hanna's, and Hanna immediately responded by moving her hand over Ava's and intertwining their fingers.

'Hanna, is Papa all right? Is he going to—'

'I don't know,' Hanna replied into the dark, before Ava could finish her sentence. 'But he's right about not being able to see the doctor. If anyone thinks he is weak, if they detect he's not as strong as he once was . . .'

Hanna didn't need to finish her sentence for Ava to understand. If her father lost his position in the party, his status, it would be dangerous for all of them.

'Come home with me on Saturday,' Hanna whispered. 'I have something special I want to show you.'

'What is it?' Ava asked.

'You'll have to wait and see.'

Chapter Twelve

Ava was always happy to be home, but never more so than she was that day. She'd been taken in her father's chauffeur-driven car – he was home for barely a few hours before he had to go back to Berlin for the night – and they'd had a pleasant family lunch together. Although there wasn't a moment when she didn't think about the family living above them, silently, in the attic, and she expected the rest of her family felt the same. Sometimes she wondered if they could simply lock all the doors and bring them downstairs to join them, but she knew it would be too dangerous.

'Ava, could you come with me please?'

Her father stopped at the kitchen as she stood talking with her mother, and she happily followed after him, curious about what he might want her for.

'Are you certain you can't stay longer?' she asked as they walked to his study. 'I miss us being together, all under the same roof. It would be so nice to have the weekend.'

'One day, when work isn't so demanding, all I want to do is come home and never leave.' She heard the sadness in his voice, and wondered if he honestly thought it would ever all be over.

She could imagine such a time, although her problem was that she was supposed to be dreaming of a life with Heinrich once the war was over. A man whose head was filled with monstrous ideas, whose bed she was going to have to share if she couldn't find a way not to marry him. She shuddered at the thought of him ever touching her again.

Her father closed the door when they were in the room and turned on his music, before indicating that she should follow him. She watched as he opened a panel in his bookcase to reveal his safe, which as a girl she'd been fascinated with and had loved seeing, and now felt a great weight of responsibility at being given the code for. He made her repeat it to him, three times, before finally nodding and reaching inside to retrieve something.

'I have identification papers in here that I want you to give Eliana,' he said. 'I have only the one set of papers at this stage, but I believe we can at least get her out of there and into our home as a legitimate guest with these.'

'Truly?' she asked, before throwing her arms around her father. 'That's wonderful news. And the others? Will you be able to get papers for them, too?'

'I fear that I won't have a solution for the rest of the family for some time,' he said. 'But I'm doing my best.'

'You think they'll have to remain in hiding until the end of the war? In our attic?'

She could tell from his eyes, the way his shoulders dropped slightly, that that was exactly what he thought.

'I wish it were different, but it's only Eliana we can help right now, and I've risked a lot doing this for her. But if anything ever happens, if for some reason I don't return or we're discovered, you must take everything from the safe,' he said. 'If I've managed to have papers prepared for them, for any of us, they will be in there. I'm trying to prepare for every possible situation.'

'You think we might need false papers, too?'

He looked away for a moment, before turning his gaze back to her. 'I think that there are officers who aren't loyal to our Führer any more, which is causing suspicion like never before. That's why young men like your Heinrich, who've proved themselves to be fanatical in their dedication to the party, are being welcomed home and transferred into new positions.'

'Papa, about Heinrich,' she began, as goose pimples rippled across her skin.

'I'm hoping he will be relocated soon,' he said. 'He's become quite the favourite of Goebbels and Himmler, and they have plans for him outside of Berlin. I had hoped to send him elsewhere, but my efforts have been stymied at this stage.' She heard the hesitation in his voice, sensing his concerns, and wondered if something had changed, if somehow his influence had waned.

'Papa, he's told me what they want for him, and he wants us to marry soon and have me move to a cottage near the, the—' She hesitated as his brow creased. 'The concentration camp. He wants me to live nearby to where he'll be working.' She remembered what Hanna had told her, what she'd read in the papers at Goebbels' office. There was no way she could live so close, knowing what was happening there.

He studied her for a long moment, his expression impossible to read.

'Turn the music up please, Ava,' he finally said, bringing the papers with him and sitting down in one of the armchairs.

She did as she was asked, and then settled down to listen to his quietly spoken words about what he needed her to do to ensure Eliana's safety, and just how he was going to delay her marriage to Heinrich. But it was something he said when they both stood, kissing her forehead as he embraced her, that she knew would forever echo through her mind.

I'm going to hell for what I've been part of, Ava, for the things I've ordered and been witness to, but I hope that this one small thing, this one family we're helping, will at least count for something.

Because it made her wonder just what her father had done in his role with the SS, what brutality he'd been part of, and how he intended on living with himself after the war. He might be her father, and she loved him dearly, fiercely even, but if she knew what he'd done? If she found out definitively that he'd had some part in what had happened to Lina? She feared that she might never be able to forgive him.

Ava spent an hour alone in her father's study, thinking through everything he'd told her, everything he'd asked her to consider. But when she heard her mother call out to her, she gathered herself and went to find her. There was no sign of her in the living room or kitchen, but then she saw a flash of movement outside and realised where they were. Ava took her jacket down from the hook near the back door, laced up her boots and went out to join her mother and sister.

'What are you doing?' she called out as she walked.

They were some way from the house, but close enough that she could see they were gardening. Hanna appeared to be wielding a shovel and was digging, and her mother was carrying plants.

'I didn't realise you were both so interested in gardening these days,' she said, folding her arms across her chest as she approached. It had certainly never been a favourite pastime of hers – she much preferred to stay indoors.

'Ava, come and help me,' Hanna called, looking over her shoulder and waving for her to join them. 'We need to do this as quickly as possible.'

'Do what as quickly as possible?' she asked. 'I'm not well versed in gardening, you know. Is this to be a new vegetable plot?'

She hadn't yet told her mother about Heinrich's mention of slave labour, although she suspected Hanna might have divulged it. Did that have something to do with their sudden interest in the garden?

'We have jars to bury,' Hanna said. 'Eliana helped me to prepare these.'

Ava absently picked one up, trying to see the contents. 'This is the surprise you had for me?'

Hanna looked lighter than Ava had seen her for some time, and she crouched down beside her, having to move closer so she could hear her soft voice.

'We created a jar for each child I've helped to save, so that one day there's a chance they can be reunited with their families. The children I've been helping to escape Berlin, Jewish children, inside is everything about where they lived, who their parents were, their grandparents . . .' Hanna paused a moment, as if she were about to cry and needed a moment to collect herself. 'Who they were before all of this.'

Ava blinked away her own tears as she gently picked up one of the jars and sat down in the dirt, understanding the weight of what her sister was a part of.

'You think it's safe to do this, in our garden?' she asked, gently. 'This is such a beautiful gesture, Hanna, I only hope that we don't regret doing it here.'

'If not here, then where?' Hanna asked, wiping her forehead with the back of her hand and smudging dirt across her skin. 'I've thought this over so many times, and I just want to make sure that every child I helped to smuggle out of Berlin has a chance at finding their family. It feels right to do this here, somewhere that can never be forgotten, can never be taken from us.'

'Mama?' Ava asked, looking up as their mother came closer. 'You're comfortable with doing this here? At our home?'

'We're going to transplant larger seedlings from the vegetable garden, as well as flowers,' her mother said. 'So long as we work quickly and bury them fairly deep, I think it's a lovely idea. No one will ever think to dig up a vegetable garden.'

Ava nodded. She wasn't comfortable with it, terrified that they might somehow be discovered and bring everything crashing down around them, but she certainly understood the sentiment. 'This will be the only record? If those children survive, if their parents survive, this information could be what brings them back together?'

Hanna nodded. 'This will be what gives them the chance to be a family again. So long as one of us survives, we will be able to dig them up and give the information to the authorities.'

And so Ava reached for one of the gardening tools and set about helping her sister, their mother digging up seedlings from another plot nearby. It seemed reckless, burying the jars so close to the house, having a permanent record that all but confirmed they'd been involved in the smuggling of Jewish children, but she knew it was the right thing to do.

'How many do we have?' Ava asked, the dirt cool beneath her skin as she tucked the first jar deep into the earth and began to cover it.

'Sixteen,' Hanna said.

Sixteen. Sixteen children who her sister had risked her life to save, who had been given a chance at living when so many others hadn't. Ava might be doing her best to follow her father's orders and memorise paperwork in the office, but it was going to take her a long time to do anything even remotely as ambitious or impressive as what her sister had already done for the cause.

'Thank you,' Hanna said, as she passed her another jar.

'What for?' Ava asked.

'For not trying to stop me.' She paused. 'Nothing has ever meant so much to me, Ava. I feel as if this is the only thing keeping me going sometimes, giving me a purpose, giving me something to focus on.'

'Then we shall bury every single jar together,' Ava said, her heart breaking when she saw the pain etched on her sister's face. 'But we must do it quickly, and then never speak of it again until the war is over. Agreed?'

Hanna nodded. 'Agreed.'

Their mother came closer and knelt beside them then, and the three of them silently buried jar after jar, until all that was left before them was a patch of tilled soil, and a pile of plants that had to be thoughtfully placed in the earth to disguise the precious records buried beneath.

'What we've done here is a beautiful thing,' their mother said. 'One day, our bravery could allow a mother to reunite with her child, and then, despite everything, it will have been worth our risk.' *If the mother and child were still alive to see that day.* Ava couldn't help but think that those were the words her mother was thinking and had chosen not to utter.

When they stood, in a line, the three of them facing the garden, Ava knew she'd just witnessed something that would stay with her for the rest of her life.

'There's something I've been thinking about,' Ava suddenly said, looking from Hanna to her mother. 'Can we not take up extra mattresses to the Goldmans?' she asked, lowering her voice. 'Surely we can do something to make it, well, to make it more comfortable up there? Can we bring them more clothes, too? More books?' *More luxuries?*

'We can't do anything that would draw attention. If we were to take a mattress from one of our beds, Zelda would notice, and if we had a new one delivered, the old one simply couldn't disappear,' her mother said. 'We're doing everything we can, but we have to be careful. Every decision we make, every item we take up there, has to be done in a way that will avoid notice entirely, which is why we're simply trying to put what was already stored up there to good use.' Her mother paused. 'But perhaps you could find more books or board games for Eliana and David? Those are the types of personal items we can easily give them.'

Ava nodded. Finding books for them was the least she could do.

That night, when the house was silent and it was just Ava, Hanna and her mother in residence, she went up to the attic while the other two prepared food for their guests – only her second time going back up since she'd discovered them living there. She was surprised how homely they'd made the attic with what little they had, although that didn't diminish the sadness she felt at seeing them all crammed into the small space. She imagined it would be like being a caged animal; pacing back and forth with no way of escape, desperate to get back out into the world again.

'Ava,' Eliana said the moment they saw her, the light from their oil lamps sending shadows around the space and making it difficult at first to see all four of them. Ava could see that her presence made them nervous, and she wished she could tell them how truly sorry she was, how much she regretted the way she'd behaved. But she knew that the way to gain their trust was to prove to them that she cared, which was what she intended on doing.

'I don't know how to begin,' she said, the words difficult to find. 'I—'

Her eyes found their way to David, who was watching her intently. She remembered him then, years earlier, when he'd carried her library books for her all the way to their apartment block. But with that memory came another, and she wished she could shut it out.

Ava and her BDM friends sat at a little table, licking their ice creams and chatting in the sunshine. Until one of the girls shrieked in horror and pulled her seat back as a well-dressed young man walked down the road, a yellow star pinned to his chest, marking him for the world to notice.

Ava knew immediately who he was, but when the other girls began to make a fuss and chant a song, as his eyes met hers, pleading, she looked away. She sung the little song beneath her breath, expecting him to hunch his shoulders and walk away, but instead he straightened, as if he couldn't hear their cruel taunts.

'Dirty Jew,' called one of the older girls, hurling her ice cream at David and hitting him square on the back, like she'd thrown a ball at him. But instead of a ball rolling to the ground, the creamy liquid stuck to his jacket and then began to dribble down the fabric. But he didn't stop, just kept on walking, his head still held high.

'My father says they'll all be gone soon,' one of the other girls said.

Ava returned her attention to her ice cream, only looking over her shoulder once to see where the boy was, to see whether the sun had baked the cream stain into his jacket, but he had already disappeared.

'My father has asked me to share some news with you,' she said, transferring her gaze to Eliana and trying not to think about the past. 'I'd also like to say that I deeply regret the way I behaved when I first discovered you here. It came as quite a shock to me, but—'

'You have news?' David interrupted. 'Please, tell us what you've come up to say.'

She glanced at him, clearing her throat while his parents moved to sit on the footstools that had been placed near the centre of the attic. She chose to perch on the floor, rather than take one of their precious luxuries from them.

'My father has returned to Berlin, but he entrusted me with these before he left.' She took the papers from her pocket and passed them directly to Eliana.

'What are you giving me?' she asked.

'Identification papers,' Ava replied. 'You are now Eleanor Müller, or Elly for short.'

Eliana's eyes widened as she examined the papers, before looking up. 'Where are the rest? You only have the one set?' She frowned. 'I'm to share your surname?'

Ava shifted uncomfortably. 'I'm sorry, but this is all he's been able to obtain so far,' she said. 'He told me that it's a painstaking process to ensure that the lineage is perfect, that no one can question who you are. He wanted the papers to be watertight, especially as you would be living as one of our family members.'

'It's because Eliana is the only one of us who can pass for not being a Jew,' David said, his voice rising in a way Ava hadn't heard before. 'Isn't it?'

She took a deep breath. 'My father wants Eliana to stay with us, as his niece, before she begins a job in the city. He believes she will be useful to the resistance, if she is willing, and that no one will think to question her lineage as a Müller.'

Eliana gasped at the same time as David glowered at Ava. 'You want to leave me to rot up here, while my sister fights? I'm to stay here and be forgotten?'

'David—' Ava began.

'I've already told Hanna, I have to do something, I have to do *anything* other than stay up here like a coward. I don't know how much longer I can stand it.'

Ava looked up at him and into clear blue eyes. 'I am telling you that if there was anything I could do, anything my father could do, he would have done it by now. But you are not a coward.' Her lower lip trembled as she paused, seeing the pain on his face, the trembling of his body as he stood before her. 'There is only one coward in this room, and it is me, not you. So please don't call yourself that name again.'

She saw the tight clench of his jaw when she spoke, knew how much it frustrated him to remain in the attic and accept his fate.

'David, I promise that we will find a way to get you out of here, but right now Eliana can help us. She can become part of the resistance in a way that you can't. And quite frankly, you're right. She can pass for one of my family members in a way that you can't, and there's nothing I can do about that.'

'Your father is adamant this will work? That she will be safe if she leaves us?' Herr Goldman asked.

Everyone looked to Ava.

'Herr Goldman, Papa wanted me to tell you that Eliana will be treated as family in the same way that Hanna and I are, due to his position and the lineage he has created for her. He said that there will be risk involved, as the family she will work for are part of the resistance, but that it is a worthy cause. Both Hanna and I are working with my father, so he said he's risking his own daughters, too, not just Eliana.'

'Please, Papa,' Eliana implored as Ava watched. 'You have to let me go. I cannot stay here knowing that there's something I could be doing to help.'

David turned away, going to the far corner of the attic as his sister stared after him. Ava watched him for a moment, before deciding to go to him – as much to speak to him as to let Eliana exchange words with her parents in partial privacy.

'I'm sorry,' she said, quietly, as she approached him. 'I am truly sorry, for everything.'

He grunted, but she saw his shoulders move up and down, as if he'd taken a deep breath.

'What if there was a way you could help? Something you could do from here?' she asked.

'Ava, there's nothing I can do from here. Don't you think I've tried to think of something? If I have to stay here, then I'm useless.'

'Useless is better than dead.' She clamped her hand over her mouth. She hadn't meant to say that. 'I'm sorry, I—'

'You were being honest,' he said, laughing despite the soberness of their conversation. 'But honestly, sometimes I wonder whether this is worth it. Because this isn't living, Ava. What we're doing up here, this is surviving, nothing more. I don't know how long I can continue like this, how long anyone could live like this.'

She looked at David, *really* looked at him, and for the first time she saw him for who he truly was. And it broke her heart. He was just one man, but suddenly, to her, he represented all the men she'd never thought about when they'd disappeared.

'Our life has gone from being full of friends, work, study . . .' He looked away, as if he were naturally turning to look out of a window, only there wasn't one, because it had been permanently covered with blackout fabric. 'I'd just begun to study to be a doctor, did you know that? I had my whole life planned out, so many dreams about what I wanted to do, about the places I wanted to work.'

Ava swallowed away a lump of emotion in her throat. 'David, I want you to have those dreams again, I do. I don't want this to be your life any more than you do, but right now, there's nothing more we can do than promise to keep you safe.'

'Then speak to your father again. At least try to get me a gun, any kind of weapon, to protect my parents if they come for us.'

'I will get you a gun, David. I give you my word,' she said, lifting a hand and hesitantly touching his arm, feeling his tense muscles soften beneath her touch. 'If that's what you need to feel safe, then consider it done.'

They stared at one another for a long moment, before he eventually nodded.

'Thank you, Ava. I will never forget the kindness shown by your family to ours.'

She was about to pull away when his hand closed over hers for the briefest of seconds.

'And you're not a coward, Ava.'

When she turned back to Eliana, all she could think about was David and how his words had touched her. He would have made a brilliant doctor, for he was clearly kind, compassionate and smart. She only hoped that one day he'd be able to put those skills to use. She also looked down at her own hand, the palm she'd touched him with, wondering how she'd ever believed it was wrong to make contact with a Jew, that somehow she could become sick or be harmed by them by virtue of their religion. It seemed ridiculous now, as if she'd woken from a dream.

'Eliana?' Ava asked, looking from her to her parents.

'Where will my sister be working?' David asked, coming to stand behind her.

'At a grocer's in the city. They're good people and they'll take good care of her. They're people who've been deeply involved in the resistance from the very beginning, according to my father.' She looked at Ava, then her parents, and finally back at David. 'My father will say that she wants to help Germans, but that she has no formal training as a nurse or teacher. It will be a good cover for her choosing to work there, for the greater good.'

'You promise me she'll be safe?'

Ava nodded to him. 'I hope so, David.'

It simply wasn't a promise she was willing to make.

137

Two hours later, after leaving Eliana with her family to eat dinner before going back for her, they stood in her room as Eliana tried clothes on. She'd always been slender, but having not used her muscles properly for so long and no doubt fretting constantly, she was swimming in Ava's clothes. They certainly didn't appear tailored, as they should have.

'I thought this might be an occasion for hot chocolate,' Hanna said, walking into the room with a tray of mugs.

'Well, we're going to be up half the night sewing,' Ava said, gratefully taking one from the tray. 'So thank you, it's exactly what I need.'

'I feel so guilty, being down here, acting like normal again while David and my parents are up there,' Eliana whispered. 'It feels so wrong. It feels like when I first left them, when I had to leave David behind in our apartment. We've always been so close, and I kept thinking then that he'd have never left without me.'

Ava and Hanna exchanged glances, but it was her sister who spoke first.

'Remember that you will be doing work that might eventually free them. If there was a way for David to join us safely, I would have insisted we utilise him, too. Perhaps we still can, actually.'

'How so?' Eliana asked.

'How is his typing?'

Eliana laughed as she turned her back so Ava could do the buttons up on another dress. 'Terrible. But he's a quick study and he's desperately in need of *something* to do.'

'Then leave it with me. I shall find a typewriter and something useful for him to do. Something to keep his mind busy, so that he can feel as if he's contributing.'

Ava noticed the way Eliana smiled, the way her shoulders straightened at the very idea that her brother might have a role, after all. If there was anything she could personally do to get him out of the attic, Ava would have, but at the very least she knew she'd find him the gun he'd asked for. All David wanted was a way to protect his family, and she intended on giving it to him. It was the least she could do.

'When do I start work at the grocer's?' Eliana asked.

'Monday,' Ava said. 'We'll have a car to take us back to the city early in the morning, and I'll take you there myself before work. You're simply to provide an extra set of hands, and if anyone asks, you are to say you didn't want to be idle.'

'And they're people I can trust? People who will know who I really am?'

Ava nodded. 'They will know you're Jewish, if that's what you're asking, and that you need to be protected. But they will know nothing of your family name or your past, to protect them as much as you.' She paused. 'And us.'

Eliana turned before them in the dress and both she and Hanna groaned. It was no exaggeration to say that it would take them all night to create a wardrobe fit for a young woman who was to be their wealthy cousin from Munich. But there was no disputing that Eliana looked beautiful, and by the time they'd coloured her hair blonde and put a little make-up on her, Ava doubted even an SS man would be able to walk past her in the street without turning his head.

Chapter Thirteen

HANNA

A few weeks later, Hanna sat behind the wheel of the ambulance, cursing Dieter for not showing up to work. No one seemed to know where he was, which was highly unusual as he'd never not shown up before, which meant that she was going to have to go out alone. She'd received a message days earlier about two children needing to be smuggled out of Berlin, and she'd been hiding their papers in her jacket ever since.

The bombings around the country had become more targeted, with factories often hit by the Allies, and the message had been clear: the next time a factory within two hours of Berlin was hit, they were to drive as close to the building as they could, and the children would be brought out for her to transport. It was a much longer drive than they were usually tasked with, which brought with it even more dangers, and it was one of the reasons she'd have preferred to have been doing it with Dieter rather than alone.

Hanna had been comfortable with the plan when it was mentioned to her, other than the fact the children were having to wait for potentially weeks to be rescued. But in the end it didn't take long for another factory to be hit – Magdeburg had been the target of so many of the Allies' air raids, after all. The problem now was that she would either have to drive the ambulance herself or risk someone realising what she was doing if another nurse or driver came with her, and it would be almost impossible to explain why she was driving so far to assist with the injured there. So she'd chosen not to tell anyone at the hospital that Dieter wasn't there, pretending he was waiting outside for her to join him, and she walked out with her nursing bag as she usually would.

She waited for a moment to check that no one else was coming out of the hospital, before starting the engine and manoeuvring her way out on to the street. She wasn't used to driving it, but one thing she did have was determination, and there was no way she was letting Dieter not turning up to work be the reason that two children missed their chance of escape.

An hour later, and clutching the steering wheel so hard that her knuckles had turned white, Hanna moved past the fire trucks and soldiers, and parked as close as she could to what was left of the factory. What had once been a building was now a smouldering pile of charred timber and ashes, reduced to rubble, but what disturbed her most were the bodies lined up on the ground. Given the number of them, she wondered if there had been any survivors at all.

'Help!' someone yelled, carrying a child in their arms and running from the closest home to the factory. It had a hole through the side, as if it were a doll's house that had an opening to peep through.

Another person appeared, carrying another child, and Hanna quickly got out of the ambulance and opened the back up.

'Bring them here!' she called.

It only took minutes for Hanna to play along and have the children put in the back, where she placed them on stretchers and covered them with blankets, smiling in the hope that she was able to reassure them they were safe.

But just as she was about to step out, a shadow fell across the back door and she saw that two SS men were standing there, watching her. The couple who'd brought the children out stood, looking at her, as if hoping she could make them go away. Hanna smiled, looking from one man to the other, refusing to cower. They didn't intimidate her in the way they did others, not when her father and many of his colleagues wore the same uniform.

'The papers,' one of the men said. 'For both children.'

'I have them right here,' Hanna said, producing two sets of identification papers from inside her jacket. 'I'd already asked to check them before I put them in the ambulance.'

She handed them over and stood as the two men looked over both sets of papers.

'You are the parents?' the SS officer asked, turning to the couple. 'We need to see your papers, too.'

'I'm sorry, but one of the children appears to have a knock to the head, and the other child isn't breathing well. It's imperative that I get them to the hospital as quickly as possible,' said Hanna.

They both seemed to consider her as she held out her hand to retrieve the papers, tugging them free.

'Since you're SS men, you'll both know my father, Oberst-Gruppenführer Karl Müller? He is the one who asked me to work as a nurse, specifically to ensure the medical care of children. They are our future, after all.'

That seemed to work immediately, and the papers were passed back to her without any fuss. She closed the back door of the ambulance and promised the parents that she'd ensure the pair received the very best of care, before settling herself behind the wheel again and driving away from the SS men who were still standing on the road.

It was the very first time she'd ever used her father's rank in that way, but it had worked, and she'd do it again if she had to. Now she just needed to get the children to the drop-off point and hope that her contact was waiting for her, because if they weren't, she had no idea what she'd do with the two frightened little children in her care.

Hanna jumped sideways when a man bumped into her as she walked back to her apartment after work, her mind still full of thoughts of the children she'd delivered earlier. She'd been so lost in her own thoughts that when the man fell into step beside her, she realised he wasn't a stranger at all. This man had bumped into her on purpose to get her attention.

'Sorry, Fräulein,' he said.

'Noah?' she whispered, recognising him when she glanced sideways. 'You're lucky I didn't hit you with my bag!'

To anyone watching it would appear they didn't know one another, the way he fell back a few feet from her as they both continued to walk in the same direction. She hadn't seen him for months now, had wondered if he was even in Berlin any more, and now here he was in the flesh and clearly seeking her out.

Noah was a rare sight in the city – a young man as handsome as could be, with the type of features so loved by the Nazis – when most of the eligible young men were either away or parading around in uniform. But Noah walked with a limp, which had made him unsuitable for service. Sometimes she wondered if it was even real, because in every other respect he appeared fit and strong, but he had the papers to prove it and it had so far prevented him from being asked to report for duty. It certainly didn't detract from his magnetism though, in the same way she supposed that Joseph Goebbels could capture a crowd despite his deformed foot.

'You're here because of today?' she asked, wondering how he knew what she'd done. Had something happened to the children?

'You breached protocol today, Hanna, going alone and driving the ambulance, but I have to say that I admire your dedication to the cause,' he said. 'But no more transfers until you're told otherwise. It's becoming too dangerous for us to operate near Berlin. There are snitches everywhere, so we need to wait until we know who they are.'

She swallowed. What would happen then to the children who were still waiting for them to help? The families who'd heard the whispers about the network that could help them, the paperwork that was already being falsified for them? Germany had largely already been purged of Jews, gypsies, homosexuals, and anyone else the Nazi Party had decided to take offence to, but there were still pockets of families and children hidden in attics and basements all over the country.

'A family was found last night in the city,' he said. 'Someone knew they were being hidden, someone reported it, which confirmed that we have a traitor in our midst. Or perhaps traitors.'

Hanna shivered, clenching her fists. 'They were taken? Last night?'

'My guess is that they're already on their way to Auschwitz, along with the family that was hiding them in their basement.' He was silent for a moment, and she knew he was about to tell her something she didn't want to hear, because his face softened in a way she'd never seen before. 'The family was that of your ambulance driver, Dieter. I'm sorry to inform you that's why he didn't come to work today, why you were forced to work alone.'

'Dieter was taken?' She gasped. 'And his parents, too?' Her heart was heavy as she imagined the terror of what they'd been through, where he might be now. He'd been as determined as her to help, but the difference between them was that he'd still been holding out hope, however small it might be, that his wife would survive the camps, that they could be reunited if the war ever ended.

He'd never confided in her that they were hiding anyone.

'Does that mean that I'm in danger? That my family is in danger, too?' She dug her nails into her fisted palm, turning her attention to what his being taken into custody might mean for her. 'Does it mean that our entire network could collapse?'

'We're all in danger, Hanna, we always have been. But if someone has turned on us, someone close to what we're doing? They'll begin to pick us off, one by one.' He gave her a sharp stare when he finally came to walk beside her. 'Or they could come for us all in the night and take us all out at once.'

Hanna focused on her breathing, trying to calm her racing heart. 'What do you need me to do? How can I help you?' She wanted to ask if there was anything she could do to help Dieter, but she knew that wasn't a question worth asking. Once someone was in one of the camps, there was nothing anyone could do.

'You can introduce me to your sister,' Noah said, as they passed the door to her apartment block and kept walking, not wanting anyone who might be watching them to see where she lived. 'I know your father recruited her, and I need her to do something for me. We have to move our timeline up, in case we need to move faster to avoid being caught.'

Hanna tucked her chin down into her scarf and drew her coat tighter around her body. 'No,' she said. 'My sister can't be any help to you. Let me do it. Whatever you need, I can do it for you.'

'Unless you have access to the personal papers of Joseph Goebbels, you can't help me with this.'

'That would be a death sentence for her and you know it. They would figure out it was her immediately if she relayed personal information!' She glared at him. 'I won't allow it. You need to find another way.'

'If you don't arrange the meeting, then I'll find someone else to introduce us.' He paused, his gaze steely as he stared at her. 'It's up to you. But I *will* find a way to meet your sister, whether you help me or not.'

Hanna watched him and knew that he wasn't calling her bluff. Noah was notorious for his ruthlessness, for using whoever he had to in order to get what he wanted. If he wanted to contact Ava, she had little doubt that he'd find a way, just like she knew that whatever he was planning wouldn't be abandoned, no matter the risk.

'Fine. Meet us at the Café Kranzler tomorrow, at midday,' she finally said, choosing a coffee house they could easily walk to, just as he was turning to walk away. 'I'll make sure she's there.'

Noah nodded, smiling as he met her gaze again. 'Sit at the table beside me, and don't greet me. We will talk and drink coffee without looking at one another, so no one thinks we're there to meet.'

She nodded. 'I understand, we'll be discreet. But Noah, you do know who her fiancé is, don't you? That he's back in Berlin? You know how dangerous it is for her to be part of this? What he'd do to you if he thought you'd involved her?' Hanna stared hard at him. 'Even being seen with you when she's engaged to a man like Heinrich could be a death sentence, for you as much as her.'

'I already know everything there is to know about your sister, Hanna. And don't forget, we are all playing a cat-and-mouse game here, it's dangerous for all of us. But if this works? Then it might be over, once and for all, and perhaps we can go back to the lives we had before.' He gave her an intense kind of look that scared her, before speaking again. 'Hanna, is your father unwell?'

She swallowed, doing her best to keep her face impassive. 'Why would you ask such a thing?'

'I've heard rumours, that's all.'

She dug her nails into her palms again, forcing a smile. 'My father is fine, but thank you for your concern.'

With that, Noah turned on his heel and walked away, and Hanna watched him go, finally letting go of the breath she'd been holding. How could anyone possibly know about her father? Unless she hadn't acted quickly enough at the dinner party, and one of the guests had noticed. She prayed that Ava hadn't been foolish enough to tell Heinrich, but then chastised herself for thinking such a thing. Ava knew who Heinrich was now, and there was no way she would do anything to jeopardise their father.

Hanna walked briskly back to the apartment, fretting as much about Ava as their father, for she knew how easy it would be for Ava to be drawn into Noah's web, only to be discarded when she was no longer of use, or to end up dead because something went wrong.

Noah had orchestrated the transport of Jewish children out of Berlin since the night of broken glass, and he'd come to her soon after her husband and son were killed, as if sensing that she was the perfect candidate to assist the cause, crossing paths with her regularly until one day he'd finally asked her outright. He'd recruited her by playing on her conscience, by knowing precisely how to manipulate her, and she'd been a willing participant, especially when he'd confessed to her that his family had been executed by the SS for housing his Jewish girl-friend and her family. But since then, he'd moved on to bigger things, being bolder in what they were doing to try to disrupt the Führer, which told her just how dangerous it was to be associated with him.

She only hoped that whatever he wanted with her sister wasn't part of that bigger plan, because then she'd never forgive herself for being the one to introduce them, for not being more forthright in protecting her. Losing her husband and son had broken her in a way that she doubted she could ever heal from, but losing her sister as well? Hanna shuddered as she walked briskly all the way around the block until she was outside her apartment again. Losing Ava was not something she could survive, which meant that she had only one option available to her.

Hanna was going to have to tell their father about Noah coming to her, and let him decide how to deal with the situation. Noah would be furious with her, but Ava was her sister and she had a duty to protect her, no matter what. If her father thought it was worth the risk, then so be it, but this wasn't something she was prepared to accept without consulting him first.

Chapter Fourteen

Ava

Ava was nervous as she walked with Hanna to the Café Kranzler for coffee. She didn't often go out at lunchtime, and when she'd been told there was someone to see her, her stomach had flipped with worry that it might be Heinrich, but thankfully he'd been too busy to call on her over the past few days. Every day that passed without seeing him was a relief, although she knew that she'd have to make time to visit both him and his family soon.

'Are you going to tell me anything about this man?' she asked her sister as they walked.

'He's someone I never wanted you to meet, put it that way,' Hanna said. 'I initially refused, but I thought it was best that I was there, rather than him approach you in a different way.'

'And you're opposed to my meeting him because . . .'

Hanna stopped walking, folding her arms across her chest. 'Because he's dangerous, Ava, that's why. He's dangerous because he will stop at nothing to change what's happening in our country.'

'So he's a revolutionary then?' Ava asked, laughing when Hanna threw her hands up in the air, clearly in despair.

'Ava, please! This is not a game, none of it is a game.'

Ava sighed and they began to walk again, falling into step beside each other as she whispered to her sister. 'I am very much aware this isn't a game, Hanna. I worry myself sick all day at my desk, certain that someone will read my mind or the SS will come for me because I've passed some piece of information on that only I could have been privy to,' she said. 'So I know how careful we have to be.'

'It's good that you're scared,' Hanna said. 'The moment we stop being scared is the moment we become complacent, and that's when we'll do something without being careful enough. That's when we'll be caught.'

'I also have the added problem of having a fanatical Nazi for a fiancé,' Ava said. 'Thankfully he's stopped talking about us getting married soon. Papa must have said something to convince him we were best to wait, because I swear Heinrich would have us married next week if he could.'

'Or perhaps Papa simply convinced him that no daughter of his would be living within a stone's throw from one of the most wretched concentration camps?' Hanna said, before taking Ava's arm and whispering in her ear. 'Look, there he is. Sitting alone at the table, at the café across the road. Don't stare.'

Ava followed her gaze, being careful not to look at him for too long. But she couldn't help but notice that he was particularly handsome; similar to Heinrich in a way, but with skin that was more tanned, as if he were used to enjoying the sun over the summer. And when they moved closer, she noticed that he had warm brown eyes, not blue.

'He looks harmless enough,' Ava said.

'Trust me, he's not,' Hanna replied, walking ahead of her into the coffee shop before muttering: 'Noah is *anything* but harmless.'

They ordered their coffees and produced their ration cards, before making their way to the table beside Noah's. Hanna managed to keep up a steady stream of small talk, which Ava did her best to keep up with, and they completely ignored Noah until their coffees arrived. He spoke only when they were both taking their first sip of the strong, bitter drink.

'I'm very pleased to make your acquaintance, Ava,' he said, sitting back in his chair and nursing his own coffee. 'It's very important that we always act as if we don't know one another, and that we always sit at different tables. If you have something for me, you will place it on the table, tucked into a napkin, and you will leave before me so that I can retrieve it after you've left.'

'What things would I be leaving for you?' she asked.

'Documents, notes that you've made, information that I've requested for you to retrieve for me.'

They sat quietly for a long moment, as Ava thought over what he'd just said. It didn't sound any different to what she'd been doing for her father. 'What if I need to contact you? What if something goes wrong?'

'You don't have a plan for when something goes wrong? Because mark my words, something will go wrong. It's only a matter of when.'

Ava glanced at Hanna, who only nodded to her in reply.

'What is it you want from me? Why are you approaching me now? Why are you coming to me directly rather than through my father?'

Noah looked at her then – truly looked at her. His eyes seemed to linger, his full lips impossible not to track with her eyes. She felt herself blush under his scrutiny.

'Because I'm told you are now the private secretary of someone very important to the cause, and that you may be the only one who has access to his diary, among other things,' he said, looking away again and lifting his coffee cup to his lips. 'I need you to give me any key dates when he might be meeting with the Führer, as well as locations. I need to know when he's going to be in Berlin, and where, and something tells me your father wouldn't want his darling daughter to be doing something quite so brazen. Although I think we both know his influence is waning.'

'Waning?' she asked, glancing at Hanna, not sure she understood. What did he mean by *waning*?

She saw the way Hanna clenched her fingers around her coffee cup, either irritated, taken by surprise, or both. 'Our father's influence is certainly not waning, despite what you might have been told.'

Noah shrugged. 'Perhaps I'm wrong then. But regardless, back to you, Ava. Are you prepared to help, or not?'

Ava had a feeling that Noah was very rarely wrong, and she carefully considered her next words, hoping that she didn't sound as naive as she felt. 'You must know that I'm the only woman in the office currently with access to his diary. If anything leaked, it would be obvious it was from me.'

'Which is why we're having this conversation,' he said. 'Everything rests in your hands, Ava. Although if we're careful with the information you gather, I disagree that fingers would immediately point towards you.'

The way he said her name, the way he glanced over at her, sent ripples through her that she wasn't entirely comfortable with. She could tell Hanna wasn't happy – it was obvious in the stiff way she was sitting, her back turned slightly to Noah – but all she could feel right now was excitement. That this man could be sitting here asking for something that only she could do.

'I've heard rumours about some of the Wehrmacht officers, that they're not as loyal as they once were,' Ava said, thinking out aloud, her voice barely a whisper. 'It could be that they think someone closer to Goebbels, someone more trusted, has betrayed him, although I'm certain I would still be a suspect.'

'Or they could realise immediately that it was you, which is a far more likely scenario,' Hanna whispered. 'You don't have to do this, and you certainly don't have to decide today. You can think about it.'

'I'll do it,' Ava said, wishing her voice didn't sound so shaky.

'Your assistance will never be forgotten, Ava,' Noah said. 'This could be the final piece of the puzzle that we've been waiting for, so thank you.'

Someone called out to Hanna then from across the street, and Ava watched as Hanna rose, touching her shoulder as she passed and murmuring that she would only be a moment. Which meant that she was suddenly left alone with Noah.

She kept her gaze straight ahead, finding it almost impossible not to look at him, to pretend they were complete strangers.

'I'd heard you were very capable, Ava, but no one told me quite how beautiful you were.'

She blushed, catching her lower lip between her teeth as she fought not to smile.

'Tell me, how do you feel, now that you've seen the truth?'

'Foolish,' she said, shaking her head. 'As if I couldn't see what was happening right before my eyes.'

'But you're not foolish,' he said, his voice deepening. 'You are clever and intelligent, which means you're the perfect asset.'

She glanced over at him, wondering how often he'd said these words, or if they were truly just for her.

'Women like you might just help us win the war.'

Hanna returned then, inclining her head as she waited for Ava to stand, keeping her back turned to Noah. 'Let's go.'

Hanna moved slightly ahead of her, and when she did Noah's fingers collided with Ava's as she passed his table, slipping something into her hand. She quickly tucked her hand into her pocket, glancing back at him, but he was looking the other way as if he didn't know them, as if he were oblivious to the two women who were leaving.

Ava left her hand there, feeling the tiny piece of paper, wondering what he'd given her and whether it was safe to carry back into work. But she didn't fancy opening it in front of her sister, so work it would have to be.

'I don't like this,' Hanna muttered as they crossed the road. 'The way he's approached you, the danger of what he's asking, I just can't stand the thought of you being so closely connected to whatever they're planning.'

'You don't have to like it,' Ava replied. 'Just as I don't like some of the risks you've taken recently. But as I see it, this is my chance to make up for my lack of compassion and hopelessness in the past. This is something that only I can do.'

They slowed as they came closer to Ava's office building. 'Ava, you don't have anything to make up for. The fact that you're helping now, that you're doing something when most simply turn their backs? That's what counts. You don't have to put yourself at risk like this – and make no mistake, Noah is playing up to your ego, he's wanting to make you feel special just to make you do what he wants. That's what he does.'

'Why is it all right for you to risk *your* life, to put *your* life on the line, but not mine? Why are you the one who gets to decide what we should and shouldn't do?'

'Because you have your whole life ahead of you,' Hanna said, sadly, the tears shining from her eyes. 'Because I have nothing to live for, Ava, and you have *everything*.'

Hanna may as well have punched Ava in the stomach, her words hit her so hard. 'You have something to live for, Hanna,' Ava said as she slid an arm around her sister's waist and pulled her close, feeling her pain. 'You have a family who adores you, who'd never be the same if something happened to you. Please don't say that again, because it's simply not true.'

Hanna made a noise that Ava couldn't decipher, so she simply hugged her even tighter, wanting her to feel just how loved she was.

'I will never be the same again, Ava,' Hanna whispered as they stood just outside the office building. 'Something broke inside of me that day, something that I will never get back, and some days I wonder how I can even breathe knowing that I'll never see them again, that I'll never hold my son in my arms or hear my husband's laughter. I can't explain how hard that makes the very act of living, but it does, no matter how much I know that you and Mama and Father love me. It's just not the same.'

Ava knew better than to tell her it would get easier, because what did she know? How could she possibly understand what it was like to lose a husband and child, to have to live with that loss every day? It was no wonder Hanna was prepared to risk so much, to do everything she could to stop another mother from losing her child forever.

'I'll be careful,' Ava said. 'I promise I will.'

'I don't know if you *can* be careful if you do what Noah asks of you,' Hanna said, taking a step back and shaking her head. 'He won't stop with just this. He is so focused on what he's doing that I don't know if he can even see the danger he's putting you in.'

The little piece of paper was burning a hole in Ava's pocket. Just knowing it was there made her feel as if she were deceiving her sister, that she had agreed to be part of something that Hanna wasn't aware of, even though she didn't even know yet what was written on it. But she didn't believe her, that Noah could be so dangerous or ruthless.

'What he said about our father . . .'

Hanna shook her head. 'He can't know. I don't believe that anyone could know.'

Ava touched her sister's arm. 'If you haven't told anyone, and I haven't told anyone, then it must simply be a rumour. But should we say something to him? Warn him?'

Hanna nodded, before embracing her. 'I'll talk to him. He'd want to know what was being said.' She held her for a long moment, before finally letting go of Ava and beginning to walk away. 'I love you, sister. Just please, be careful.'

Ava watched her go, experiencing the strangest feeling, as if Hanna were saying a final goodbye to her. But then she hurried inside the office building and went to the bathroom, closing the door to ensure her privacy before sliding the piece of paper from her pocket. She unfolded it, her heart thumping when she saw that it was an address.

She shut her eyes and thought of Noah; the way he'd looked at her, his smile, the confident manner in which he'd spoken, the sparkle in his eyes. He might be dangerous, but he was also incredibly magnetic, too, and so passionate about the work he was doing. There was a knock on the door, someone else wanting to use the toilet, and Ava read the address again, committing it to memory before putting the piece of paper in her mouth and forcing herself to eat it.

The paper was clumpy and wet in her mouth, despite how small it was, but she forced herself to swallow it down and then opened the door, smiling brightly at the secretary waiting on the other side.

Would I ever be brazen enough to visit him?

She straightened her shoulders. Of course she would. They had an agreement whereby she was to help him, nothing more. Thinking that he could want to see her for any other reason than the cause was her being foolish.

Ava took a deep breath before lifting her hand to knock against the door. She'd walked to the unfamiliar apartment block straight after work, becoming more and more nervous with every step, and now that she was here, her heart was hammering. Perhaps she shouldn't have come. It was completely out of character for her to even consider being with a man alone, especially one who was essentially a stranger to her, but if she wanted to work for him, then she was going to have to stop questioning herself.

But when the door opened, her heart almost skipped a beat.

Noah was dressed in the same clothes as earlier, only this time he was holding a glass of something alcoholic, and his two top buttons were open to show a glimpse of his chest. If she'd thought he looked handsome before, she didn't even know how she'd describe him now. There was a confidence about him that she found herself drawn to, because it seemed so different to the other men she knew.

'I didn't know if you'd come,' he said.

'I didn't know, either. I'm not exactly used to this type of subterfuge.'

He looked out, brushing against her as he peered down the hallway. 'You weren't followed?'

Her eyes widened. 'I don't think so. Should I have been checking?'

Noah just laughed. 'You have much to learn, little butterfly, but this is why you're so perfect. No one would ever suspect you'd be involved in anything with that innocent face of yours.'

She wasn't sure whether to bristle or smile, but given the way Noah was grinning at her she decided to take it as a compliment. When he stepped aside and indicated that she should come in, she did, taking her coat off and folding it over her arm as he locked the door behind him.

'Does anyone know you're here?' he asked.

She was tempted to lie and say yes, given that she was alone in a strange man's apartment, but instead she shook her head and told the truth. 'No.'

Noah walked across the room and took down a glass from a kitchen cabinet, picking up a bottle and pouring some liquor into it, as well as topping up his own.

'Drink?'

She barely ever consumed alcohol. The last time had been when she'd found the Goldmans in her attic and her father had asked her to join him in his study.

'Yes,' she replied, despite her nerves. Perhaps it would help to settle them?

Noah came closer, too close if she was honest, before inviting her to take a seat across from him.

'This is where you live?' she asked, looking around the apartment and thinking that it felt more like a family home than that of a bachelor.

'I don't stay for more than a few days in the same place,' he said. 'The longer I'm involved in all this, the more paranoid I get that someone will give me up to the authorities. So I'm constantly moving from place to place.'

She studied him, taking a sip of her drink and trying to stop her eyes from welling up as it burned in her mouth and throat. She doubted she'd ever get used to drinking straight liquor no matter how many times she tried.

'My father is the same, he's always paranoid about listening devices at home.'

'Your father has every reason to be cautious. He's surrounded by some of the most powerful men in the country, who'd love nothing more than to see him fall and take his place. Including your fiancé.'

She paled. 'Heinrich?' *What does he know of Heinrich?*

He held her gaze. 'Surely you must know how dangerous an ambitious young SS man can be?' He laughed. 'And don't look so surprised, I know everything there is to know about you. I wouldn't trust just anyone to work for me.'

She took another sip of her drink so she didn't have to answer.

'Ava, why did you come here?' he asked. 'You're engaged to an SS man, you have a good job, you're the kind of young woman the Nazi Party loves. Why did you decide to become involved in any of this?'

'Perhaps I'm trying to right my wrongs.' She swallowed.

He smiled. 'Perhaps.'

She took a deep breath. 'My sister told me that you're ruthless. That no matter what you say, you don't care about how many people you have to lose in pursuit of the greater good. She wasn't happy that I'd agreed to help you.'

'She said that?'

Ava cleared her throat. 'She told me that you could be as dangerous to a woman as Adolf Hitler could be, just for different reasons. That you would stop at nothing to further your goals.'

'And did she tell you what those goals were? Did she explain why I am both nothing and everything, like our esteemed Führer?'

Ava took another tiny sip of her drink as Noah edged closer, leaning forward on the armchair that he was sitting on. She watched as he downed what was left in his glass before holding it between his fingers, his elbows on his knees as his eyes met hers, making it impossible for her to look away. Had her instincts been wrong in coming to see him?

'No,' she whispered. 'She did not tell me those things.'

'Your sister is right, I will stop at nothing to eliminate the evil in our country and help to restore it to the Germany we were before this war *and* the last one. If that means losing some good people along the way, then so be it, it is the cost of war. There are millions

159

rotting in camps, being killed by the thousands, so I'm constantly reminded of the bigger picture. That sometimes, in order to achieve greatness, we have to make sacrifices along the way.'

She had the most overwhelming feeling that she shouldn't have come then, even though she was powerless to get up and walk out of the door. Noah was magnetic, and despite the fear rising inside of her, she stayed seated, her gaze locked on his.

'I am like Hitler in that I will stop at nothing to get what I want. But unlike him, I will not tolerate hate nor lies. I want all people unified, not one race promoted as being better than another.'

'Why?' she found herself asking. 'Why do you think so differently to everyone else?'

'Because I've lost people I loved very dearly. Because I have seen the pain in the eyes of those taken against their will.' He placed his glass on the low table beside him. 'And because I'm one of the few people who spent time in one of the camps and lived to tell the tale. I also don't believe that I'm different to everyone else, I believe that many others feel the same as me but are too scared to do anything.'

Ava forced herself to finish her drink, taking a moment to feel the heat pooling in her belly. Perhaps she could get used to it, after all.

'Then what exactly are you planning to do?' she asked as he pulled his chair even closer to hers. 'Why do you need me to look at the diary? What am I even looking for?'

He smiled and reached up to brush a stray hair from her face, his fingers whispering gently across her skin. 'We are trying to create a fresh start for Germany,' he said. 'An end to the war.'

'And you think that the information I gather for you will help you to do that?'

His eyes darted to her lips and back again. Ava found herself waiting for him to close the distance, her breath catching in her throat as she tilted her face upwards. Heinrich couldn't have been further from her mind.

'Yes,' he whispered. 'You, Ava Müller, could help us to change everything.'

She swallowed. 'I think I should go now.' Her voice was a whisper as his breath warmed her skin.

'You're free to go whenever you like. I'm not keeping you here.'

But Ava didn't want to go, and when he finally kissed her, she slipped her arms around his neck, lost in his embrace, wondering how she'd ever thought she was in love with Heinrich, because his kisses had never made her feel like this.

Chapter Fifteen

Eliana

Eliana stood in the store and looked around. It was just before opening, which meant the shelves had been stocked, and despite the people already lined up outside, it was still quiet inside. Silence had become normal for her during her months in the attic, the constant quiet so hard to adjust to at first, fuelled by a fear that had been all-consuming. If they made any noise, they could be found, which had led to them moving about like mice.

But despite all that, it hadn't taken her long to adjust to being back in the world, albeit in a different world to the one she'd left behind. No one saw her now. She was able to move about the store, talk to customers, live a life that hadn't been hers to live for years. She felt as if she were both visible and invisible at the same time – women she recognised as mothers from her old school had passed her and even spoken to her, without seeing her. The blonde hair and change of appearance hadn't truly changed what *she* saw in the mirror when she looked at herself – the same eyes blinked back at her, she wore the same expressions – but it had been enough to stop anyone from recognising her. Or perhaps it was simply that no one expected to see a girl like her any more; they clearly thought all the Jews had been well and truly eradicated from polite society. Regardless, she was no longer scared that someone might know who she was. The more days that passed, the more confident she became.

'Eliana?' Ethan called to her and she turned, seeing that he was carrying more goods into the store. His blue eyes caught hers, and she couldn't help but admire his broad shoulders and strong arms as he hefted the box in front of him, his dark hair lifting from his forehead as he tilted his head back.

She ran over to help him, only too pleased to be of assistance. He'd been so kind to her since she'd arrived – he was shy but polite, warm yet a little nervous – which was incidentally exactly how she was feeling being around his family and in the store. It was the first time she'd ever had a proper job, but all those years helping her father had helped her settle quickly into her new role. She was just grateful Ethan was such a patient teacher.

Eliana helped Ethan to place the flour on the shelves, knowing how quickly it would disappear as soon as the doors opened for the day. By the time they were down to a few sacks, fights would begin as those queueing realised there wouldn't be enough for everyone waiting. Because according to Ethan, there was never enough, no matter how much they started with each day.

'How are you?' he asked, glancing at her as they both placed the sacks of flour on the shelves.

'I'm fine. Grateful, above anything else.'

He smiled, catching her eye. 'You don't have to pretend with me. I know you must be missing your family.'

She hesitated. 'You know about me, don't you? About how I came to be here?'

His smile was warm, and she found it so easy to be around him. The fact that he was the same age as her was refreshing too, after so long having only her parents and brother for company. She hadn't realised how much she'd been craving the company of others.

163

'I know enough,' he replied. 'But you can talk to me, when it's just the two of us. I promise that I'm very good at keeping secrets.'

Eliana laughed. 'Well, I have a lot of them. Are you sure you want me to offload everything on you?'

Ethan laughed, too, and Eliana found herself wishing for more time with him as his father came in and called out that he was opening the doors. In other words, the chaos of the day was about to begin.

'Ethan, has there been any news?' she whispered, as they readied themselves behind the counter. 'Of what happened to all the Jews? Those that survived the first waves of violence?'

The laughter that had lit his eyes earlier was gone now. 'No news that's good. There are multiple concentration camps where they're holding German, Polish and French Jews by the sounds of it. They've rounded them up all throughout Europe, and it's still happening.'

She shivered as she saw the sadness in his face. 'You've lost someone you loved, to one of the camps?'

They both straightened as his father called out that everyone should make an orderly line; people she knew who were fervent supporters of Hitler's regime stood merely feet from her. It sent an initial shiver of panic through her, before she remembered they couldn't see her, her confidence returning at being able to stand before them, unseen.

'I have,' he murmured. 'And I don't believe they'll ever be coming home.'

Hours later, and with barely a grain of food left in the store, Eliana watched as Ethan closed the door and locked it, turning the sign to 'Closed'. His father and uncle were in the main storeroom,

164

receiving a delivery and getting everything prepared for the next day, which meant that it was just the two of them again.

Which meant it was also time to find out if any messages had been passed to Ethan during the day.

Eliana stretched and then found her way to the smaller store-room that was hidden behind the others, waving to Ethan's father as she passed him and receiving a nod in reply. It was barely bigger than a broom closet, but hidden beneath a pile of old food sacks was a typewriter and reels of paper. Her job was to type up any information that needed to be shared with other members of the network that the Müller family were involved with, but most often she was simply to receive any messages and take them home with her for Karl. To begin with, from what she understood, they'd wanted to take over what the White Rose had begun – spreading information far and wide by leaflet drops, in an effort to tell every-one throughout Berlin the truth of what was happening. But the risk of being discovered had been too great, especially when the SS were so ruthless at unearthing those who weren't loyal.

'I thought you might like this,' Ethan said, appearing in the doorway with two slices of bread covered in jam. Her stomach rumbled at the sight of it. 'There is something to be typed tonight.'

'Thank you,' she said, carefully taking the food from him. The last thing she needed was to get sticky, jammy fingers on the paper, especially when it was the first day there'd been something for her to do. 'I thought jam was almost impossible to get these days?'

'It is,' he replied, 'unless you own a grocer's and keep enough hidden to last for years.'

They both laughed, and Eliana was reminded again how easy she found it to be around him.

'Apparently there are stocks of all sorts of luxury items for the high-ranked officers and their families,' he said. 'Coffee, jam, chocolate . . . everything you can think of.'

Eliana finished chewing her mouthful and looked up at him. 'It's true, what you've heard,' she said. 'I've been hidden somewhere, so life has been very bleak, but we had the best food we could wish for. The family helping me seemed to have access to everything they needed.'

'And you trusted them?' Ethan asked. 'If they were eating like kings, I can only guess what their involvement in the party is.'

'We had no choice but to trust them. But honestly, I think they're different.'

'Or they're trying to ease their conscience by helping one family and pretending they're not monsters like everyone else?'

Eliana looked up at him, suddenly losing her appetite as she digested his words.

'I'm sorry, I should never have said that. Please forgive me.'

'No,' she said, setting the slice of bread down on the plate. 'You should have said it. You don't have to hold your tongue around me, I appreciate your honesty.' *Even if that honesty is hard to swallow.*

Ethan leaned against the doorframe, his eyes darting away before coming back to meet hers. 'Well, I should have at least waited until you'd finished eating, so I didn't put you off your food.'

Eliana grinned back at him, shaking her head. He was impossible not to laugh at, or laugh with in this case, and she appreciated his efforts to make light of what was an awful situation.

'So, other than jam, tell me what you miss the most, from your life before,' Ethan said.

She loved that he'd swiftly changed the topic away from the Müllers. 'I don't even know where to start. My mother's roast chicken, or her latkes, or her matzo ball soup.' She sighed. 'And sweets. I keep dreaming of ice creams or chocolate, but mostly just ice cream.'

Ethan groaned. 'I keep thinking about my mother's pork cutlets. I think I could eat them every night for the rest of my life.'

'Do you ever think about what we'd be doing, if the war hadn't happened?' she asked.

'You mean do I think about all the dances, all the long summer days swimming in the lake, all the films we'd be watching?'

Eliana watched him, seeing that he missed it all just as much as she did, even though he'd been afforded a freedom throughout the war that she hadn't. She hadn't thought about dancing in a long time, but now that he'd mentioned it, dancing was something she missed deeply, too.

'Yes,' she finally said. 'All those things. Even just lying in the sun, reading a book and laughing with friends.'

'Eating ice cream?' he teased.

She laughed. 'Yes, eating ice cream. Of course.'

Ethan slid to the floor, his back against the doorframe, as they spoke. 'Sometimes it's hard to believe how quickly things changed.'

They sat in silence for a moment, until he spoke again.

'When there were still Jews in the city, we had to turn them away, even though they were starving. The women would stand there with their little children, begging us for food, and all we could give them was whatever was left at the end of the day. A bit of stale bread was often the best of what we had. But then we weren't even allowed to give them that.'

'If you hadn't followed the rules, you'd have been arrested,' Eliana said, seeing the anguish on his face, the memories that clearly still haunted him. 'You'd have filled their stomachs for one meal, and then you and your parents would have disappeared in the night.'

'Sometimes even knowing that doesn't help, though. It doesn't make what we did any easier to accept.'

'No, but it's the life we've been forced to live. And there is no black and white, good and evil. There are many people who are having to exist in the grey, just to preserve their own lives.'

They were silent for a time, with Ethan keeping watch as she finished her bread and then dusted her hands together to rid them of any breadcrumbs. Then she set up her workstation, using an apple box as her makeshift desk, positioning her typewriter and sitting cross-legged on the floor. She had a sack beneath her, but the cold still managed to leach through to her bones, making her shiver almost instantly.

'I almost forgot to give you this,' Ethan said, standing up and slipping a piece of paper from his pocket.

The note had been passed to Ethan at some stage during the day, tucked inside a ration book, which meant that there was something important to share with the network. She'd been told she could go weeks without having to type anything, so this meant something was happening.

'I think they're planning something that could end it all,' he said, when she looked up.

'What sort of something?' she asked.

He shrugged and went back to his position by the door, to keep a lookout. 'I don't know. But there seems to be a lot more activity than usual, and someone said that Noah was back.'

'Who's Noah?'

'He's been instrumental in our entire network from the very beginning, but I don't know him personally.'

She nodded and placed the piece of paper to her left so she could begin typing. But before she did, she looked up and smiled at Ethan, who was still watching her.

'One day we'll be dancing again, Eliana. One day you'll be able to eat ice cream every day if you so desire.'

She imagined meeting him at a different time, wondered whether perhaps he might have invited her to one of those dances. 'I certainly hope you're right.'

Ethan held her gaze for a moment before looking away, staring out of the door to make certain that no one was coming. They had a plan whereby she would hide the typewriter and put any paper into a sack if someone came, before the two of them would lie down on top of it and pretend to be two young lovers, caught kissing. The theory was that no one searching would think to ask them to stand up, but she wasn't so sure it was a fail-safe plan.

Eliana smiled to herself as she began typing. *It might not be fail-safe, but I wouldn't mind an excuse to cuddle up to Ethan.*

Two hours later, when Eliana had finished typing, she stretched and indicated to Ethan that she was done. Because they didn't have a printing press, she had to type multiple copies of each page, and by the end of it her fingers were aching and her back was sore.

She left the stack on the apple crate, thankful when Ethan came to lift the heavy typewriter for her. They both hid it, and when they went to stand, she could see that his back was as stiff as hers from sitting in the doorway.

'I think we deserve a cup of tea and something hot to eat,' he announced, taking out a sack and filling it with the papers for his father to come and collect later. 'Would you like to come back to the house with me?'

Eliana hesitated. If she'd had her own parents to go home to, she knew she would have declined, knowing she needed their approval first. And that very fact stopped her now, thinking of them still locked away in the stuffy attic. She wanted to behave in a way that they would approve of.

'I would love to, but I'm so tired,' she said. 'Would you mind walking me home though?'

He nodded. 'Of course.'

'I'm so scared of the bombs,' she admitted, as she put her coat on and they walked through the dark store. Ethan checked the doors and collected his own coat, and she took his arm as they walked to the front, where he let them out on to the street. It wasn't far to walk to the Müllers' apartment, but she was grateful to have him accompanying her, especially when so many buildings had been reduced to rubble around them.

'Ethan, earlier today, you mentioned you'd lost someone,' she said, hoping she wasn't being too nosy. She realised then that her arm was still looped through his, but she decided to leave it there, feeling safer with him close, especially in the dark. It was almost impossible not to be scared of the SS, even with papers in her pocket to prove her identity – or of bombs lighting up the sky or falling around them.

'I lost many someones,' he said. 'First, our teacher disappeared, and that was my first real understanding of what was going on, that people in our lives could be there one day and disappear the next. And then my uncle's wife was taken, our doctor, and then . . .' He took a deep breath, and for a moment she wondered if he was even going to tell her who else had gone. 'And then my best friend.'

'He was arrested?'

'Rounded up with other families in our neighbourhood and loaded on to a train. I hid and watched. I knew it was dangerous but I needed to see what they were doing with him, where they were taking him. I watched him and his brothers until they disappeared from sight, and I just knew that it was the last time I'd see them.'

'You were a member of Hitlerjugend?' she asked.

'I was.'

'And even so, you remained best friends with this boy? Throughout it all?'

'His name was, *is*, Ezra,' Ethan said. 'Remember our conversation earlier, about grey areas?'

She nodded.

'Well, I didn't have a choice about being in Hitlerjugend, but I did have a choice about how I treated those around me. Even though we had to see each other secretly, so no one else saw us, he remained my best friend.'

Ethan was a rare man, she'd give him that, and it only made her like him all the more. He'd clearly been raised by good parents, kind parents; people who wouldn't accept what was going on around them, but knew they had to at least appear to play by the rules to avoid detection.

'How have you managed to avoid being called up for service?' she asked.

Ethan's arm fell away from hers then, and she watched as he patted the breast pocket of his coat and listened to his sigh. 'I haven't,' he said, taking something out and passing it to her.

She squinted in the almost-darkness, trying to make out what it said. But after reading the first sentence, she knew what it was.

'Do your parents know?'

He nodded. 'Yes.'

'You were able to avoid being called up until now, because of the grocery store?'

'I was. But apparently they need every man they can get now,' he said. 'I had pneumonia as a child, and it damaged my lungs, so in the beginning that was another reason for me to stay home, because I didn't pass the medical. But now it seems they're taking any man, no matter what.'

'I'm sorry,' she whispered, taking hold of his arm again, hating the thought of this gentle, caring man being sent to fight a battle that he didn't believe in. 'I'm so sorry that you've managed to stay clear of the fighting for so long, only to be called up now.'

'So am I.'

'Who will they send to replace you in the store?'

He cleared his throat, holding her gaze. 'You. You are my replacement, Eliana.'

She gasped. 'Me? I'm the reason you've been called up?'

Ethan shook his head. 'No, you are the reason my parents will have help when I'm gone. If it weren't you, it would have been someone else. My papers had already arrived.'

They walked the rest of the way to the Müllers' apartment in silence, and when they got there, Eliana turned to Ethan, blinking away tears that this beautiful man in front of her would soon be gone.

She slid her arms around him, refusing to be shy now that she knew how little time they had together, drawing him close and placing her head on his chest, closing her eyes when his arms went slowly around her. They stood like that for a long while, until she finally stepped back, looking up at him, hoping he knew what he'd come to mean to her in such a short time. Given everything that had happened to her and her family over the past few years, genuinely kind, good people had been in short supply, which made her appreciate Ethan and his family all the more.

'You're a good man, Ethan. I feel so privileged to have met you.'

He hesitated, watching her, as if deciding what to do, before placing a warm, slow kiss on her cheek that she felt all the way down to her toes. It was as close to a first kiss as she'd ever had, and she couldn't have imagined it being better if she'd tried.

'Goodnight, Elly,' he murmured against her skin.

'Goodnight, Ethan.'

And with him watching, his eyes burning into her back, she ran up the steps to the door and let herself in, finding it almost impossible to wipe the smile from her face as she ducked her head down, not wanting anyone to see her. She was acutely aware that, despite her change in appearance, someone who'd known her from before might recognise her.

'You must be the Müllers' niece!' came a shrill woman's voice that took her completely by surprise.

Eliana breathed a sigh of relief that the woman was a stranger, before glancing back to see if Ethan was still there. To her disappointment, he was already gone. She turned back to the woman standing at the foot of the stairs with a young girl whom Eliana presumed was her daughter tucked into her side. They were well dressed, with the woman wearing a thick fur coat that for some reason looked familiar to her, even though she knew that was a ridiculous thought.

'I am,' she said, remembering the role she was to play, fixing her smile just as she'd practised in Ava's bedroom when she'd been trying on her clothes and preparing to become someone else. 'I'm very fortunate to be staying with them, although I have to say that I'm still getting used to the air raids here.'

The woman was smiling brightly, but Eliana felt like she was about to be interrogated.

'I don't think any of us will ever get used to those. But remind me, your parents are . . .'

Eliana held her smile, as difficult as it was, trying to push away the fear that was rising inside of her. 'My father is an officer, posted outside of Germany, and my mother . . .' She looked away and cleared her throat, finding it particularly easy to make tears form in her eyes. After so much loss, it wasn't hard to find something sad to fixate on. 'My mother was killed by an American bomb. I wasn't home, and I came back to find our house destroyed and my mother—'

'Oh dear, please, you don't need to continue,' the woman said, holding her hand to her heart and then rushing forward to engulf

Eliana in an awkward hug. 'I didn't realise you'd suffered so much loss, and your poor father, losing his wife when he's away bravely leading our soldiers.'

It was a lie of course, but this woman had likely already heard all of this before and was simply trying to see if her story matched up, to make certain that Eliana was who they said she was. From what Hanna had told her, everyone was suspicious of everyone else now, trying to find fault, trying to find traces of a lineage that wasn't pure enough, their terror at someone having Jewish blood at fever pitch.

Eliana nodded, dabbing at her eyes with the backs of her fingers. 'Thank you. Everyone has been very kind, but especially my aunt and uncle. I don't know what I'd have done without them, and I know it's been a great comfort to my father too, knowing he doesn't have to worry about me.'

'I haven't seen your aunt recently. She's not staying here?'

Eliana could tell how insincere this woman was. She'd switched from concern over Eliana's mother to questioning her about Frau Müller, barely pausing for breath. If it had been any other time, Eliana wouldn't have given her the time of day, and she certainly wouldn't be letting her interrogate her so brazenly.

'She's staying at their country house. My uncle likes to return home there and know she's safe, and my cousins would be there, too, if they didn't have such important work to do in the city.'

The little girl peered out from behind her mother then, and that was when Eliana realised what she was wearing. It was the Jungmädelbund uniform. Of course, children as young as ten were being indoctrinated now, to ensure they hated Jews and everyone else who wasn't part of the 'master race', when they were barely old enough to think for themselves. Eliana wondered if this little girl already had such hate running through her blood and her mind.

These children had never been around Jewish boys and girls – it was probably impossible for them to imagine a mixing of religions and cultures.

'Well, we must let you get home, sorry to keep you,' the woman said. 'It was just such a wonderful coincidence to run into you like this, especially after hearing all about you from your uncle.'

Eliana began to walk up the stairs, not realising they were on their way up, too. She'd expected them to be leaving, which now that she thought about it didn't make sense at all given the hour.

'You're here to visit the Müllers?' Eliana asked, glancing at the girl again, who appeared to be studying her intently.

'Oh no, we moved into the apartment upstairs over Christmas,' the woman said. 'You should see it, it's absolutely stunning, and we have the most beautiful art! Some days I can't stop staring at it all, I have to pinch myself that it's all ours. And look at this coat! Would you believe I found it hanging in the wardrobe for me? I haven't taken it off since we arrived.'

Eliana's voice caught in her throat, her smile impossible to hold as she failed to respond, as she realised why the beautiful fur coat had seemed so familiar. What was she supposed to say to that? How was she supposed to react to this woman proudly announcing that she'd moved into an apartment that didn't belong to her, that had been Eliana's home? *That still has my papa's precious artwork on the walls! That had my mama's fur coat still hanging where she left it in the wardrobe?* Did these people even wonder how these homes became available? Did they ever think of the people who had lived there before them, or the lives that had been ruined? Or did they simply think that anything that had once belonged to the Jews should be redistributed among them all?

'I – I . . .' She could feel her face turning red, knew that both the woman and her child were staring at her.

'Are you all right?'

'No,' Eliana said, shaking her head and holding her stomach, doing her best to feign illness. 'I think something has upset my stomach, I'm feeling quite unwell.'

The woman took hold of her arm and helped her up the last few steps, and even the feel of her skin against Eliana's and the brush of her mother's coat made her want to scream, made her want to turn and grab the woman by her shoulders and shake her, to push her down the stairs and watch her tumble to the bottom. She'd never had violent thoughts before, but in that moment, she truly felt as if she were capable of murder.

But instead she fumbled for her key, her fingers shaking as she pushed it into the lock, mumbling her thanks as the woman called out behind her, trying to hold the facade together for just a moment longer until the door was shut.

Eliana ran through the apartment to the bathroom, bile rising in her throat, burning in her mouth as she doubled over the toilet, emptying the contents of her stomach until there was nothing left. She cried as she kept being sick, as her tears fell, as pain rippled through her body.

'Eliana?'

She heard Hanna's worried call but couldn't respond, wiping her face and falling back to her knees when she tried to stand, curling up on the cold floor tiles as her entire body trembled, as she fought not to scream.

Before she knew it, Hanna was behind her, her body moulding to Eliana's as she wrapped her arms around her and held her tight, soothing her, instinctively seeming to know that Eliana needed to be held. And then Eliana cried so hard that her stomach hurt, her cheeks ached, her heart broke. Even her bones seemed to ache with her pain.

'They're living in our apartment. They're living my life as if it was theirs to steal.' She sobbed as she tried to breathe, gasping for air. 'When will it ever end? When will we ever get our lives back? When will they stop taking what isn't theirs to take?'

Hanna didn't say anything, but Eliana could feel her silent tears falling against her neck, wetting her skin. She kept her arms wound tightly around her as they lay and shivered on the cold bathroom floor.

'It has to get better,' Hanna eventually whispered. 'It has to, Eliana. It can't be like this forever.'

Eliana closed her eyes, Hanna's arms still wrapped around her. She only wished that she could believe her.

Chapter Sixteen

Ava

It had been months since Ava was last home, which meant that some time had passed since she'd seen her mother. Under normal circumstances they would never have been parted for so long, but with the Goldmans needing her mother's care, they'd had to devise a series of excuses as to why her mother chose to stay at the country house. They predominantly centred around her father preferring to know she was safe and well away from any bombing, which was why he liked to send his daughters back home whenever he could, too.

That afternoon, with her mother downstairs in the kitchen and Zelda gone for the day, Ava took food up to the Goldmans and invited them to come down to the top floor of the house and stretch their legs. They were never quite brave enough to ask them downstairs, but she knew how much any reprieve from the attic meant to them, especially David.

'Do you have any news from Eliana?' he asked, looking relieved when she reached into her pocket and produced a letter.

'I do. She made me bring this for you, and she said that you must read it out loud to your parents.'

He nodded and put it in his pocket. 'Thank you. You wouldn't believe how much I miss her.' He grunted. 'How much I miss everything.'

Ava didn't know what to say; she could only imagine how difficult it would be for him, being stuck up there without his sister, with only his parents for company.

'I know it won't help your boredom, but I made you a promise, David, and I wanted to make good on it.'

His eyebrows lifted in surprise, as if he hadn't expected her to ever follow through with her promise.

She reached into the bag at her feet and lifted out a pistol to give him. 'My father told me to give you this. He understands your need to feel safe, to be able to protect your family.'

David stepped forward and took it from her, looking over his shoulder at his parents who were stretching their legs properly by walking up and down the hallway.

'Would you mind if I took the bag, too?' he asked. 'I don't want to worry them any more than they already are, so it would be best to keep it hidden from sight.'

Ava handed him the bag. 'Of course. But he said to tell you that there are six bullets loaded, and a handful more in the bag.' She cleared her throat and leaned a little closer to him. 'He also said that if they find you, if anyone makes it up to the attic for whatever reason, that you are not to hesitate to use it.'

David's gaze was still trained on the gun, but when he finally looked up at her, she noticed a steeliness to his stare that she'd never seen before.

'Tell him that I have no intention of hesitating. But I'd prefer to be of use elsewhere. He still hasn't found something for me to do?'

'Other than typing the notes he's given you?'

David sighed. 'Having a typewriter delivered and being asked to type his notes wasn't what I had in mind when I asked for a job.'

'Yes, but it will be a factual account for after the war, of what has been happening here. To someone, one day, it will be important.'

Her mother came upstairs then with a tray of food, and when she disappeared up to the attic with David's parents, the pair of them started to walk. Ava noticed that he seemed less relaxed today.

'Eliana is thriving, you know. She's loving her job, and she told me that it's the most surreal feeling, to be able to work among people and have no one recognise her.'

He smiled. 'I can only imagine how she must feel in her disguise. I'm happy for her. Even though I miss her terribly, I'm so happy that she has the chance to live.'

'Will you go back to your studies, if . . .' The rest of her question hung between them.

'I hope so. The only thing I've ever wanted to be is a doctor – a surgeon actually.'

Ava smiled. 'You know, I remembered something about you the other day, from my childhood. I remembered seeing you with a little dog, throwing a stick for him down by the river.'

'Ahh, yes. He was a wonderful little dog. He belonged to my grandparents and they used to bring him with them when they came to stay. That's something else I can imagine, having a dog by my side one day.'

'Well, I shall imagine you as a surgeon with a little dog at your feet, then,' she said with a laugh. 'How does that sound?'

He laughed back at her, and she realised it was the first time they'd ever had such an easy conversation.

'Tell me about you. About what you're involved in,' he said. 'I overheard our fathers speaking.'

Ava was taken aback. 'About me?'

'Yes. Something to do with being worried that a certain young man might be taking advantage of you. I believe they were talking about the resistance movement.'

'Taken advantage of?' She shook her head. 'Noah has been very upfront about the risks involved, and I made the decision to do what he asked. No one is taking advantage of anyone.'

David stopped by the steps to go back up to the attic. 'So he is putting you in danger?'

She didn't want to argue with him, but she also needed him to know that she'd chosen to be part of this world, and that Noah was very much one of the reasons she'd changed her perspective.

'I'm choosing to help the cause, David, the same as anyone else in the resistance is doing. The same way that Hanna is choosing to help.'

His eyes were sad, and she knew that it would take her a long time to forget the way he was looking at her. 'I'm just saying that I would want to keep you from danger, Ava. I don't like the thought of him taking advantage of you, especially when it's clear you have feelings for him.'

'We're not romantically involved, it's a professional relationship and nothing more,' she said firmly. The last thing she wanted was for anyone to know how she felt about Noah, not when she was engaged to Heinrich, even if it was only David who'd figured it out. 'But I appreciate your warnings. Thank you for thinking of me.'

David nodded, but she wasn't certain she'd convinced him.

'I'll see you again soon,' she said, as he began to climb back up to the attic.

He turned and looked at her. 'Keep asking your father if there's something more for me to do,' he said. 'Tell him there's only so long I can stay cooped up here. And Ava, please stay safe.'

'Perhaps he'd rather protect you than let you risk your life?'

David smiled, albeit sadly, before disappearing from sight. Once her mother had come back down, they secured the attic staircase and went downstairs to the kitchen. But Ava was deep in thought, and it appeared her mother was too, because they took their dinner to the table and ate in relative silence, as she thought about the Goldmans moving about two floors above them.

'Is your sister keeping well?' her mother finally asked.

'Yes, Hanna's fine.' Or at least Ava thought she was. They hadn't seen much of each other in the past couple of weeks, since she'd been seeing more and more of Noah.

'And Eliana? She's adjusted to the change?'

Ava nodded. 'She has.

They continued eating, but she noticed that her mother pushed her stew around on the plate a lot, doing more moving than eating.

'I overheard some of your conversation with David earlier,' her mother eventually said.

Ava waited for her to continue, setting down her spoon.

'I don't want to interfere, but he's right about no young man asking you to do things, using his relationship with you to—'

'David was ill-informed. That is not the case,' Ava replied, bristling. 'There is nothing for you to worry about.'

'But if it were the case, you need to remember how careful you must be. Your father's involvement – well, he's always tried to be as careful as possible, to do things that could easily be blamed on another.'

Ava's mother set her spoon down, too.

'If whatever this man has asked you to do is something that will lead straight back to you? It's not only you who's in danger, whether you're in a romantic relationship with him or not. You'd be endangering all of us, the Goldmans included.'

Her words washed over Ava, and she knew her face was reddening as her mother watched her. How typical of her mama to say the one thing that she knew she couldn't argue with.

'I know what's at stake,' Ava eventually said. 'But thank you for the reminder. I shall keep what you said close to my heart.'

They both picked up their spoons again and resumed eating, although Ava found each mouthful hard to swallow. Because, despite what she'd just said, and despite understanding the risk, she'd already agreed to do something for Noah that would very much be something that only she could be blamed for, should the deceit be discovered. Her world had changed after her first afternoon with Noah; and when he'd asked her to access the diary, to obtain information that only a few people would know about, she'd realised there was nothing she wouldn't do to help him.

'Ava! There you are,' Hanna said, rushing to her and helping her off with her coat, at the same time giving her a panicked look. It had been a week since she left the country house, and the first night she'd returned to the apartment to find her sister there. They were more likely to see one another as they bumped around in the dark, hurrying down to the cellar during an air raid. 'Heinrich has been here waiting very patiently for you.'

Ava shot the same kind of panicked look straight back at her sister. *Heinrich is here?*

She took a deep breath and fixed her smile, hurrying into the sitting room to find him with Eliana. She glanced at Hanna and saw the tight set of her face, and then noted the high colour on Eliana's cheeks.

'Heinrich! What a lovely surprise,' she said as he stood. 'I wish I'd known to expect you. I would have come home sooner.'

'I went to your office but was told you'd already left for the day, so I came here,' he said, as his eyes ran up and down the length of her body before fixing on her face. 'But you weren't here, either.'

'Well, first of all, I see you've made the acquaintance of my delightful cousin,' she said, stalling as she tried to put a story together in her mind. 'But yes, you're quite right that I left work a little early. I had some errands to run, for my father.'

Heinrich frowned. 'That's strange, because your father—'

'Papa!' Ava exclaimed as her father entered the room, holding two drinks that she presumed were for himself and Heinrich. 'I went and visited your old friend Otto, at the hospital, and I managed to find him some fruit as you'd requested. I know you said not to visit him until later in the week, but I was able to leave early today so I went straight there. I'm sorry I didn't tell you.'

She smiled sweetly at Heinrich, but he seemed more interested in her father and watching his response.

'Thank you, Ava, although you would have saved us all some worry if you'd simply told me you were going today.'

'Sorry, Papa,' she said, before going to sit beside Heinrich, forcing herself to take his hand. 'And I'm sorry for any worry I caused you, too. It's very unusual for me to go anywhere other than home, work and to the grocer's, as you well know.'

She noticed the way Heinrich was looking at her blouse, and she glanced down to see that she'd missed one of the buttons. Heat rose in her cheeks, and she turned away from him slightly to do it up. But when she turned back, he simply smiled and took her hand again, and all she could do was pray that he didn't smell another man on her skin, for it was all but impossible for Noah's aftershave not to have clung to her hair or her clothes.

She looked over at Eliana, who was showing great interest in some of her mother's knitting she'd left behind the last time she'd been at the apartment. And even though Ava was almost positive that Eliana didn't know how to knit, she certainly made it look like she knew what she was doing, her head bent as she avoided having to so much as look at the devil seated so close to her.

'Speaking of the grocer's, I hear your cousin Elly here is working there.'

Ava nodded and glanced up at Hanna, wishing she'd known what had already been discussed. But they all knew the story they were to tell, which meant that nothing she said would contradict what her sister or even Eliana herself had already said.

'That's right. We all have to help where we can, and I'm told Elly has fitted right in.'

'Herr Müller, I didn't know you had a sister in Munich,' Heinrich said, as he took a sip of his drink. 'I thought your family were all in Berlin.'

Ava's eyes flitted to her father, who sat back in his seat, smiling broadly. 'Most of them are, but one of my sisters went against my family's wishes and married a man not of their choosing. We saw little of them over the past two decades, but when my sister was killed, I was hardly going to turn away my niece.'

'It's been so lovely spending time together,' Ava said. 'Although between our work schedules, all of us here are like ships in the night.'

Heinrich nodded, but she shifted uncomfortably as he looked at her father.

'And you're well, Herr Müller?'

Ava noticed that Eliana stopped knitting, and that Hanna went stiff in her chair.

'It's very kind of you to enquire about my health, but I'm as fit as an ox. Other than a bad cold that very nearly went to my lungs, I feel like a man half my age.'

Ava placed her hand on Heinrich's knee and smiled at him, hoping she was able to distract him. 'Heinrich, it would be so lovely to see your mother and sister. Do you think they'd have time to meet you and I for lunch one day? I'd love to discuss the wedding with them.'

With those words, he finally softened into the seat beside her, as Hanna rose to pour him another drink.

'Where were you?' her father asked, his eyes never leaving hers as she shifted uncomfortably before him once Heinrich had left. 'Were you with him?'

She looked at the floor. There was no point in lying. 'Yes.'

'Ava, you're playing a dangerous game here,' he said, and she watched as Eliana and Hanna quietly left the room, clearly not wanting to be drawn into whatever argument she would be having with her father. 'If Heinrich suspects anything, if he finds out, you will have put all of us at risk, do you understand that? For a young man who will discard you as quickly as an unwanted pet as soon as you're no longer useful to him.'

Ava didn't need to be told what a precarious position she'd put Eliana in, but she hadn't known that Heinrich would call on her unannounced like that. Especially when the last time she'd seen him, he'd been preparing to go away for a week or longer – she hadn't even known he was back in the city.

'I think you're wrong about Noah, I think—'

'You think he would risk his life to save you, if Heinrich discovered your duplicity?' her father muttered. 'Because I can answer that for you: he won't.'

She disagreed, but didn't dare say her thoughts out aloud to her father, not when he was angry.

'Whatever he's asked you to do, whatever you've agreed to, Ava, it had better be worth it.'

She stood and watched her father go, downing his drink before slamming it to the table as he passed, leaving her alone in the sitting room. That was when she began to shake, her body trembling violently as she sat down on the sofa that had once been filled by Heinrich, remembering the curious way he'd looked at Eliana, while she imagined what he'd be capable of if he ever figured out who she was.

Whatever Noah had planned, it couldn't come soon enough.

Later that night, as the air raid siren wailed endlessly, and she lay on a temporary mattress down in the cellar between Hanna and Eliana, the family who'd taken over the Goldmans' apartment merely inches from them, she couldn't stop thinking about what had happened earlier that day, what she'd so brazenly done.

Noah had asked her to look for anything in Goebbels' diary that pointed to a meeting with Hitler, to commit to memory anything that was discussed in her presence or in the diary notes that she typed every day for her boss. She'd been carefully searching for weeks now, for anything that could be of value to Noah, and it was the reason she'd gone to visit him instead of coming straight home that night.

He'd told her little about what they had planned, and she hadn't even tried to guess, afraid to know.

Hitler was to meet with his top military aides at the field headquarters in Rastenburg, East Prussia, the following month. She'd been privy to the information owing to her elevated position typing Goebbels' personal diary each day, and she hadn't hesitated in sharing the information with Noah – she'd gone straight to the café where they were to meet, leaving a note beneath her napkin as he'd instructed her to do, saying she had to speak with him.

He'd eventually caught up with her and given her an address as he passed, and after pausing to sit in the sun and walking some more to ensure no one was following her, she'd gone to him, eagerly telling him what she'd discovered.

He'd asked her to repeat everything numerous times, before leaving her and asking her to wait, but when he came back he was smiling from ear to ear.

'Ava,' he'd said, as he'd cupped her face and looked into her eyes. 'There are very few civilians involved in this coup. And yet it is you who has given us the piece of information that we needed. This is what we've been waiting for.'

'What should I do now?' she asked, as he pulled her close to him.

'You keep your eyes and ears open, in case anything changes, even the most minute detail. You come to the café after work if you need to tell me anything else.'

She nodded. 'I will.'

Then, she'd basked in Noah's attention, excited by what she'd done, believing that no one could ever catch her or know of her involvement. But now, as their basement rattled from bombs falling above, she wondered if she'd simply been naive. And she couldn't stop thinking about the way Heinrich had looked at Eliana, the way he'd questioned her father. It had terrified her.

But the rational part of her brain told her that if Heinrich truly suspected anything, he'd have already returned with his SS friends to take them all in for questioning. Because she had a feeling that he wasn't intimidated one bit by her father any more, and the fact that the man she was engaged to marry could feel superior to her own papa sent shivers of terror through her that would make it impossible for her to sleep. The only thing worse was imagining what he'd do to Noah if he ever discovered someone else had already been to bed with his fiancée.

Chapter Seventeen

It didn't matter how many times Ava saw Noah, he always managed to make her heart skip a beat, and tonight was no different. What was different was the way he scooped her up into his arms and swung her around the moment she was through the door, his lips on hers.

'You did it,' he whispered, to which she pressed her mouth to his in return. She could taste the alcohol on his breath, knew that he'd been out celebrating without her, but she didn't care. She only hoped that they had the night together without being interrupted by air raid sirens – she wanted to spend as much time in his arms as she could.

'You did everything I asked of you,' he said. 'I always knew my little butterfly would be clever enough to do it, and now everything is set to happen on Thursday.'

Ava shrugged out of her coat and threw it down on the chair, spying a bottle of brandy that was open in the kitchen. She saw two discarded glasses but didn't ask who they belonged to – she doubted he would have told her, anyway. Jealousy rose inside of her, wondering who else he'd been celebrating with, but she chose not to ask. Instead, she crossed the room and poured a small amount into each glass; she may not have been able to stand the taste only months earlier, but she'd quickly become accustomed to it over the past few weeks. Tonight she needed it to settle her nerves – being in the office this week had been nerve-wracking, as she'd spent every minute worrying that her deception had been discovered – but it was almost over now. Although for what, she still didn't know.

She passed one to Noah and he downed it in one gulp, before placing it down and then fixing his gaze on her again. She took a few sips as he rained kisses on her neck and started to unbutton her shirt, making it impossible for her to finish her drink, before taking her hand and leading her to the bedroom. She had so much she wanted to ask him, so many questions about what would happen next, about where he would live and what their lives would look like once it was all over, but those questions could wait, for he was clearly in an impatient mood and she was only too happy to oblige.

They could talk about their future after.

'Slow down,' she said with a laugh as he pushed her backwards on to the bed.

But as usual, Noah chose not to listen.

—— ∼⧉∼ ——

'Have you heard any more about what's being planned?' she asked, as they lay in bed together. She propped herself up on one elbow to look down at him. 'Is there anything you can share with me yet?'

He stroked her cheek. 'It's safer for you not to know. But you've done very well, little butterfly, very well indeed.'

A tingle of excitement ran through her. 'So the information I gave you, it was—'

'Exactly what we needed to follow through with our plan,' he said, mirroring her pose and lifting his head. 'You did very well, Ava. It's not an exaggeration to say we couldn't have done this without you.'

She smiled, secretly thrilled that she'd been involved and able to help with such important information.

'It will be so nice to see you in public once all this is over, instead of having to sneak around,' she said, drinking in his beautiful face, the strong angles of his jaw and his warm brown eyes. 'Can I choose the first place we go to dinner?' She imagined that men like Heinrich would be arrested as the regime collapsed and everything changed. 'I can imagine us dancing all night until our feet ache, eating as much food as we can consume and drinking champagne.'

'That sounds like quite the picture,' he said, smiling down at her. 'And I would love to go dancing with you, but Ava, I don't want to think I've misled you.'

'Misled me?' She bristled. 'I don't think I understand.'

'It's not that I don't care about you, but if what we have planned works, once the Führer has gone . . .'

She swallowed, realising for the first time what she'd been a part of. It wasn't that she regretted what she'd done, because she didn't, but just hearing him say those words, that the Führer could actually be gone, told her that it could be in part because of her.

'I will never say no to seeing you, but I simply don't want you to start dreaming of a life with me, of some sort of fairy-tale ending. Marriage, family, staying in one place, it simply isn't me.'

'You mean to say that after all this, that once the war is over, once the Nazi regime has come to an end . . .' Her voice trailed off as she saw the expression on his face.

Suddenly it all made sense, suddenly she realised what a fool she'd been to imagine a life with Noah. She couldn't even blame him for using her to get what he wanted, because she'd been a willing participant – and he was right, he'd never made her any promises.

'Don't look at me like that, Ava,' Noah said, running his finger down her bare arm. 'I've never hidden who I was to you. I thought you understood, that you knew what this was. It doesn't mean that I don't care for you, because I do.'

She glanced away for a moment, not wanting him to see her tears. 'I thought there was something more between us, I thought—' Ava stopped speaking when she saw the look on his face. She did not want to be the object of his pity. In fact, she refused to be.

'This has been fun, *very* fun in fact. But you didn't expect me to—'

'Of course not. I'm still engaged to Heinrich, I always knew this wasn't anything serious.' She was lying of course; in her mind she barely acknowledged the fact that she was still engaged to be married, and she'd thought Noah had fallen for her, as she had him. She'd dreamed of spending the rest of her life with Noah once all this was over, had imagined spending every night in his arms instead of only for stolen moments.

Hanna had tried to warn her, and so had David, but she'd refused to listen to them, believing that they simply didn't under-stand. It appeared that she was the one who hadn't understood. Noah had needed her, and now he didn't. It was as simple as that, no matter how he tried to sugar-coat it.

Ava stood, taking the sheet with her and keeping it wrapped around her body, no longer wanting him to see her naked. Her skin was crawling, making her wish she'd never given her body to him, never fallen for the sweet words that had fallen so casually from his lips.

'Come back to bed,' he said, reaching an arm out to her.

'Can I ask you one thing?' she said, turning back to look at him.

Noah placed a cigarette between his lips and lifted a match to light it. He propped himself up on the pillow as he blew smoke into the air.

'If I hadn't been able to access information for you, if I hadn't—'

'Ava, don't. Don't ruin what we had by saying things like that. I don't want this to be the last time we see each other, I was only trying to explain—'

She shifted uncomfortably, unsure what to think, or how to feel.

'Ava, come here,' he said, patting the bed beside him.

When she didn't move, he smiled, his face softening.

'Please.'

She hesitated for a moment, clutching the sheet tight to her chest as she slowly walked forward and sat, careful not to touch him. But when he reached up to stroke her hair, and then trailed his fingers down her face, she found it impossible to pull away.

'Tell me, do you believe in the cause? In what we're doing?'

Ava nodded.

'And you want our country to change? You want this war to end? To rid Germany of evil?'

'Of course.'

'I didn't deceive you into doing anything, Ava. I always told you the risks. I approached you because you were already part of this world, and I thought that I could encourage you to do more.' Noah grinned. 'I've loved every moment I've spent with you, but I'm trying to be honest about who I am. Don't let that taint what we shared, just because we both see different things in our future.'

It didn't necessarily make her feel any better, but he was right. She had been a willing participant, and if she'd only done it all to please him, then she was the fool, not Noah. He hadn't made her any promises; she'd simply fantasised about the life they could have together, believing that he would want the same as her. She could see now that she'd simply been naive.

'I will never forget the part you played in this, what you risked to help us.' His smile was kind. 'You may well be the bravest woman I'll ever meet.'

She wished she didn't feel so heartbroken, but she couldn't help it. He was right, she had done this because she believed in putting an end to fascism, but it didn't stop her from wishing that Noah felt for her the same way she felt for him.

When he leaned forward and pressed his lips to hers, she didn't pull away, savouring the taste of his mouth as it lingered over hers, knowing it would be the last time.

When Ava arrived home, she let herself quietly into the apartment and started to walk directly to her bedroom. But she hadn't expected someone to call out to her from the dark.

'Ava?'

She stopped and squinted, making out Hanna sitting in one of the armchairs.

'What are you still doing up?' she asked, pleased it was dark so that her sister couldn't see her tear-streaked face.

'I was waiting for you,' she said. 'Papa has gone to bed, he wasn't feeling well, but—'

'What happened? Did the morphine work like last time?'

'It did, but I don't know how long it will keep working for, or how long we can keep hiding what's wrong. He needs to see a doctor.'

She moved closer to Ava, seeing how worried she looked.

'Ava, he was angry about the work you're doing with Noah. He wouldn't tell me what was going on, but he said Noah had asked too much of you, that you shouldn't have—'

'When he asked me to join you all, to change sides and support the work you were all doing, he never said there would be a limit to my involvement.'

'Maybe not, but he expected the chain of command to be followed. He expected to be in control of whatever you were being asked to do.' Hanna sighed. 'Please can you tell me what you're involved in? Father wouldn't tell me, and I can only guess that it's something big.'

The last thing that Ava wanted was to argue with her sister, especially after the night she'd had.

'I honestly don't know, Noah never told me. He said it was better if I didn't know, but I'm starting to wonder . . .'

Hanna grabbed her hand. 'Wonder what? Ava, tell me!'

She took a long, slow breath. 'I think they could be planning to assassinate the Führer,' she whispered into Hanna's ear. 'I don't know for certain, but everything Noah said, the information he wanted on where Hitler would be, it all points to that.'

'How many other people have access to the diary?' Hanna asked, standing now. 'How many others, with the exception of you, will be questioned if whatever is planned goes wrong? You truly believe that's what they could be planning?'

Ava nodded.

'What if Papa can't take the fall for you on this?'

Ava took a deep breath. 'I don't want him to take the fall for me,' she said. 'I knew what I was doing, I—'

'But did you? Know what you were doing?' Hanna asked, sounding exasperated. 'Did Noah truly explain to you how dangerous whatever all this was, did he truly—'

Ava couldn't hold back her emotions any longer. She burst into tears, turning away from Hanna, embarrassed that she'd broken down in front of her.

'Ava!' Hanna's arms were around her, holding her, loving her as her sister's legs threatened to give way. Ava clung to her sister, needing her now more than ever despite how much she'd tried to push her away. 'What's wrong? Tell me why you're crying.'

'It's over between me and Noah.'

Hanna was quiet for a while, but her hands kept moving in circles on Ava's back.

'I have every reason to believe he cared for you very much, Ava,' Hanna eventually said. 'But Noah is complicated. Sometimes men like him, who are so focused on the work they're doing, they don't have the ability to commit themselves or fall in love.'

'I can't even hate him,' Ava said. 'How can I hate a man who's trying to put an end to such evil?'

'Would you have done it if our father had asked you to?'

Ava nodded. 'Of course. Without question.'

'Then that's what you need to remind yourself. You did this because you believe in the cause, because you've chosen to be part of this. It didn't matter whether Noah asked you, or Papa, or someone else. And eventually, you might even remember your time with him fondly, when it doesn't hurt so much.'

She nodded. Hanna was right. The fact that Noah had broken her heart had nothing to do with what she'd been part of; she needed to grieve him without losing sight of how influential she'd been in helping the resistance.

'I'm still angry with you,' Hanna whispered, pulling her close again and hugging her. 'But I'm proud of you, too.'

'Will Papa forgive me?' she asked, when Hanna finally let her go.

'I think he's incredibly proud of everything you've done,' she said. 'He only wishes that you weren't so involved. I think he regrets ever asking you to help.' Hanna stared at her for a long moment.

'Hanna, I keep thinking about the way Heinrich asked Papa the other night whether he was well,' she said. 'You don't think he knows Papa's sick, do you? Do you think he suspects something, or that he's trying to find out more about Eliana?'

She saw the shiver that ran through her sister's body. 'I hope not. If that man turns on us, if he finds out anything that would point to us being traitors . . .'

Hanna didn't need to finish her sentence for Ava to imagine what would happen. But when her sister cleared her throat, she realised she had more to say.

'Ava, that night you discovered the Goldmans in our attic, you asked me whether I was hiding anything else from you,' Hanna said, her eyes wide as she met Ava's. 'I didn't tell you the truth.'

Ava waited, holding her breath as her sister's eyes filled with tears. She watched as she blinked them away, wondering what other secret there could possibly be.

'The car that killed Hugo and Michael . . .' Hanna began, her voice faltering until Ava put an arm around her, knowing how hard it was for her to talk about her son and husband. 'Goebbels was there. It was his driver, him and another party official, and they drove away as if they'd hit a stray dog in the street. I watched as he inspected the scene and then left.'

Ava's heart ached as her sister cried, and she held her, wishing she'd known but also understanding how much pain Hanna was in by recounting that day.

'Mama and Papa know the truth?' she asked. 'You've told them.'

Hanna nodded. 'I'm sorry. They felt it was better than we keep it a secret, but I can see now that it was a mistake to keep it from you.'

Ava refused to be hurt. So much had changed over the past few months; she was a different woman to the one she'd been then. 'Does he know? That it was your family that day?'

Hanna shrugged. 'Honestly? I don't know. Sometimes I think that he does know, almost as if he's taunting me with it, waiting for me to say something when I see him. But in truth I think that's my imagination.'

'Thank you for telling me,' Ava said, as Hanna held her hand. 'No more secrets though. From now on, we tell each other everything.'

Hanna squeezed her fingers, blinking away fresh tears. 'No more secrets. I promise.'

Chapter Eighteen

Eliana

Eliana knew something was wrong when Ethan stayed behind the counter long after the shelves were bare and the store had emptied of people. She crossed the shop to the front door and turned the sign to closed, locking it and pulling down the blinds – all things that Ethan would usually do himself.

'Tell me what's wrong,' she said, looking around to make certain that they were the only ones there.

Ethan's face was pale, his skin devoid of all colour as he came out from behind the counter towards her.

'Come with me,' he said, taking her hand and hurrying her out to the storeroom where she usually worked.

'Do I need to get the typewriter out?' she asked, breathless from his dragging her along at such a fast pace. 'Is there an urgent message we need to transmit?'

He closed the door behind them, which gave her an uneasy feeling in her stomach. Not because she didn't trust him alone with her in such confined quarters, but because he'd never done it before. Which meant he had something important, or secret, to tell her.

'I was given a message today,' he said, his hand shaking as he passed it to her. 'At first, I didn't believe it.'

She quickly opened it.

Happening tomorrow. Be ready.

'What does this even mean?'

'It means there is to be an assassination attempt on Hitler's life tomorrow,' he whispered. 'We have to be prepared to spread the information as soon as we have word.'

'An assassination?' she repeated. 'You're certain that's what this note is referring to?'

He nodded. 'Yes, I'm certain, they've been planning it for some time. The conspirators aren't who you'd expect, either, but officers close to the Führer, politicians, German nationalists who know we will be defeated in this war and want to save our country. Perhaps some of them simply want to preserve our morality while they still can. Either way, they all seem to want the same thing, and they no longer believe we'll be victorious without overthrowing the party.'

An unfamiliar warmth spread through Eliana, but she couldn't understand why Ethan looked so nervous.

'What is it? You must be thrilled that this could happen before you're to report for duty on Monday?' She reached for his hand and took it, threading her fingers through his. She'd thought of little else other than his leaving since he'd told her.

'Eliana, if this doesn't work, if it's not a success . . .'

She searched his face. 'What are you worrying about? We can only hope and pray that it will be. This is a chance for you to stay home, for the war to end, for—'

'Ava is involved.'

Eliana's breath caught in her throat. 'Involved?' She'd known that Ava was working for the greater cause, but hearing Ethan say her name still came as a shock. 'How involved? How do you know?'

'One of the reasons they've been able to plan this all so meticulously is because of her access to information. From what I understand, her friend Noah convinced her to access information for him. He's one of the few civilians involved in the coup.'

'You're saying he's been using her affection towards him to make her do things? That he's willingly put her in danger?' Now it made sense why she'd heard Ava and Hanna arguing about him; clearly Hanna didn't approve.

Anger rose inside of her, and she knew her face would be beet red, her heart thumping loudly in her chest.

'I don't want to presume, but I do know that he recruited her.'

'There's nothing we can do?' she asked. 'To ensure that she's not in danger? Should I say something? Should I encourage her to leave the city, to flee somewhere safer?' But where would be safer? Where could she go that they wouldn't find her?

'What's done is done. We just have to wait now and hope that it's successful, that it doesn't fail, because if she flees now it will only confirm her guilt.'

'But you believe that the trail could lead back to Ava, in the case that it isn't a success?' Eliana asked.

Ethan squeezed her hand. 'I fear that everyone with access to high-level information will be questioned, that there will be a witch hunt for all involved.' He took a step closer. 'But there is every reason to believe that won't happen. I only wanted you to understand the risks involved, given how close you are to the family. And I wasn't certain how much you knew, whether you were even aware she was doing so much for the cause.'

'No, I wasn't aware. Although I did overhear Hanna warning her about Noah. I thought her father was being careful with her level of involvement.' Did Herr Müller even know? Now she wasn't sure what to do – did she go behind Ava's back and confess what she knew to Hanna, or even their father? After everything Karl had done for her family, she almost felt she owed it to him to tell the truth.

She shut her eyes for a moment, imagining the Müller house being searched, imagining her family being found – the implications of Ava's involvement stretched far beyond Ava's own family. There was a chance that Eliana could hide, that she could somehow find a way to survive with her papers, but just as David had always said, her family were sitting ducks up there in the attic. The only consolation was that Ava had given him the gun he'd been asking for, although that would only stop a handful of SS men. Then where would they go, if they escaped the house? How would they hide? Or was there a chance that everything might change if Hitler was, in fact, killed?

'I wish I hadn't worried you,' Ethan said, pulling her from her thoughts.

'I'm pleased you did. It's better I understand the risks, especially for those I'm close to.' She sighed. 'Ava is like family to me now, I couldn't imagine losing her.'

They stood for a moment, before Eliana pulled away from him, wrapping her arms around herself.

'Will you still have to go?' she asked, looking up at him. 'If this succeeds, will the war end? Will our soldiers surrender? Could this actually all be over?'

Ethan shook his head. 'I honestly don't know. Who knows how long it could be until the fighting is over?'

She understood. He still expected to have to leave on Monday. He didn't truly think that this would change anything – not immediately anyway. The only thing they hadn't discussed was whether he could find a way to disappear instead of report for duty, but she knew he'd likely be too fearful of the repercussions for his family if he did that. That was one of the reasons she liked him so much – he respected and cared for his family as much as she did hers – which meant that if he thought they would be punished for his actions, he wouldn't even consider such a thing.

'After everything you've done for me, Ethan, I want you to know that I'll fight for you if I have to. I'll never stop searching for you if you don't come home. I promise.' She paused, looking into his eyes. 'We have ice cream to eat together, remember?'

Ethan's smile was tinged with sadness as he stepped towards her, closing the distance between them. He touched her cheek with his palm, cupping her face with his hand. His eyes were locked on hers, shining brightly.

'And I will never stop searching for you, either. I'll never forget you, Eliana. You're like a bright light in the midst of absolute darkness, and I'm so grateful that our paths crossed.' He grinned. 'And I haven't forgot about that ice cream. After the war, I'll buy you one every day for the rest of our lives.'

When his lips touched hers, she willingly kissed him back. Her lips moved softly against his for a heartbeat, and when it ended, he held her in his arms, pressing her against his chest. All she could think was that being held by him felt like home; it reminded her of when she was growing up, and not worrying about what the next day would bring.

'Should I start typing the leaflets now, so we're prepared?' she asked, her cheek still pressed against him. 'Is there anything else we have to do?'

'No, all we can do is wait. But when the Führer is dead, we will work through the night together, making certain everyone knows what has happened. They're going to begin by immediately arresting high-ranking Nazi leaders right here in Berlin, so the news will spread fast.'

Eliana squeezed Ethan even tighter, her arms wrapped firmly around him now. Part of her was filled with fear, but the other part, for the first time in longer than she could remember, was filled with hope. Hope that there would be a future in which she and her family wouldn't be persecuted; hope that she could walk the streets as herself; and hope that maybe, just maybe, there was a future for her that might involve Ethan.

Chapter Nineteen

Hanna

Hanna knew the moment she arrived that she shouldn't have come. Something was wrong. She hadn't been involved in a pick-up since finding out that Dieter had been taken and Noah had warned her from continuing, but when she'd heard about a little boy who needed urgent transportation, she hadn't hesitated in saying yes. The moment she'd heard that his papers had come through, she'd prepared for how to get him out, volunteering to both drive the ambulance and provide the triage care, given the shortage of nurses at the hospital. Thankfully, no one had questioned her.

She hadn't personally seen Noah for weeks, and as much as she knew that she should have heeded his warning, the people she worked with were as motivated as she was, and they had all agreed to proceed.

This one is for you, Dieter. He'd been on her mind constantly since he'd disappeared, and she only wished she didn't know so much about the camps. Otherwise she might have been able to pretend that he was all right.

Hanna turned into the street and slowly picked her way past rubble, changing her route as she came across bomb damage, relaxing a little once she'd left the city behind her. This rescue was a little different, because it was a boy who'd been left orphaned and cared for by a non-Jewish family. They were leaving Berlin and couldn't take him with them without a passport, so her job was to find a way to move him safely, so they could eventually reunite. It seemed to her the most certain reunion that she'd been part of – because deep down she was beginning to wonder whether the other children she'd helped would ever have the chance to see their parents again.

After driving for almost thirty minutes, Hanna was forced to slow down when she saw a SS blockade ahead on the road. *What is all this about?*

She came to a stop and rolled down her window to speak to one of the officers. 'Can I pass through?' she asked.

'Papers,' he asked, holding out his hand.

She leaned over and took her papers from her bag, passing them to him. 'Why is the road blocked? Is there bomb damage ahead?'

He looked up at her and then at her papers, before passing them back to her.

'You'll need to open up the back of the ambulance.'

Hanna stared at him for a moment, before realising he was deadly serious. 'Can you not simply let me on my way so I can do my job?' she asked. 'I have patients depending on me.'

'Open up!' he shouted, banging his fist on the side of the ambulance.

Hanna reluctantly got out and opened the back doors, waiting where he told her to as he climbed in and searched the interior, turning things over and carelessly knocking medical supplies to the ground.

'My father is Karl Müller,' she said. 'Oberst-Gruppenführer Müller.'

The man just looked at her as if he couldn't have cared less, which made Hanna's skin crawl. Something was very, very wrong if he didn't have any reaction to her father's name. Every SS man in Berlin should have withered at the very mention of his rank. She thought of Ava's suspicions regarding Heinrich, and about what Noah had said.

'Where are you travelling to?' he asked.

'An assembly plant in Brandenburg. I understand there were multiple casualties after the air raid last night, and I've been sent to provide care and transport any patients that need to go the hospital.'

'Will you be coming back this way?' he asked, surprising her when he didn't ask why she was travelling so far when there must have been closer ambulances that could have responded.

'Yes,' she replied. 'I have to return to the hospital.' Suddenly what she was doing seemed like a very bad idea.

'Then we will search you again then,' he said, gesturing that she could walk ahead of him. 'No one is passing through without being searched.'

'May I ask what you're looking for, exactly?' she asked, as politely as she could, as if she couldn't imagine what he was possibly searching for.

'Traitors,' he replied. 'We are looking for cowards and traitors to our great country.'

Hanna swallowed and wished him good day, before climbing back into the ambulance and driving slowly through the SS blockade. Something told her it wasn't the worst thing that would happen to her that day.

She carried on, careful not to drive too fast or do anything that might attract attention, and within another twenty minutes she neared what was left of the assembly plant. But the place was crawling with SS; there was another patrol that she'd have to pass if she turned down there, and she knew that it wasn't worth the risk. As much as it broke her heart, as surely as the tears ran down her cheeks, there was no way she could attempt to rescue a Jewish child under such scrutiny – not knowing whether she would be searched as soon as she tried to drive away.

She only wished she knew what had happened for so many patrols to be in place.

Hanna turned the corner and drove away, deciding to drive directly to her rendezvous point where she was to meet the other ambulance. The last thing she wanted was for them to be sitting waiting for her, risking discovery, when she wasn't coming. But when she finally reached the meeting point, after an hour of driving, no one was there.

What do I do? Do I pull over and wait, or do I keep driving?

She passed the spot where she should have stopped, trying to imagine what Dieter would say if he were beside her, whether he would be brave enough to pull over, and suddenly she could almost hear his voice in her mind.

Trust your instincts, Hanna. You've been doing this long enough. If it doesn't feel right, then keep driving. You can't help anyone if you're caught.

And so she did. She drove further up the road until she could find a safe place to turn around, which was when she saw them. The two contacts whose names she didn't even know were standing on the side of the road, the doors to their ambulance open, as they faced two SS men.

Hanna gripped the steering wheel, heading straight on, not turning as she'd planned to do but deciding to drive an unfamiliar route just to avoid having to go past them again. But as she passed, she allowed herself a quick glance sideways, saw that one of the SS men was holding his pistol in his hand, and that was when the woman's terrified eyes met hers, and she shook her head ever so slightly. It was a very slight movement, a signal that Hanna understood. She was to keep on driving, no matter what. She wasn't to stop, or try to help them, or do anything other than drive past and get herself to safety.

She blinked away her tears, not taking her hands off the wheel to wipe away those that had escaped and were slipping down her cheeks. Hanna didn't stop until she was well out of sight, and when she did she took out a map to figure out how exactly she could get to their country house from where she was.

She needed to get home and warn her mother that something was happening.

'Mama!' Hanna called as she leapt out of the ambulance, leaving the door flung open as she ran up to the house. 'Mama! Where are you?' she called.

Hanna almost fell into Zelda's arms as she opened the door.

'Hanna, we weren't expecting you,' Zelda said, steadying herself by catching hold of Hanna's arms. 'What's the matter?'

'I need to know where Mama is,' she panted. 'Please, is she here?'

'Your mother is—'

'Hanna?' Her mother stood at the top of the stairs, rushing down when she saw how flustered her daughter was. 'Come with me, into your father's study.'

Hanna took her hand and dragged her mother with her, closing the door behind them. She knew that Zelda was probably listening, so she kept her voice low and walked her mother all the way over to the window on the other side of the room.

'Mama, something has happened,' she whispered. 'There are SS everywhere, I was stopped by a patrol and—'

Her mother kept hold of her hand, their eyes locked on each other's.

'My contacts were stopped on the side of the road, and I don't think they fared as well as I did.'

She watched as her mother looked out of the window. 'You are alone? There's no one in the ambulance with you?'

Hanna nodded. 'I'm alone. I couldn't pick up my patient, there was no way I could get to him.' *That child will never leave Germany now. There won't be another way for him to escape.*

'Your father warned me that something was happening today,' her mother finally whispered in reply. 'It must not have been a success.'

'What was being planned? What success are you speaking of?' Had Ava been right about it being an assassination attempt?

She studied her mother's face, saw the way it fell, the way her lip quivered and her hands began to tremble.

'Mama?'

She watched as her mother crossed the room, turning on the gramophone and pouring herself some brandy, swirling it around before drinking it in two quick gulps, her shoulders slumped forward.

'There was a plot to assassinate the Führer,' she eventually said, turning back to look at Hanna, her eyes filled with sorrow. 'At the Wolf's Lair in East Prussia. Today was the day that Hitler was supposed to take his last breath.'

Hanna gasped, her hand flying to cover her mouth. 'What should we do? Where should I go?' She began to tremble. 'Do I need to go to Ava? What if someone discovers her involvement?'

Her mother poured herself another drink as Hanna watched.

'We return to our normal lives, we act as if we know nothing, as if nothing about our lives has changed,' she eventually said. 'The only reason we'll be suspected of wrongdoing is if we appear guilty, and your father is already worried that he's under suspicion.'

'So I should return to the city, then? To the hospital?'

Her mother passed her the drink, clearly thinking her daughter needed it more than she did, as Hanna stood beside her and downed the brandy.

But all she could think was that perhaps her mother had it wrong. Perhaps the Führer had been killed. Perhaps it *had* been a success, and the news simply hadn't reached them yet?

Or perhaps that was just wishful thinking.

Chapter Twenty

Ava

'Ava.' Her father placed a hand on her shoulder and leaned down, his breath whispering against her cheek he was so close. 'I need you to listen without showing any emotion.'

She looked up, heart hammering as she felt the weight of his palm against her skin. He didn't remove his hand, and that told her everything she needed to know. Something had gone wrong.

'There was a failed attempt on the Führer's life today.'

She trembled, thankful for her father's touch as she realised what a dangerous position they were now in.

'Hundreds of men are being arrested, and there will be more tomorrow,' he whispered, directly in her ear, so low that she had to concentrate hard to hear him. 'Noah is to be executed for treason.'

Her body stilled as her eyes filled with tears, her heart began to thud and the room swam around her. She dug her fingernails into her desk, leaning back into her father as he kept his hand on her back, steady, comforting her. He knew how much Noah had come to mean to her.

'There must be something you can do to stop it,' she whispered back.

'There is nothing I can do,' he murmured. 'I'm sorry. They're all to be executed by firing squad.'

A tear escaped the corner of her eye and she lifted her chin, fighting the emotions that were rippling inside of her. Noah had known the risks, and so had she, but for him to be caught and arrested so quickly? She couldn't stop seeing it happening in her mind, his body being ricocheted by bullets, slumping over, his beautiful brown eyes lifeless as he fell to the ground.

Her father squeezed her shoulder, standing beside her for another moment before walking away, and she sat there, numb, digesting the fact that it had all been a failure. The risks she'd taken, the risks Noah had taken; it had all been for nothing.

'Is something wrong?'

Ava blinked and quickly wiped her eyelashes with her finger, braving a small smile as she looked over at Greta, who was studying her with a puzzled expression on her face.

'My father had news of a family friend who's just passed away,' she said. 'It took me by surprise, that's all.'

It wasn't even a lie. As far as she knew, Noah *was* already gone.

'Well, let me know if I can take over some of your typing for you,' Greta said. 'I can see how much it's upset you.'

Ava only smiled and nodded, not trusting her voice. But as she shuffled the papers to her left, she saw that her hands were trembling so much there was no way she could resume her typing. She closed her eyes for a moment and took a couple of deep breaths, seeing Noah in her mind, remembering the last time they'd been together.

Noah had made it clear that he didn't love her the way she'd fallen in love with him, but it didn't stop her heart from breaking knowing that she would never see him again. And then her heart began to pound all over again as she looked up at the door, wondering if anyone was going to come in and look for her, wondering how long it would take for the SS to point the finger internally and ask who had access to information within the ministry.

Lieutenant Schwägermann entered the room, then disappeared into Goebbels' office without pausing to look at or speak to any of the secretaries. He was in there for some time before storming out in a hurry.

'Do you think something has happened?' Ava overheard one of the other women whisper.

She closed her eyes again, trying to breathe, fighting against the feeling that she should walk out the door and run for the safety of their apartment. But she knew that if the SS wanted to find her, they would search for her everywhere, which meant that nowhere was safe. They knew where she was, they'd know where to find Hanna at the hospital, and they would know exactly where to find her mother, too.

Ava had held herself together for the rest of the day, but as she glanced at her wristwatch she was relieved to see that it was almost time to finish. There had been a steady stream of uniformed men coming in and out of the building for hours, but so far nothing had been said. And no one had come looking for her.

She had tidied up her papers before standing and reaching for her bag, when she felt someone watching her. Ava looked up and saw that Heinrich was standing in the doorway, his gaze trained on her.

She put her bag over her shoulder and collected her coat, before going over to him. He was smiling, but she still felt nervous, as if he might know something.

'Heinrich! What a lovely surprise,' she said, hating how false her voice sounded.

'I was called back to Berlin,' he said. 'Have you heard what happened?'

She shook her head. 'What has happened?' Ava hoped he bought her look of innocence. 'We've all wondered what's going on, as there's been a lot of activity in the building today but no one has told us anything. Is something wrong?'

'Look after this one,' Greta said as she passed them, leaving for the night. 'She had some sad news today.'

Heinrich looked down at her, his eyebrows drawing together. 'Sad news? What is she talking about?'

Ava's pulse ignited as she looked up at him. 'A family friend passed away. Father came to tell me earlier, he'd had news.'

'This friend, was that the man you'd been to visit that evening I came looking for you? The one you took fruit to?'

She nodded, touching his arm and trying to distract him. 'Yes, that was him, but Heinrich, you had something to tell me. I'm certain it's more important than the news of my father's old friend passing.'

Her smile and warm touch seemed to catch him off guard, just as she'd hoped.

'There was an attack on the Führer's life,' he told her, as she began to walk with him, through the building and down the stairs, still holding on to his arm.

'There is always someone trying to take down our mighty Führer, is there not?' she asked. 'It's a wonder they haven't all realised they can't succeed by now.'

'I didn't tell you it was unsuccessful,' Heinrich said, stopping once they'd stepped out on to the footpath.

She looked up at him, at the strange way he was staring down at her, at the way his eyebrows were drawn tightly together as he studied her face.

'You didn't have to,' she said, tugging him along while her heart began to race. 'Heinrich, if it had been successful, our country would already be in mourning! That's not something that would have been kept secret all day. I might be naive at times, but I'm no fool.'

He began to walk again, and she leaned into him, as much as it made her feel sick to be so close to him, her head on his shoulder, doing everything she could think of in order to appear as an adoring fiancée. Her heart raced at how easily she'd almost been caught out.

'Heinrich?' she asked, blinking up at him when she realised he still hadn't said anything.

'Of course, you're right, I just—'

'He's not hurt, is he? I wasn't too bold in believing no one could hurt him, was I?'

'He's fine, barely a few scratches as far as I heard. The bomb was in a briefcase, and it blew out the windows nearby, but it was blocked from killing him thanks to a thick wooden table leg.'

'A bomb?' she asked. 'They tried to kill him with a bomb? How awful.'

'Hitler was in East Prussia, for a secret meeting, and they were supposed to be in an underground bunker, the place they call the Wolf's Lair,' he said, seeming to enjoy the way she was hanging on to his every word. 'But it was so hot that they decided to change location and use an above-ground bunker instead. It sounds as if the change saved his life, although two of the men closest to the bomb weren't so fortunate. If they'd been in the original location, there would have been no windows, and likely everyone at the meeting would be dead.'

Ava smiled, nodding along as if she were as relieved as he was, but inside, her heart had never been heavier. She had known precisely where he was going to be, for she'd been the one to relay the information to Noah. And to think that it was weather that had caused its failure – that had cost Noah his life.

'Did they say who might be responsible?' she asked. 'Do they have any leads or anyone in custody?'

'Some of his closest advisors were responsible, from what I understand. They even thought they'd killed him, would you believe? They started having SS officers arrested right here in Berlin, thinking they were about to overthrow anyone loyal to Hitler! That's why it was so chaotic in the office for you today, although I am surprised you all weren't advised what was happening.'

Ava fought back a fresh wave of tears. They'd been so close, so close to putting an end to Hitler's reign of terror. She might have loved and admired the Führer once, but she wouldn't have spent a moment mourning him if the plan had been a success.

When they reached her apartment block, Heinrich took her hand and lifted it, pressing a kiss to her knuckles.

'I know your father wanted us to wait, but I cannot wait so much as another month, Ava,' he said. 'I've informed him that we are to be married at once, and I'd be lying if I didn't admit to having more influence than him right now. I dare say he won't fight me on this one, not any more.'

She smiled through her pain, struggling not to slap his face away when he brazenly kissed her on the mouth, right there on the street. Where Noah's lips had made her giddy, the feel of Heinrich's made her want to be physically sick, and to hear him speak that way about her papa . . . Her stomach turned.

Ava forced herself to lift her hand and placed it gently to his chest, pushing him back as softly as she could.

'I would very much like that, although I do not want to show my father any disrespect,' she whispered, trying to encourage him at the same time as turning him down. 'Why don't you and I decide on a date, and you can leave telling Papa to me.'

She didn't invite him in, kissing his cheek to make sure he didn't feel rebuffed, before saying goodbye and letting herself in. It wasn't until she was safely inside with the door of their apartment locked that she slumped to the floor, crying harder than she'd ever cried before.

Noah was gone.

Hitler was still alive.

And tomorrow more questions would be asked, and she had a feeling her name would be at the top of the list.

The door opened then, banging into her where she lay sprawled on the floor.

'Ava?'

Hanna dropped her keys as she pushed the door shut behind her, gathering Ava up in her arms and drawing her close. She couldn't hold her tears back then, couldn't stop the pain that echoed through every bit of her body.

'I risked everything for nothing,' she cried. 'He's still alive. Their plan was a failure.'

Hanna rocked her back and forth, her lips whispering against Ava's hair as she held her.

'I should have listened to you,' Ava whispered, 'I should never have done what he asked. I should have told you what was happening, what it was all for.'

She could almost see them coming, could picture herself being handcuffed or simply dragged by her arm from their home or the office.

'Father will never let anything happen to you,' Hanna murmured, as if she could read Ava's mind. 'Everything will be all right, I promise.'

Ava didn't believe her. How could their father keep her safe, when they might be coming for him, too? When Heinrich had indicated that he couldn't even put an end to their wedding plans?

She'd chosen to be part of this, and now she would have to deal with the consequences, whatever they were. Heinrich had said himself that they suspected some of the men closest to the Führer, which meant it was only so long before her father was implicated.

'We need to let Mama know what's happened,' Ava said, pushing back her hair and sitting up. 'We need to keep her safe.'

'I've already been home. She knew more than I did about what was going on.'

'She's safe?' Ava asked.

'As safe as any of us can be right now,' Hanna said. 'But unless they arrest Father, there's no reason for them to trouble her. She told me that we must go on as normal, to not do anything outside of our usual routine, in case we're being watched.'

'How did you know what had happened? How did you even know to go home and warn her?' Ava asked.

'Because it's not just in the city that men are being arrested, it's everywhere,' Hanna said, and for the first time, Ava saw fear reflected in her sister's gaze. 'I had to leave a child behind today. There were SS everywhere, they were arresting people and . . .'

Ava took hold of her sister's hands.

'I'm scared, Ava,' Hanna finally said, her eyes swimming with tears. 'I'm truly, deeply scared.'

Ava's breath shuddered from her and tears began to slide down her cheeks again. 'I'm scared, too.'

'But we can only be scared inside these four walls,' Hanna said, clearing her throat, her voice sounding strong again. 'We can't do anything that will draw attention, we have to go about our lives as if everything is fine. We can't let anyone see the cracks.'

Ava nodded and quickly wiped her cheeks. Hanna was right – continuing on was the only thing they could do, along with praying that no one ever found out about their involvement.

Chapter Twenty-One

Ava had never known the office to be so tense. The silence was almost impossible to bear, all of them with their heads down, getting on with their work while everything around them seemed to be in a state of chaos. Hanna had been right, those involved had believed their plan to be a success, and Colonel von Stauffenberg, a man who had been friends with her father for many years – and someone Ava would have least expected to be involved – had flown back to Berlin thinking he would be able to take control. They'd even begun to arrest some of the SS men, but it had only been a matter of hours before the uprising they'd planned was defeated. She'd typed the papers herself – there were a handful of high-level colonels and lieutenants who'd already faced the firing squad for what they'd done.

Her father walked from Goebbels' office just then, accompanied by Lieutenant Schwägermann, and Ava noticed how pale his face was as he changed direction and came towards her. She found herself holding her breath, seeing the strain around his eyes, hoping that he wasn't about to have one of his episodes, especially when Hanna wasn't near to assist him.

'Sorry for all the extra work today, ladies,' he said, smiling as all the women looked up at him, before coming around to Ava's side of the desk.

'Is everything all right?' she asked, not hiding her concern. Everyone was worried; it was all any one was whispering about in the bathrooms now that the news was out.

'Everything is fine. There is a lot of activity, that is all.'

He smiled and leaned down over her, reaching for her pen, which she'd placed beside her typewriter. She watched as he turned the piece of paper over, kissing her cheek as he always did, perhaps so that no one noticed what he was doing, before standing and squeezing her shoulder, the same way he had when he'd broken the news to her about Noah.

And that was when she read what he'd written.

RUN.

Ava quickly turned the piece of paper over, her breathing shallow as she watched him walk from the room as if nothing had happened, as if he hadn't just written that one terrifying word on the letter she'd just typed.

She fixed her smile, deliberately making her actions as unhurried as possible as she reached for her bag, deciding to leave her coat so it wasn't obvious that she was leaving the building. She would walk to the bathroom, and instead of going in she would dart down the stairs and run. *Just stay calm. Don't let anyone know anything is wrong. Keep smiling and walk as slowly as you can.*

But that was almost impossible, given that she didn't know who she was running from. All she knew for certain was that her father wouldn't have written that word unless he needed her out of that building immediately. Someone was coming for her, or for him, or perhaps even both of them. He'd warned her, he'd told her that if they were found out, the SS would come for every member of their family, and all she could think about was that she and her father were the only ones who knew it was about to happen.

As Ava turned to step out from behind her desk, she heard boots on the stairs and, echoing up through the building, the unmistakable blare of an air raid siren. The first long drone sounded as all the women leapt to their feet and grabbed their coats and bags.

'Ava, your coat!' Greta called, thrusting it at her, giving her a strange look when she saw that she was holding her bag, as if wondering where she might have been going. 'Quickly!'

Ava shrugged into her coat, her bag held tightly under her arm as she ran with the other secretaries down the stairs as quickly as they could. Everyone else from the building was hurrying with them, all heading down to the basement that they used as a bunker, to avoid having to race down the road to the public shelter. But as the crowd continued on, Ava darted out to the side, making a run for the front door.

She only hoped that her father had been able to use the diversion to his advantage and had disappeared into the street as well.

Ava didn't stop running until she reached the road, looking both ways before crossing and heading directly for their apartment. She would go there and wait, hide in the basement perhaps if she made it in time, and figure out what to do. Her father would come for her, he would tell her what to do, he would have a plan to get them all to safety.

But as the siren continued to scream, the sound filling her ears in a way that was impossible to block out, and the far-off explosion of a bomb falling made the concrete rumble beneath her feet, Ava stopped running. She stood across the road from her apartment building, holding on to a lamp post to steady herself as she looked at the two black Mercedes parked outside, blocking the street. There were two SS men stationed by the door, their expressions formidable, standing guard. She could only imagine that there were more of them upstairs, looking for her or her father. Perhaps he had managed to get away, and that was why they'd gone there to look for him, or maybe they were wanting to arrest her entire family. Maybe they had orders to take them all.

She looked back and saw a haze of smoke or perhaps dust in the air, the type that told her a building had been reduced to rubble as the sound of planes flying low almost drowned out the siren.

Ava knew that she should go to the nearest shelter, knew she should find a way to stay safe. But when she looked across the road one last time at the men standing there, she also knew that the only way she was going to be safe was to get as far away from them as she could.

And so she did what her father had told her to do. Ava ran, as fast as she was able, her heels clacking on the deserted city road, her bag thumping against her hip. Then she turned right down the next road. She would never forgive herself if she left without warning Eliana, because for all she knew they were looking for her, too.

She'd turned her back on her once, and would never forgive herself if she did it again.

Chapter Twenty-Two

The knot in Ava's stomach had never been tighter. She hurried down the pavement, head down, glancing up only to cross the road. At any moment she expected someone to shout out, and to hear the heavy fall of boots pounding on the concrete behind her – her only hope was that the chaos caused by the bombings would work to her advantage. Seeing those men stationed outside her apartment block had confirmed her worst fears – they were looking for her family, which meant that nowhere was safe. It wouldn't take long for word to spread around the office that she'd disappeared; as soon as they emerged from the basement they'd see she wasn't there, and she remembered only too well how quickly Lina had disappeared when she'd been blamed for the missing papers. If they found her? She didn't even want to imagine the interrogation that would follow, or what the sadistic SS men could do to her in an effort to extract as much information from her as possible.

She paused outside the grocer's, glancing around to make sure no one was watching her. The last thing she wanted was to lead the SS straight to Eliana. She was almost certain that no one could know about Eliana's real identity, and she wanted to keep it that way.

Ava waited for another moment to be certain, before pushing past the queue of people with their ration books in hand. They were so desperate for food that even the air raid siren hadn't made them move, for fear of losing their place in line.

'Excuse me,' she said, as many people grumbled at her and tried to block her from moving past. Ava held up her hands. 'I'm not shopping, I'm looking for someone. Please, let me through.'

It took her only a moment to spot Eliana once she was through the crowd – she was busy restocking a shelf, her back to Ava. It appeared that the goods were going faster than she could restock, the food supplies in Berlin much more restricted than they'd been even a few months earlier, and Ava could see the desperation in the eyes of those waiting. She expected that she didn't look out of place – only her wide-eyed desperation was for another reason entirely.

'Eliana,' Ava hissed, ignoring more muttering from behind her as she pushed through the smaller line gathered inside the store. 'Eliana!'

Eliana turned, smiling when she saw Ava. But she must have immediately read the expression on Ava's face, for her smile disappeared and her eyes widened, and she quickly stepped down from the little ladder she was on, brushing her hands on her apron as she came towards her.

Ava inclined her head towards the other side of the store, grabbing hold of Eliana's arm and pulling her close as they walked to the furthest point, so no one could overhear them.

The way Eliana looked at her, the fear on her face, made Ava want to pull her close and hold her, to reassure her that she would keep her safe. But if she did that, she'd be lying. There was no one who could keep them safe now, no one who could rescue them – they were on their own. If her father's work had been compromised, which she had every reason to believe had happened, then she doubted even he could find a way to help, to follow through with his plan to take the fall for all of them. Ava cleared her throat as emotion pricked at her eyes, thinking of her beloved papa. *Will I ever see him again?*

'They know.'

'They're looking for you?' Eliana visibly swallowed. '*For me?* They know what we're involved in? What your—' She leaned even closer, her lips whispering into Ava's ear. 'What your family has done?'

'We have to presume they know everything, that they will be seeking to arrest me, Hanna and my mother,' Ava whispered in reply. 'I'm certain I wasn't followed, but if they know about my family's involvement, about my involvement, if they know about my father—'

'Then they could know about *my* family. And me.'

'Yes, or they could simply want to arrest anyone connected to us, which includes you because they think you're our family. And they could very well be on their way to the country house now.'

'The apartment has already been compromised?'

She nodded. 'There were SS men stationed outside. We have to leave the city; they won't stop looking for us.'

Ava gripped Eliana's hand tightly, wishing things were different, that they could have had longer, that everything had worked out as it was supposed to. She also wished that there was some way they could warn Eliana's family, because right now the Goldmans were in grave danger with nowhere to go. The attic was the first place they'd look if they stormed the house, and there was only so far David could protect them with one gun.

'We have to leave now, Eliana. There's no time.'

Eliana pulled her hand from Ava's and disappeared from sight. Ava looked around, nervously considering everyone in the queue, although no one seemed interested in two young women with their heads bent, whispering. They were all far more concerned with their stamps and peering around to see what was left on the barely stocked shelves. Food had a way of doing that – before the war, all the old ladies would have been craning their necks to hear what it was they were whispering, and now they argued over sausage meat and bread, their growling, aching stomachs all they cared about.

When Eliana reappeared she was hand in hand with Ethan, who had turned a ghostly shade of white. Ava watched on as Eliana stood on tiptoe to kiss his cheek, wishing they had the luxury of time so that she could let them say goodbye properly. Ethan was a good man, and he didn't deserve to lose Eliana like this – it was obvious to anyone watching that they'd fallen in love in the short time they'd had together.

'I have family just outside Cologne,' he said, as Ava moved closer to them, his voice only loud enough for her and Eliana to hear. 'If you make your way there, they will give you somewhere to stay, even if it's just for a night to rest. You can trust them, I promise, and as far as I know their home is untouched by the bombing, so they should still be there.'

'Thank you,' Ava said. She needed to thank him for so much – for not only taking Eliana in, but for the help he'd provided to others, and for risking his life. But there was no time, and so she settled for giving him a quick hug once he'd scribbled the address on a piece of paper.

'Look after her,' he said.

'I will,' Ava replied, tucking the note safely inside her brassiere so that no one would find it. 'There's nothing I wouldn't do to save her.'

Eliana switched her hold from Ethan's hand to hers, and the two women hurried from the store, pushing past the line of people who were far happier to move aside for people leaving than they had been to let Ava through when she'd arrived. But they'd barely set foot outside when Ethan ran after them, calling out.

'Wait!'

Ava turned, her palm still pressed to Eliana's.

'Take these,' he said, breathless as he thrust a set of keys at them. 'Take the delivery truck, no one will think to stop you if you're driving that.'

They both looked at the truck, only just visible from where it was parked around the corner.

'Ethan, if they find us in your truck, they could link us back to your store, and then—'

'Please,' he said, giving the keys to Ava, his eyes trained on Eliana. 'Take them. I need to know you have a way to leave the city. Go and save your family.' He paused. 'I'll find you, Eliana, after all of this, I promise. But you'll never get out of the city in time if you don't take the truck.'

Eliana threw her arms around him as Ava glanced away, kissing him, her fingers tangled in his short curls, until he pulled away and began to walk backwards.

'Look after her, Ava. Please keep her safe, I'm trusting you with her life.'

Ava nodded, clutching the keys in her palm, and watched as he ran back to the store, turning at the door to look at Eliana one last time. She doubted either of them would ever forget Ethan's kindness; there were good men, and then there were great men, and Ethan was certainly one of the latter. If there was anything else he could have done for Eliana, Ava didn't doubt for a moment that he would do it.

'You take the truck,' Ava said, pressing the keys into Eliana's hand. 'You need to drive to the hospital to warn Hanna, and then meet me at the house once you have her. They will know exactly where to look for her, so you must go quickly.'

'What about you? How will you get there?'

Ava wrapped her arms around Eliana, hugging her tightly. 'I'll find a way. Please don't worry about me, just get yourself and my sister to the house. All I want is for you to be safe.'

'You're certain we shouldn't stay together? That we wouldn't be better—'

'Eliana, there were men waiting outside my apartment block.' *Our* apartment block – that was what she should have said. Only, Eliana's family were living in her attic, and a Nazi family had been moved into the Goldmans' apartment, surrounded by their beautiful furniture and priceless art collection. 'They know who I am, they're expecting to find me, but chances are they won't know what you look like. It's safer for you to be alone.'

Eliana didn't look convinced when she broke their embrace. Tears shone from her eyes and she started to slowly back away – so slowly, as if she still wasn't convinced that she should go.

'You're certain?'

Ava forced a smile to reassure her. 'I am.'

'Tell my family that I love them,' Eliana said. 'If you get there before me, tell them I'm coming.'

Ava nodded. 'I will, and I'll keep them safe, I know what I have to do when I get there.'

Her father had warned her what could happen, had told her how to react if there were any signs that their work had been detected or if there were suspicions about the Goldmans, only he'd always expected that his work would be discovered, not hers. But everything had changed now that she was on the run. Executing the plan once she got home wasn't the problem; it was how to get there that she was struggling with.

She looked around, spying a bicycle leaning against a storefront. Ava had never stolen anything in her life before, and she most certainly couldn't pedal all the way to Bogensee, but it was a start. Hopefully once she made it so far, she could find a faster mode of transportation to travel the rest of the way.

She stood for a second as she heard the rumble of an engine, knowing that Eliana had started the truck, before walking quickly to the bike and taking it, wheeling it for a second, then throwing herself up on to the seat and riding away. She pedalled as fast as her legs were capable, praying that no one would see her and cry out that she'd stolen it, or chase after her and alert the authorities, but once she'd travelled a few blocks, she was confident she'd gotten away with it.

Now all I have to do is get home. Which was easier said than done. *Without the SS seeing me, without someone recognising me, without being caught.* Without the Goldmans and her mother being found at the house before she got there.

For the first time in her life, Ava wished she had a gun, because if it came to protecting herself or her mother she didn't doubt that she'd be able to use it.

She pushed even harder on the pedals, panic propelling her forward, sweat curling over her lip and across her forehead as her breath came in fast pants. And that was when she saw a farm truck rumbling along the road, slowing down and then coming to a complete stop at a corner.

Ava saw her chance and changed direction slightly to catch up to it, pedalling up fast behind and managing to jump off her stolen bicycle and launch on to the back without the driver seeing. She tucked down low when it started up again, looking out only to check they were going in the right direction. With any luck, she'd only have to walk part of the way, although she wasn't entirely certain how she'd disembark if he didn't slow down near her turn-off.

Chapter Twenty-Three

HANNA

Hanna touched the boy's forehead with the back of her hand, concerned that his fever still hadn't broken. Her shift had ended almost an hour ago, but she'd chosen to stay and look after those who needed her. She never liked leaving the children, not when she had no family of her own to go home to. She adored her sister and her parents, but they could never replace what she'd lost.

She was walking down the ward to check on her other patients when she heard the sound of tyres crunching over gravel outside. It wouldn't have alarmed her usually to hear a vehicle arrive – they had ambulances arriving throughout the day after all – but to have three cars pull up one after the other . . . She patted one of the children on the leg as she moved around the bed, leaning over to part the curtain and look out of the window. The hairs on her arms rose as she heard the sound of multiple doors closing and realised who their visitors were.

There were three unmistakable SS vehicles parked across the entrance to the hospital, effectively blocking it, and six men were marching briskly towards the door. Hanna's blood ran cold. Either there was a medical emergency or they were looking for someone.

And she had the most overwhelming, gut-wrenching feeling that they were looking for her.

They're coming for me. There's no one else here they could be looking for. Run. I have to run!

Hanna fled the room, walking as quickly as she could so as not to alarm the children, but when she reached the hallway she began to run. Fear knotted in her stomach as she heard the heavy thud-thud-thud of boots, and she propelled herself forward even faster, the doors and doctors she passed a blur as she raced for the back exit, crashing into one of the doctors and not even pausing to apologise as she stumbled on.

I just have to make it to the door. I have to get home. I have to warn Mama. This cannot be the end, not yet.

'There she is! The Müller girl is there!'

The sound of boots chasing after her became louder, but Hanna could see the door now, all she had to do was make it through and she could hide outside, it would be so much harder for them to find her out there. She'd known this day might come, but now that it was here, her fear was greater than she could ever have imagined, her desperation to not be caught driving her forward.

Five more steps. One. Almost there.

Hanna almost slammed into the door as she reached for the handle, but just as she thought she was about to escape, a hand caught her hair, yanking her backwards, pulling her clean off her feet and dropping her on to the floor. She sat up, frantically trying to push her back against the wall so she could at least face her captors, but a black boot came down hard on her stomach, pressing so hard, so heavily, that she could barely breathe, her lungs feeling as if they'd been crushed.

'Put the handcuffs on her.'

Hanna didn't bother trying to fight; she didn't try to proclaim her innocence as one of the men stood over her and spat in her face. But she also didn't react when the boot pressed harder into her abdomen, even though the pain was sharp and immediate, even though she began to see black as her vision swam. She'd been prepared for this, she'd known all along that she could lose her life for the work she'd done, but it had been worth it. All she cared about was finding a way to convince them that the rest of her family hadn't been involved in any way. Protecting Ava, her mother and the Goldmans was all that mattered to her now.

'Traitor bitch,' the SS man who cuffed her said as he hauled her to her feet, the metal cutting deeply into the flesh around her wrists. 'Just like her father.'

She considered fighting and flailing, spitting back at them like a wildcat and kicking with all her might, but as nurses and doctors came to stand in open doors to see what the commotion was, she simply hung her head. There was no point fighting against the inevitable, and she didn't want to make a scene that her patients could hear, that would make what was happening any worse for those who were watching.

It's over. Her only regret was that she wouldn't be able to rescue any more children, or help any more Jewish families and children still hidden in the city. She wouldn't be there for her sister, or for Eliana. A tear slipped down her cheek. *It's all over for Papa now, too.*

'We've got them both,' the man striding ahead of her, the one whose boot had been pressed to her body, called out triumphantly. 'We caught the other one looking for her.'

And just as Hanna was wondering who they were talking about, just as she lifted her head to look, everything changed.

Someone further down the hall screamed. It was unmistakably a woman, the sound piercing and heart-wrenching all at once, and when the man in front of Hanna moved slightly to the side, she saw a scene that broke her heart.

'No!' Hanna cried. She saw Eliana, her hands in cuffs behind her back, as one of the men used the back of his hand to smack her across the face, his knuckles leaving a smear of blood on her pale skin. She dropped to her knees, her nose dribbling red.

Please God, no. Not Eliana.

'Let me go!' Hanna screamed, snatching her hands away from the man holding on to her, trying to escape, forgetting all about not making a scene.

But she was no match for the men surrounding her, no matter how hard she kicked or thrusted. She frantically tried to bite one of them when he pressed his thick, ugly arm around her neck, but she received a sharp slap to the face in return that sent blood dripping from her mouth, one of her teeth rattling loose.

'Hanna!' Eliana cried.

Hanna fought again, so hard she feared the cuffs were going to cut through her wrists to the bone, not certain whether the screams she could hear were coming from her or Eliana. All she knew was that it was her fault Eliana was here – the only reason she could possibly be in the hospital building was for her. She'd come to warn her, and instead she'd been captured.

'Keep her still!' a man yelled, just as the butt of a pistol connected with the side of Hanna's head, sending her reeling sideways. The ground came up to meet her and everything went black.

Chapter Twenty-Four

Ava

Ava stood beside the driveway to her family home, careful to conceal herself behind the cover of trees while she watched the house. There were no cars outside, and she couldn't detect any movement or anything out of the ordinary, so she decided to run up the driveway and go through the back door, just to be certain.

The only sound outside was the occasional chirp of birdsong, and Ava slipped through the door, closing it quietly behind her and then standing, dead still, to listen out. Her heart was beating so loud, her breathing was so ragged, that she could barely strain her ears to hear anything else.

'Ava!'

Zelda dropped the folded stack of bed sheets she was carrying, her shriek making Ava almost jump from her skin.

'I'm so sorry,' she said, bending to help Zelda collect the fallen load. 'I've come home because I'm feeling unwell, and I had to pause there a moment to catch my breath. I didn't mean to take you by surprise.'

Zelda put her hand over her heart for a moment, before shaking her head and laughing at Ava. 'Well, now that I've recovered my fright, let me make you some soup to help you feel better. You go on up to bed.'

'Oh no, please,' Ava said, handing her the sheets. 'I don't want you to go to any trouble. In fact, you should go home for the rest of the afternoon.'

'Home?' Zelda looked as if Ava had suggested something most absurd. 'I have beds to make and—'

'Please,' Ava said. 'I wouldn't want you catching this, it would devastate my mother if you became unwell and couldn't help her with her dinner party this weekend. My father told me today that she will be hosting some senior party members this weekend. Has she told you?'

Zelda's eyes widened. 'This weekend? You're certain it's this weekend?'

'I believe the date has just been set. I overheard talk today at the office.'

Ava touched Zelda's arm, trying her best to stay calm even though her heart was racing. The SS could arrive at any minute, and she needed to find her mother and get Zelda out of the house as quickly as possible so she wasn't drawn into whatever was about to happen. She wanted to believe that they wouldn't suspect her mother of being involved, but she had no way of being certain.

'Now, where is my mother? If she doesn't yet know, then I'll have to tell her all about it.' Ava hoped her lie was convincing Zelda.

'Your mother isn't here, Ava. She left in a hurry late this morning.'

Ava balled her fists, digging her fingernails tightly into her palms. 'Did she mention where she was going?'

Zelda shook her head and turned as if to go up the stairs. 'She didn't tell me.'

'Zelda, please!' Ava said, taking the sheets forcibly from her. 'I shall take these up. Take the rest of the afternoon off, and perhaps you can plan what you will serve for dinner this weekend? Mama will be most impressed if you have a menu for her to look over when you arrive in the morning.'

Zelda threw her hands up in the air, muttering something beneath her breath.

'I promise I'll tell her that I sent you home, that it was all my idea. See you tomorrow.'

Ava stood at the foot of the stairs, watching as Zelda moved almost painfully slowly, gathering her bag and then eventually letting herself out. The moment she was gone Ava dropped the sheets and ran to the door, locking it and then running to the front door and locking that too. She glanced around, making sure there were no windows open, before sprinting up the stairs as fast as her feet would carry her.

She stopped beneath the attic door, fumbling around for the catch to pull the stairs down.

'David! Herr Goldman!' she called. 'We have to go! Quickly!'

She hurried up the stairs, her eyes adjusting to the dim light, and the first thing she saw was the fear written all over the faces staring back at her. They'd been playing a game of cards from the looks of it, and they were all frozen, cards still in hand.

'What do you mean we have to go?' David asked, dropping his cards to the makeshift table.

'I'll explain as we move, but quickly. Gather up warm clothes and follow me.' She paused. 'We might not be coming back, so we need to prepare for colder weather, too.'

She rushed back down the narrow stairs, waiting impatiently at the bottom as Frau Goldman came down first, followed by the men. Ava took her arm, realising how frail she'd become in the time she'd been up in the attic.

'Ava, tell us what's happened. Where are you taking us?' David asked.

'Where is Eliana?' Frau Goldman asked, her face almost contorted as she fretted about her daughter.

'I don't know what's happening, I don't know what they know or what they're going to do, but—'

'What who is going to do?' David asked, moving to block her way.

'David, we have to hurry!' she said, pushing her way past him. 'We have a bunker in the field, just out from the garden, and we have to hide there. Papa told me that if anything happened I was to hide you there. That we were all to hide there until he came for us.'

'Ava, what danger? Please, what has happened?'

'They know,' she said, pausing at the door to unlock it and turning to face David. 'I don't know what or how, but my father warned me – there were SS at our apartment, and I came here as quickly as I could to make sure you were safe. I don't know how long we have before they get here, or which of my family members they're even looking for.'

'Where is my daughter?' Herr Goldman said. 'Is she in danger, too?'

'Eliana has gone to get Hanna, they'll be here soon,' Ava said. 'But for now, we have to get to the bunker. It's the only place we'll be safe.'

'The SS are coming here, aren't they?' David asked.

'Yes,' she replied. 'I think so.'

The moment the words were out of her mouth, David grabbed hold of his father's arm and moved even faster across the back garden than Ava.

Ava felt as if she'd been watching the house all day, when in fact she knew it couldn't have been for more than two hours. Her legs ached from being in the same position for so long, and her heartbeat hadn't settled since she'd left the office that morning. Now, darkness was slowly starting to creep across the sky, and she had no idea what to expect, what to do.

'Do you hear that?' David asked.

'Yes, I hear it.'

She wished she had binoculars so she could see what was coming, but her ears told her that it was more than one vehicle travelling up the road or already turning into their driveway. Their home was secluded and surrounded by trees, which meant they were able to hear any motor vehicle approaching.

A flash of black confirmed her fears – the SS had arrived, so there was no chance Eliana and Hanna were going to be joining them anytime soon. She only hoped they would realise before it was too late, and manage to turn around instead of being accosted by the men when they arrived, or by a patrol on the road.

'Is there any chance that could be your father arriving?' David asked her.

She moved closer to him, wanting to make certain she was completely obscured from sight. 'I don't know.' If she were being truthful, she didn't think there was any chance it could be him. Her father had managed to warn her, but she doubted he'd have been able to escape the city, and if he had, he certainly wouldn't be in an SS motorcade. Her greatest fear was that he wouldn't come at all, and then she wouldn't know what to do.

Ava watched as two men stepped out of the first car, but it was the second car that captured her attention. The driver turned to open the back door of the car, and she couldn't imagine who their passengers might be. *Could* it be her father?

No. No, no, no!

'Eliana,' David whispered, at the same moment as Ava murmured her own sister's name.

She watched in horror as they were dragged from the car to the house, the men pounding on the door before kicking at the timber until it gave way, and then disappearing inside.

'What do we do now?' David asked, turning to her.

Ava blinked away her tears. 'We wait,' she said. 'If we try to go in there now, they'll only kill us both, and then we won't be any use to anyone.'

She reached for David's hand, intertwining their fingers as they stood together and watched the house. She dropped her head to his shoulder as she tried not to imagine what they were doing to her beautiful sister, and to the girl who'd become her best friend.

Ava woke with a start, scrambling to her feet as she realised she'd fallen asleep. Everything came rushing back to her then, as David reached out a hand to steady her. *Hanna. Eliana. Mama.* She was grateful he was holding her as she stared at the house.

'You should have woken me,' she mumbled. 'I don't know how I fell asleep.'

'You were barely asleep for thirty minutes,' he said, and it was then she realised she was still holding his hand. He must have noticed too, for he looked down and then let go of her, their fingers slowly parting.

'Has anything happened?'

'Two of the SS men just left,' he said.

She looked at the house, wishing they were able to get closer without being seen. 'So you think there's only two of them left in the house? No one else has arrived?'

David nodded. 'That's right.'

Ava stood for a moment, thinking through what her father would do in this situation, what Hanna would do, if she were in her shoes. She imagined Hanna would be far better at coming up with a plan, would have no doubt already thought through exactly what to do if she were faced with this very situation.

'You didn't see any sign at all of my mother?' she asked, knowing it was unlikely that there'd been a sighting of her in the short time she'd been asleep.

'No,' David replied, his face falling. 'No sign at all.'

Ava didn't want to acknowledge the fact that she could have been taken already. Zelda had said she'd left in the morning, so what if she'd gone to the apartment to wait for her daughters, and been accosted there by the men Ava had seen? 'I think we should go through the woods, get as close to the house as we can, and then make our way inside through the back door.'

'It's our one chance to get Eliana and Hanna,' David said. 'I agree.'

'If we wait, if more men return when we're in the house . . .'

'We move quickly,' he said. 'We watch the house, see where the guards are, and then find them.'

Ava swallowed, looking at David, who appeared as uncertain as her, despite his words.

'Do you have the gun?' she asked.

He reached into his waistband and took out the pistol she'd given him. 'I do.'

They had only one gun between them, but this was her home, which meant she knew how to get in and move around inside without being seen. It was her only advantage, and she had to hope that it was enough.

After making their way through the woods and near the back door, Ava was confident that they could get inside undetected. There was only one car parked outside, and she knew that the longer they waited, the greater the risk.

'You go in,' David whispered. 'I'll go around the front.'

'No!' she hissed. 'You need to come with me. We go together.' She was already terrified of going in with him, let alone on her own.

'Someone needs to keep a lookout. If they hear you, if they leave their posts, I can do something to get their attention. You need to go alone.'

'David, they'll kill you if they see you.'

He looked into her eyes. 'You think they'll treat you any differently? I'm as scared for you as you are for me.'

Ava knew he was right, even though she was loath to admit it. 'Be careful,' she murmured, moving to stand from her crouched position, knowing she had to be brave and do this. If it were her inside, she had little doubt that Hanna would risk everything to save her.

'You too.'

She didn't wait around to second-guess herself, running as fast as she could to the door. She waited for a moment, listening, before slowly turning the door handle. She'd locked it the day before, but thankfully it opened and she closed it behind her as quietly as she could. Ava could hear the two men talking, and she inched along the wall on tiptoe before darting along the hallway and going up the stairs. She was going to search upstairs first, and she took each step carefully so as not to make the floorboards squeak.

Every breath, every placement of a foot, sent a fresh wave of terror rolling through her body, but she forced herself to keep going, wishing there was some noise in the house so that every tiny movement didn't sound so loud. What worried her most was that she couldn't hear anything coming from any of the rooms, which made her wonder if Hanna and Eliana were even up there. Could they have escaped without her or David seeing? Or left with the other SS officers? A shudder ran down her spine. Were they downstairs? She doubted they'd escaped, because the SS officers would have sent for dogs and she knew the men would have searched the forest and hunted the girls down, not stopping until they'd apprehended them.

She reached the top of the stairs and pressed herself against the wall, her heart pounding so loud she was convinced it was audible outside of her body. Ava inched her way along, peering into her bedroom. No one was there. She moved slowly to the next door, a closet, and then tiptoed to her sister's room. She swallowed, trying to calm her breath as she continued on. There were only three rooms left to check, and she hurried down the short hall that led to her parents' bedroom.

Hanna.

Ava almost forgot she was supposed to be silent. She ran to her sister, taking in the dishevelled state of her hair, her ripped blouse, her undergarments showing as she fought against her restraints. But it was the cloth stuffed into her mouth and her cuffed hands that upset Ava the most.

She reached her sister, tears falling down her cheeks as she thought of all the hours she'd been up in the room alone, of what might have happened to her while Ava herself was hiding, safe, away from the house. She should have come sooner, should have fought for her the moment she'd seen her arrive.

'Hanna,' she whispered. 'I'm going to get you out of here. We just have to find Eliana, we—'

Hanna fought to speak, groaning as Ava's fingers worked as fast as they could to untie the crudely tied rag across her sister's mouth.

'Ava,' Hanna croaked, her eyes wild with fear in the way that a cornered animal's might be, knowing their life was about to be taken. But it was only then that she realised her sister wasn't looking at her, but past her. 'Ava—'

The hairs on the back of Ava's neck lifted when she sensed someone behind her, and suddenly understood her sister's panic. She froze, fear pulsating through every inch of her body. The sound of a heavy boot-step made her turn, her fear turning to panic as she saw the man standing in the doorway, his lips pulled tightly together. He narrowed his eyes, staring at her. But it wasn't the anger of his expression that terrified her so much as the pistol he was aiming at her chest.

Heinrich.

She had no doubt that he'd kill her without a second thought. A man she'd once loved so fiercely, but whom she now despised as much as he clearly despised her. And that's when she saw the half-naked woman in the adjoining room, took in Heinrich's untucked shirt, watched as Eliana lifted her head from behind him, her nose crusted with thick blood.

'Heinrich, please,' Ava began, drawing her gaze back to him, but even she could hear the tremble of fear in her own whisper as she tried to reason with him. 'Please put down the gun. We've done nothing wrong, this has all been a misunderstanding.'

Ava heard her sister move behind her, knew that he would kill both of them in an instant if she didn't do something to stop him. If only she'd managed to rid Hanna of her restraints, if only they had something to defend themselves with.

'Heinrich—'

'Shut up!' he screamed, the whites of his eyes flashing as he spat on the carpet in disgust.

'Heinrich—'

'You don't speak to me, you Jew-loving bitch!' Spittle formed in the corners of his mouth, a deranged man if ever she'd seen one.

Ava knew the only advantage she might have would be taking him by surprise; he was staring at her with so much hatred that she knew he wouldn't hesitate in pulling the trigger, but if she could just wrestle the gun from him or knock him off balance, at least her sister might have a chance.

She lunged forward without hesitation, diving to the side as the gun fired, lowering her body and quickly scrambling to her feet and charging at him with her shoulder, reaching desperately for the gun, her hands flailing while she struggled to connect with it.

He was so much bigger than her, so much stronger, and even as her fingers wrapped around the pistol, even as she fought with every bit of strength in her body to pull it from his grasp, she knew it was useless. Heinrich was going to kill her and her sister and Eliana, and then he'd find her mother, too.

When he wrestled the gun free from her grip, she only had a moment to find her feet before the butt of the pistol connected with the side of her head, sending her reeling. Ava staggered backwards, hand raised to her face, watching through blurry eyes as he cocked the gun once more, smiling as he did so, and she tried to focus on him through her blurry vision.

I'm going to die. He's going to kill all of us.

There was a cracking sound when Heinrich squeezed the trigger, the sound of her sister screaming behind her echoing through the room, and Ava looked down at her stomach, expecting to see crimson blood staining her top. She dropped to her knees and the room swam around her.

But that was when she realised that the scream piercing the air in the room wasn't coming from her sister. She scrambled backwards while Heinrich collapsed, the gun falling from his hands as Ava began to scream again, and the blood she'd expected to see on her own body pooled under his. She began to shake uncontrollably as she crawled across the room, tears streaming down her cheeks.

For Heinrich's wasn't the only fallen body in the room.

Chapter Twenty-Five

Ava's hands were shaking as she crept around Heinrich, bending down to pick up his pistol and trying not to be sick while his expressionless eyes stared back at her. She gave him a quick kick with the point of her foot, wanting to make sure he was dead without getting any closer to him, then she dashed around to David, to the man who'd so bravely killed Heinrich, who'd saved her life with so little thought for his own.

He was sitting up now but slumped over to the side, blood seeping through his shirt, and Ava didn't know what to do. She heard a moan and looked past him to Eliana, torn between running to her and helping David.

'Untie me!' Hanna cried. 'David, put pressure on the wound. Keep your hand there.'

'Get the keys,' David groaned. 'You need keys, for her handcuffs.'

Ava's stomach turned. That would mean groping around Heinrich's dead body looking for them. Her heart started to pound as she thought about the other men downstairs. In all the commotion, she'd forgotten entirely about them.

'The guards,' she panicked, looking at the door, expecting them to come bursting through at any second. 'We have—'

'They're gone,' David said, his voice low, his hand pressed hard to his side as he groaned again.

Ava didn't even want to think about what David had been forced to do. All she cared about was that no one else was coming for them. Yet.

She bent down low over Heinrich, having to grab hold of him and heft him to the side in order to fumble for the keys. She unclipped them from his belt loop and let his body go, backing away from him, wondering how she'd ever loved him, how she'd ever planned to marry him and have children with such a monster.

Ava turned back to her sister, using the edge of her blouse to wipe a splatter of blood from her cheek, her hands shaking as she undid the cuffs and freed her hands. Hanna gave her a quick, hard hug before darting across the room to David. Dropping to her knees, she took his hand away to inspect his wound.

Eliana. Ava's legs wobbled as she ran back across the room and through the connecting door to Eliana, who was hunched forward now, her knees drawn up to her chest, her body trembling. Ava took in the scene before her, knowing instinctively what Heinrich had done to her friend. She sat down and gently put an arm around Eliana, holding her as she cried, pushing the hair from her face. What she wanted was to take her to the bathroom and carefully bathe her, before wrapping her in warm blankets and holding her while she slept away the pain and trauma of what had happened. But they didn't have the luxury of time – the other two SS men could be back at any moment, and she didn't even want to think what they'd do if they came into the house and found three of their own shot dead. She only hoped that Zelda didn't arrive and unexpectedly end up part of the commotion.

'I'm going to get you a fresh change of clothes,' Ava said.

'David?' Eliana whispered, looking up at Ava, more child than young woman in that moment.

'David is in good hands,' Ava murmured. 'Hanna will look after him.'

Tears began to leak from Eliana's eyes once more, and Ava pressed a kiss to her forehead and quickly hugged her again, before letting go and standing up.

'Don't leave me,' Eliana whispered, her eyes wide with fear. 'Please don't leave me, Ava.'

'I'm only going to get clothes from my room for you. I'll be right back.'

As Ava passed David, he reached out his hand and she clasped it without hesitation. She knew she'd never know how to properly thank him for what he'd done, for the way he'd so selflessly risked his life to save theirs, but she hoped he could sense her gratitude.

'Thank you,' she said, knowing it wasn't enough but saying it anyway.

He grimaced, his other hand covered in blood, pressed to his bullet wound again. 'I would do it all over again,' he said, his breath catching, his breath hissing out of him when he tried to move, 'if it meant keeping you all from harm.'

Something warm and deep swelled inside of Ava. She stared down at David, keeping hold of his hand just a moment longer than she should have. It dawned on her that there were two men in this room, two men who'd been part of her life these past months, and the one who'd pledged to spend the rest of his life with her had been the one who'd tried to kill her.

'Is she going to be all right?' David asked, looking past her to Eliana.

Ava nodded. 'It'll just take time. She's been through a lot.'

David looked away, as if he couldn't stand to even acknowledge what they might have done to his sister.

'Where's Hanna?' she asked, suddenly realising that her sister wasn't there.

'Getting supplies,' David groaned, slumping back down again.

Ava wished she could lower herself to the carpet and cradle him through his pain, but she needed to help Eliana first. She had begun to walk across the room when she heard the unmistakable creak of the stairs.

'Where did Hanna say she was going?' Ava whispered.

David looked up at her. She knew he'd heard the noise, too. 'Down the hall. To fetch water, and a needle and thread.'

Ava glanced at the pistol, sitting on the bed where she'd left it. She didn't doubt that she'd be capable of squeezing the trigger and taking a life if it meant saving David or Eliana, not now.

She lifted the gun, standing protectively in front of David, her breath shallow, her heart racing.

'*Mama?*' Ava put the gun down when she saw her and ran forward, opening her arms and throwing herself at her mother.

'Ava!' Her mother's hug was tight. 'Where's Hanna? Where are the Goldmans?' She gasped. 'What happened to David?'

Ava stepped back, pushing her hair from her face as her mother took in the scene in the room. 'Eliana is in the next room. She needs you. I'm going to get her new clothes.'

'And Hanna?'

'I'm here, Mama.' Hanna had returned with towels, a dish of water, and a needle between her lips, her words mumbled from trying not to drop it.

'Make those clothes warm ones, Ava, just in case. We need to leave now.' She turned to Hanna. 'You'll have to work fast.'

Ava hurried, pulling clothes from her wardrobe and taking them to Eliana. She let her mother tend to Eliana and went back to look for more things, realising that they all needed to change if they were going to be on the run. They couldn't walk around in bloodstained clothes without being noticed, and her mother was right – who knew how long they might be on the run for? They would need warm layers, particularly if they were to be moving around at night or sleeping rough.

'Where's Papa?' Ava asked when she came back, dropping to her knees to assist Hanna, who was preparing to take out the bullet lodged in David's flesh. His guttural groans made Ava flinch, hating to see him in so much pain. 'He warned me but then I never saw him again.'

'Your father is gone,' her mother said, her voice so low that Ava wondered if she'd misheard her.

'Gone?' Ava echoed. *Am I truly never to see Papa again?* It seemed like only hours ago that his hand had been so warm, his touch light as he'd whispered in her ear, had passed her the note in a move that had ultimately saved her life. 'He's already gone?' What did she even mean by *gone*?

'They've already executed him for treason, but he has forged papers in his study, locked in his safe for all of you.' Her mother cleared her throat, clearly trying not to cry, to be brave for them. 'We have to leave as soon as Hanna has that bullet out of David, and we must save our grief for later. Your father would want us to be safe, he'd want us to do anything we could to stay alive, do you understand?'

Ava understood. No one was coming to save them. If their father was truly gone, then it was all over. The resistance network valued them, but she'd seen first-hand how ruthless they could be, which didn't give her any hope that they might risk coming to help. She refused to cry, knowing that her mother was right. They would have to wait to grieve – that was what her father would have wanted.

'It will be a death sentence if we stay,' Hanna said, looking up at Ava, as if she could read her thoughts.

'We need to go and get Frau and Herr Goldman,' Ava said, looking away as her mother dressed Eliana, not wanting to see the ugly purple bruises on her skin, caused by a man she'd once willingly let touch her. 'They will have heard the gunshots and they'll be terrified out there.'

While Ava was downstairs rifling through her father's drawers and opening his safe to find the documents, her mother called out that she was going to get Herr and Frau Goldman, and they were to meet in the kitchen in five minutes' time. Ava found the identity papers hidden away for all of them, and she also took the money from the safe, a diamond necklace she'd never seen before, and a loaded pistol. She hated the idea of carrying a gun, but she figured it was better if they had two.

Ava went to the kitchen, quickly finding a bag and putting together two small sacks of food and filling some bottles with water. It wasn't much, but it was something, and they could all take something else to eat with them on the way.

Eliana appeared in the kitchen first, her arms wrapped around her body, which was covered in a bulky coat that looked too thick for her slender frame. David and Hanna followed, and Ava paled at the sight of David, who grimaced with each step. She had no idea how he was going to walk far with his injury.

'Here are your papers,' Ava said, passing a document to each of them. 'Memorise your new name and birth date until they're your own.'

She thought of the final set of papers inside the safe, the ones that had clearly been intended for her father to use. Part of her had wanted to take them, but she knew she had to leave them behind, in case her mother had been wrong and he came back. She wasn't going to give up hope until she knew for certain that he'd been taken from them.

The back door opened and suddenly everyone was in the room. The Goldmans were all hugging one another, happy to be reunited, and her mother came to stand beside her.

'Every minute we're here, we risk being discovered,' she said. 'You need to go now.'

'Yes, we need to go. I have food packed and—'

'No, *you* need to go, Ava,' her mother said, reaching up a hand to stroke her face, her eyes filled with an expression that Ava didn't want to see. 'I'm staying here.'

'Mama, *no*,' Ava said, shaking her head. 'I can't go without you! I can't, I—'

'We are also staying,' Frau Goldman said. 'We will stay hidden and let the four of you go.'

'But we have papers for everyone,' Ava said. 'We can all go, we can't leave you here. *I* can't leave you here.'

'We will only slow you down,' Herr Goldman said, 'and it will be much harder for us to pass as non-Jews. If we go, we'll all be caught.'

'Papa,' Eliana said, her eyes filling with tears as she clung to her mother.

'We have decided,' he said. 'But now it's time for you to go, while you still can. All this time hidden, it can't be for nothing.'

Ava knew there was no point in arguing; her mother's chin was raised, her shoulders were squared, and the Goldmans looked equally as resolute.

'I will stay also,' Hanna said.

'Hanna, no! I won't leave you, there is no reason for you to stay,' Ava said.

Hanna smiled, leaving David to lean on his father and coming to hug Ava. 'Yes, you will,' she said. 'I'll find you, I promise, we can meet in Cologne. Eliana has told me that's where Ethan told you to go. But you must get Eliana and David to safety, you have to do this for them, to finish what Papa started.'

'Hanna,' Ava mumbled, burying her face in her sister's hair, hugging her so fiercely she wondered how she'd ever let go.

'You can do this, I know you can. Please, do it for me, and for Mama and Papa, too.'

'You promise you'll find us?' Ava asked, wiping her cheeks; Hanna stood beside their mother. 'You promise you'll follow when you can?'

She didn't miss the hesitation in her sister's voice before she finally spoke. 'I promise. Now go. Make Papa proud.'

Ava looked from her mother to her sister, before finally nodding and collecting the small sacks of food. For the first time in her life, it appeared that she was in charge – the destiny of others rested squarely on her shoulders.

'We shall head directly for Cologne,' she said. 'We will stay hidden there for a day with Ethan's family, maybe two, while we form a plan to leave Germany. We might even be able to get to the Netherlands with these papers.'

Her sister nodded, and her mother took her hands in hers, lifting them to press a kiss to her skin.

'Stay safe, my love.'

Ava looked to David and then Eliana, knowing that she had to be brave, for them. 'I will. I'll see you both soon.'

Even as she said the words, she wondered if she would ever see her darling, sweet mother or her impossibly brave sister again.

Chapter Twenty-Six

HANNA

Hanna returned to the house, having secured a very tearful Frau and Herr Goldman in the bunker. She didn't know what might happen to them, but she'd left them with oil lamps, warm blankets and food, and all she could do now was wait and see who came for them.

Her mother had made coffee for them both, and they sat down in the two chairs closest to the windows in the front room so they could watch the driveway. Hanna couldn't help but wonder if it would be the last time they sat like this together in the house they both loved so much.

'You should have gone with your sister.'

Hanna kept her coffee cup in her hands, finding the warmth soothing. 'Mama, I will never leave Germany,' she said, staring out, looking down the long line of trees that flanked the entrance to their property. 'My husband is here, my son is here.' She didn't bother holding back her tears, not now, not with only her mother beside her. There was nobody she had to be brave for any more. 'This was their home, and I will never leave them. And now Papa is here forever, too.'

She glanced at her mother and saw that she, too, had tears in her eyes. 'We both have our husbands to stay for. I understand that more than anyone, my love.'

'What will we do? When they come?' Hanna asked.

'We do whatever we have to do. But I won't let them take me alive.'

Hanna wiped her eyes and sipped her coffee again, just as three big black cars began to roll up the driveway, one after another. As much as it broke her heart to hear her mother speak in that way, she felt the same. After what she'd been through, after what she'd seen them do to Eliana, she wouldn't let them take her alive, either. Not again.

'They're here.'

Both women stood, embracing before collecting their guns from the table. They both held SS pistols, and her mother also had a rifle slung over her shoulder – one they'd kept on the property for hunting purposes for most of Hanna's life. Neither of them had ever fired it before – hunting had always been her father's interest, not theirs – but she didn't doubt for a moment that her mother would use it.

The sound of dogs barking sent a shudder through Hanna, and she met her mother's gaze. The canines could only mean one thing; they'd come to search for someone.

They positioned themselves by the door, peering out, but instead of approaching the house as she'd expected, the men moved straight out towards the garden. She'd thought they would be coming directly to the house to take them, but they didn't even send one of the men to the door.

'They know about the bunker,' her mother whispered.

'How?' Hanna asked, panic rising inside of her, her skin prickling. 'How could they know?'

'We all had them built around the same time, to ensure our families would be safe in case of bombings. They must suspect we're hiding someone, and someone must have sent them specifically to search it.'

Hanna didn't think, she just ran, bursting through the front door and holding her gun high, taking aim and shooting at the closest SS man. She got him squarely in the back, and she watched in horror as his body crumpled to the ground, as the other men all turned, guns drawn. She'd never taken a life before, but as gut-wrenching as it felt, she knew she was capable of doing it again.

'No!' her mother screamed from behind her, and she ran out, moving past Hanna as she fired again, and again and again.

Hanna lifted her pistol once more, taking aim, hitting another man in the shoulder. But at the same time she saw her mother stop, the pistol she'd been holding falling from her fingers. Hanna paused only for a second, only long enough to see the crimson stain of blood spreading across her mother's dress, covering the front of it, the sound of the SS officers yelling, the dogs barking, the rush of air as she ran forward again, screaming.

Hanna fired her pistol over and over, until there were no shots left, until she tripped as something pierced her shoulder, sharp and violent, as even more pain exploded in her stomach. She looked back, as everything began to spin around her – seeing her mother face down in the dirt, her hair like a golden fan around her. And all she could think, as she felt herself slipping away, was that she hoped Herr Goldman had enough bullets to finish off what they'd started.

Chapter Twenty-Seven

AVA

Ava paced back and forth, trying to decide what to do. They'd stayed two nights in Cologne, and another night in a hay barn outside of Düren, but all Ava could think about was what Hanna had said to her, about where they would meet.

'I'm going back to look for her,' she said, reaching for her coat. 'What if she's there waiting for us and she doesn't know where to go?'

David stood, and she didn't miss the way he gestured to Eliana, who quietly disappeared from sight.

'No,' David said. 'I can't let you do that.'

'What do you mean, you can't let me? You heard what she said, she's my sister and Hanna—'

'Gave me this letter,' he interrupted, as he reached into the pocket of his jacket. 'Ava, Hanna gave me this before we left. She also asked me to stay with you while you read it.' He gently touched her arm. 'I promised her I would, so please don't make me break that promise.'

Ava looked up at him, confused, but there was an expression on his face, a pain there, that took her by surprise. 'Why are you looking at me like that? What else did Hanna say?'

He nudged the letter into her hands. 'Please, just read this. You'll understand once you've read her words.'

'She's not coming, is she?' Ava closed her eyes, feeling the weight of the paper in her fingers. *She's not coming. I believed her when she said she'd follow, but she had no intention of coming after us.*

David didn't answer her, he just watched her, as if waiting for her to fall, waiting to catch her, waiting for her to read something that she already knew she didn't want to read.

The letter was folded in two, and she slowly opened it, immediately recognising her sister's handwriting. David didn't move away and neither did she, as her eyes quickly scanned the words, wondering if Hanna had decided on a new plan that for some reason she'd wanted to keep secret. Perhaps they were to meet somewhere else, perhaps she'd been wrong in thinking she wasn't coming.

Dear Ava,

I've never been very good at saying goodbye, and so I thought it would be easier to write you a letter. David promised me he'd give this to you once it was too late for you to come back for me – please don't be angry with him, because I gave him no choice.

Ava, I want you to live a wonderful life for both of us. I want you to fall in love, get married, and grow old. Those things were taken away from me when Michael and Hugo died, which is why I was always prepared to sacrifice my life to save others, to save families and keep those children safe. It was also why I was prepared to sacrifice my life for yours. I will fight until my very last breath to protect those who need protecting, and I understand the consequences of that decision, even though I also know how painful those words will be for you to read.

There is something I need you to do for me though, Ava. Once the war is over, once there is no more fighting and hate left in the world, if that time ever comes, I need you to dig up every jar that we buried. I need you to dedicate yourself to reuniting those families, to giving answers to those mothers who were forced to leave their children, to sharing the information I saved with the authorities. And if the parents have perished, which has always been my greatest fear, I want those children to know how much their parents sacrificed to give them a chance at life. I want them to know that there was nothing they wouldn't have done to save them. I need you to find them and tell them that.

I love you, Ava, so much that it breaks my heart to write to you. But one day I hope you'll understand what I've done, and why.

With all my love, Hanna.

'No,' Ava said, shaking her head as she stared at the letter. 'No!'
'Ava—'
'You knew?' she cried, shoving David backwards, the heels of her hands slamming into his shoulders. 'You knew she wasn't coming? All this time you knew and you didn't tell me?'
'Ava, please—'
'No!' she cried, beating her fists against his chest. 'I will not let her do this, I won't. I'm going back for her!'

'Ava,' David said again, gathering her into his arms, ignoring her protests as he folded her tightly against him, his hands firm against her back.

She fought his hold until a shudder of tears forced her to give in, and she buried her face against him while he rocked her, and held her through every gasp and cry. It wasn't his fault, she knew that, but to think that Hanna wasn't coming, that she'd hugged her for the very last time, that she'd never see her again, and that David could have told her . . .

'Did you really know?' Ava asked, once she'd caught her breath. She pushed back from him and looked up into his eyes. 'Did you know she wasn't coming? I need you to tell me the truth.'

'I suspected as much,' he said, gently brushing her hair from her eyes, his fingers soft against her skin when he wiped away her tears. 'But no, I didn't know for sure.'

'Do you think she's already—' Ava choked on the word, finding it almost impossible to expel. 'Gone?'

David nodded. 'I think there's a chance they're all gone by now,' he said, pulling her close again, her head tucked beneath his chin. 'I don't see how they could have survived what was to come. They sacrificed themselves for us, to give us time to put distance between ourselves and them.'

'But there's a chance? There's a chance they could have made it, that they're in hiding, that—'

'Yes, Ava, there's always a chance. There is absolutely always a chance.'

But Ava knew, deep down, she knew. There was an ache inside of her, a bone-deep pain that she'd never felt before. Yesterday, she'd had a family, and now, she had no one.

Ava looked up at David, at the kindness in his expression, at the pain in his eyes. They'd both lost so much.

'I'm sorry,' he said.

Ava reached for his hand, her palm against his. Her breath shuddered from between her lips, and she forced herself to lift her head instead of wallowing in her pain.

'We have to survive, for them. We have to escape and not return until it's all over.'

Eliana stepped out of the shadows, and Ava held out her other hand, clasping Eliana's when she reached her.

'Their lives can't have been for nothing. The three of us, we are survivors,' Ava said, looking from David to Eliana, a strength forming that she'd never felt before, pushing against the tide of grief that was raging inside her. 'And we will survive until the bitter end. We have no choice, we have to survive. For them.'

I promise you, Hanna, I will survive to reunite those families. I will make sure everyone knows your name, that they know what you sacrificed to give others the chance to live. I will do this for you until my very last breath.

Epilogue

Ava

the Müller Estate, Bogensee, Germany

July 1946

Ava held David's hand tightly as she stood at the open door, looking out over the garden. There had been times over the past two years that she'd wondered if she'd ever have the chance to return, whether she'd ever be able to come home and carry out her sister's wishes. So much time had passed since she'd last stood at that door, terrified and wondering how they were all going to survive. Since they'd fled and left her mother and sister behind.

David squeezed her hand, and she looked up at him. Whatever pain she was feeling, whatever trauma echoed through her memories, she knew it was only equal to what he was feeling. The day they'd left Bogensee had been the day they'd unknowingly said goodbye to their families, to everything they'd known and loved, but the time that had passed since then had slowly begun to repair their pain.

'Shall we take him out to the garden?' David asked, and Ava watched as he bent to scoop their son into his arms.

Their child had just begun toddling, his unsteady little legs marching him about all over the place, and as soon as he was held high, he was wrestling to get down again.

'Let him walk,' she said. 'He can hold my hand and tire those little legs out.'

Ava held David's hand on one side and her son's on the other as they walked out and then down the few steps that led to the grass and garden beyond. It was overgrown now, with haphazard plantings sprouting every which way; something that made her think of her beloved Papa. He would turn in his grave to see the property in such a dishevelled state. The interior had fared better, despite the soldiers who'd used it while they'd been gone, although Ava hadn't yet been able to set foot upstairs, despite the time that had passed since she'd last been in there.

'Are you thinking about them?' she asked, glancing over at David.

'Of course. Are you?'

She nodded, taking a moment to let her emotions settle, not wanting to cry in front of their son. She'd cried enough tears to last her a lifetime, but even so her eyes still filled with moisture whenever she let her mind go back to the last day she'd kissed her mother and held her sister's hand.

'I keep thinking about what it was like for them, after we left. How long they fought for, what they did to give us the chance to be free.'

She could see David swallowing, clearly trying as hard as she was not to break down. If she'd been a mother at a different time, she wondered if it would have worried her, for her child to see her cry. But after everything they'd been through, after all the tears and heartache, Max was their little miracle, the child who had lit up their world and helped them to find their smiles again, and she didn't want anything to stop him from his happy babbling and joy at life. *At a life we are so very fortunate to have.*

Everyone they'd loved had gone. From what she could gather, her mother and sister had died within hours of saying goodbye and sending them on their way, fearless until the very end to protect those they loved. Her father had been executed for treason, but her mother had been wrong; that day, when everything had changed, he'd still been alive, tortured and then sent to Sachsenhausen concentration camp, where he'd been killed within days of arrival. And David's beautiful, kind-hearted parents had eventually been discovered and sent to Auschwitz, where they'd survived for some months before perishing just before the camp was liberated. She'd even found out what had happened to her old friend Lina, who'd also ended up losing her life at a camp.

These were stories of the past, stories that Ava didn't often let herself think about, but being back home had brought everything rushing back. She paused, looking out towards the field, remembering the bunker, remembering the walks she'd taken with her father, the first time he'd told her what he was involved in. Ava could barely remember the girl she'd been then, and she only hoped that her actions in recent years went some ways to making up for her ignorance during that time.

'She's here.'

Ava turned at David's words, letting go of his hand and her son's. Eliana, suitcase still in hand, was standing by the house. Her heart fluttered at seeing her old friend, still finding it hard to believe that all three of them had made it.

'Eliana!' she cried, rushing to her and engulfing her in a hug. 'It's so good to see you. I can't believe you're really here.'

Eliana hugged her back just as fiercely.

'I can feel your bones,' Ava said. 'We need to spend the weekend feeding you.'

Eliana laughed and stroked Ava's hair, smiling at her in a way that two people could only do when they'd been through so much together, when they knew one another better than they knew themselves.

'Is it strange to say that this feels like home?'

'It is home,' Ava said, linking her arm through Eliana's as they slowly walked back to the garden and down to David. She tipped her head to rest it on Eliana's shoulder. 'This will always be your home. *Our* home, for all of us. Forever.'

They stood for a moment, watching David run around chasing Max, making him giggle in a way that warmed Ava's heart. She felt Eliana soften beside her, and knew that it was having the same effect on her.

'He's the most beautiful child,' Eliana said with a sigh. 'You two make such wonderful parents.'

'We try our best. All we want is for him to be happy.'

They stood in comfortable silence for a little longer, gazes fixed on the scene before them. Ava didn't need to tell Eliana the responsibility she and David both felt to live their lives with gratitude, to make the most of every day and never take for granted the gift of simply being alive. Everything they'd been through, everything they'd fought for and lost, had bonded them in a way that was as strong as blood.

'Has there been any word of Ethan?' Ava asked.

Eliana cleared her throat. 'No. I haven't been able to find out anything.'

'So he's still officially listed as a missing person?'

Eliana nodded. 'He is. Although I was able to find records for his parents. It appears their involvement was discovered soon after we left, and they were shot. Even after everything we've already lost, hearing that they were gone, people who'd risked so much to keep me safe and alive, was almost impossible to believe.'

'I'm sorry.' Ava looped her arm even tighter through Eliana's. 'I know how much they meant to you. But don't give up on searching for Ethan. Surely miracles are still possible, even here in Germany? Even after everything?'

'Of course they are,' Eliana said. 'Miracles are always possible.'

'I would feel that way if it were David,' Ava said shyly, watching him as he looked up and caught her eye, his smile just for her. 'I would walk until the end of the earth to find him if I lost him, so you must hold on to hope. There is every chance that Ethan is still alive.'

As David and Max began walking towards them, Ava turned to Eliana and clasped her hands, trying to hold back her tears while she prepared to say something she'd been waiting for so long to say.

'I know so much time has passed since we were girls, but I want to say sorry to you, Eliana. I want to apologise for the way I treated you, for the unforgivable way I turned my back on you at the beginning of the war.'

'Ava, please—'

'No, let me. No matter what has passed since then, no matter what we've been through, I want you to know that I'm sorry. I wish I could have seen what was happening right in front of me, and instead I chose to be part of it, and I also wish that I'd been brave enough to apologise to you that very first night in the attic, when you shared your story with me.'

'The difference,' Eliana said, clasping her hands back just as tightly, 'is that you changed when most did not. But if you need to hear it, then so be it. I wholeheartedly accept your apology, and there is no need to feel guilty for not saying it earlier. Your actions spoke louder than any words.'

Ava's breath shuddered from her. 'Thank you.'

'Eliana,' David said as he reached them and embraced his sister. 'I'd say it's good to see you, but you seem to be making my wife cry. Please stop.'

They all laughed, and Ava scooped Max up into her arms and brought him close so they could all bend their heads together, all so relieved that they'd made it. She closed her eyes, remembering though at the same time trying so hard not to, for when she did, all she could see was Hanna's face as she'd said goodbye. As she'd so bravely sent Ava on her way, knowing that she was never going to leave herself, that they'd likely never see each other again.

Hanna's letter was still in her pocket; she had carried it every day since David had given it to her. But after today, she would find somewhere safe to keep it, once she'd fulfilled her sister's wishes. Until now, she'd wanted to keep it close as evidence of her intentions.

I made you a promise, Hanna, and I intend on keeping it. After today, your final wish will have been fulfilled.

Later that day, Ava stood in the back part of the garden that was partially hidden by a low stone wall. The last time she'd stood here, she'd found her sister, on her knees, with two glass jars beside her, tears streaming down her cheeks. Now it was Ava who was crying, her eyes filling with tears as she placed her shovel down and dropped to her knees.

David had offered to help her, but she'd asked him to stay at the house with Max so she could have a moment alone. She wanted to remember Hanna, to cry without being self-conscious, to feel the strength of her sister on her own as she followed through with what she'd started. But as she placed her hands on the cold ground, she'd never felt so alone. She'd wistfully hoped that she'd feel Hanna's presence, that she'd feel as if her sister were kneeling beside her in the dirt as she dug up the earth, but instead she'd never missed her more nor felt her absence more keenly.

There had been a time when Ava had truly believed that she'd be able to reunite the children Hanna had saved with their families. For months, she'd imagined passing the information to the authorities and felt certain they'd slowly be able to locate families as they came forward, looking for those they'd been forced to leave behind or send away. But it hadn't taken long after the war had ended for the atrocities against the Jews to become clearer. The losses had been in the millions, the number of people murdered as part of the Final Solution greater than even she could have imagined, the chance of family reunions almost impossible. Which had given her the very real understanding that any children who had been saved would no longer have parents looking for them; there was very little chance that those parents would still be alive. Nor their grandparents, aunts or uncles even.

Ava pushed her shovel into the dirt, thinking little of the plants her mother had carefully placed there in order to hide what was hidden beneath. She was focused on one thing only now, and that was digging up those jars. She had to be careful as she excavated, conscious that the glass could break, and the moment she heard even the softest of clinks, she would begin to dig by hand, the dirt caking beneath her nails and dampening her skin as she frantically fought to uncover the precious gifts below.

The first jar brought her to the ground, her body trembling. She carefully took it out, falling to her elbows when she saw the handwritten note inside. *Hanna buried this. Hanna gave her life for this. My sister was the last person to touch this jar.*

She sobbed into the earth for the longest of moments, before forcing herself back up, picking up the shovel again and beginning to dig once more. Soon, she was surrounded by jars, piling them up behind her as she kept digging. Ava didn't know if Hanna had buried more than the sixteen she'd helped her with, and she didn't want to miss even one, not when the information inside of each one was so important. Not now she was a mother with her own child, her own precious son; a son who, had he been born then, may well have ended up being a name in a jar. An orphan with no one left to come looking for him.

'Ava?'

When she heard David say her name, she couldn't look up. She hadn't wanted him to see her pain, but when he knelt beside her and wrapped his arms around her, she took refuge in them, wishing he'd been there with her all along.

'I'm never going to be able to reunite them,' she cried. 'All these jars, all these families, they're never going to find one another. There's so little chance that any of them are even alive now.'

David rocked her in his arms, his lips to her hair as he soothed her pain.

'Ava,' he finally said, when she sat back on her haunches and looked at him through eyes still blurred with tears. He gently stroked her hair, gazing at her with such tenderness that it hurt. 'I want you to imagine that we were one of these parents, that we had risked everything to save our son, to give him a chance at a life that we knew he would never have in Germany.'

She shuddered at the thought, but nodded to David in reply anyway.

'In their hearts, they knew that they would likely never see their children again. I think all of us Jews knew that nothing was going to get better for us, not here. But they sent their children away anyway in the hope that they would have the chance to live a full life far from Berlin.' David touched his hand to his chest. 'Their hearts were full of so much love, that they chose to let their children go. And what's important here is that Hanna cared enough to preserve this information, and that you care enough to pass that information on. It's all you can do.'

'So why doesn't it feel like I've done enough? Why do I feel as if I've done nothing at all? As if I've failed?'

David pulled her towards him again, holding her and rubbing circles on her back. 'Because you're trying to make up for the evils of so many, and you are just one woman,' he whispered. 'Sometimes we have to know when we've done our best.'

'But have I?' she whispered. 'Done my best?'

She felt his smile. 'Yes, my love, you have most certainly done your best.'

They stayed like that on the ground for a long time, until the chill coming up from the earth reminded Ava it was time to go back to the house. She sat back and surveyed the jars, confident that she'd located every last one, but at the same time knowing she'd likely come back again and again over the coming days, just in case there was one she'd missed.

'Would you have believed there were so many?' Ava asked.

David stood and walked in a small circle as he looked at the piles she'd made. 'Never. I could never have imagined she'd saved this many children.'

'Will you help me carry them all back to the house? I will carefully empty each one there, and make a record of the contents of each letter so that we retain a copy here.'

'And perhaps we could save all the jars? We could think of something special to do with them, to remember Hanna by?' David suggested as he began to fill the wooden crate that Ava had brought out with her. 'It will be a way to show Max, too, to make sure he understands the power of each jar and what it contained.'

'Thank you,' Ava said, pausing to look up at him for a moment.

David only smiled, before lifting the crate to bring it closer to her. He was often a man of few words, but when he spoke he usually did so to make her smile or share something worthwhile, and today he'd done both. And despite her sadness, she closed the distance between them and took his face in her hands, kissing him gently on the lips, hoping he knew what he meant to her.

She'd made many mistakes when it came to matters of the heart, but David wasn't one of them.

ELIANA

There had been a time when Eliana had not known if she could ever forgive Ava for the pain she'd caused her. When Ava had found them in the attic, Eliana had wondered if there would ever be friendship between them again, whether she could ever forget the way Ava had looked at her or treated her.

Eliana's father had called it Hitler Fever. He had a theory that even those who wouldn't usually be caught up in such nonsense couldn't help but catch it from those around them, as if it truly was a fever that could spread unwittingly among people, and he'd also had a not so pleasant analogy about those that turned a blind eye to Adolf Hitler. *So long as the dog doesn't defecate in their garden, they don't care about the dog. So long as their families are safe, they won't do a thing to help us. Until the dog comes into their garden; that is when they will realise their mistake.* And he hadn't been wrong, for that was precisely what had happened.

She looked up then, pulled from her thoughts as Ava and David stood in the fading light outside on the patio. The glass jars that had been recovered from the garden had been cleaned and filled with candles, and as Eliana looked up at them, they reminded her of the fireflies she'd seen with her family while on holiday once, as a young girl. Only these weren't fireflies; they were reminders of all those names, all those children, all those families who hadn't survived.

Ava had asked for the jars to be repurposed; they were the only decorations she'd wanted, as a way to feel her sister's presence, and Eliana could see from her wide eyes that she loved them.

And as Eliana watched, the only witness to their wedding vows, *she* remembered. She remembered every moment of pain, every sacrifice, every loss, but she also remembered the love that had carried her family through all those hours and days and months trapped in the attic. She remembered her first gasp of fresh air when she'd eventually left the house, the way her breath had caught when she'd met Ethan for the very first time.

And as she looked at her brother, and saw the way he was looking at Ava, at the woman he'd loved for so long without Ava even knowing it, Eliana thought about how much her mother and father would have loved this moment, seeing two people who had once been on such different paths reunited in the name of love.

Eliana glanced to her left, seeing Ethan, remembering him, imagining him beside her. She held out her hand and felt his presence, could imagine the way he'd take her palm in his and wrap his fingers around it, the way he'd catch her eye and smile at her like no one else could. The way he'd gently lift her hand and press a kiss to it.

Tomorrow, she would tell them the truth. Tomorrow she would be honest with Ava and tell her that Ethan had perished along with his family, dying just days before the camp he'd been sent to was liberated. But today was a day for happiness and love; and for that, she would forever be grateful.

AUTHOR'S NOTE

This novel is a work of fiction; however, like all my novels it is based on actual historical events. My characters were inspired by the true stories of Germans who opposed the Nazi regime – some actively, some more passively – by saving the lives of Jews, spreading information and being part of a resistance network.

I think it's easy to look back on history sometimes and believe that there was evil in every household in Nazi Germany, rather than taking the time to research and understand what living under that regime was truly like. Many people wholeheartedly embraced Hitler and believed in his vision for the Third Reich, but many simply did what they had to do to keep their families safe, and some did everything they could to oppose what was happening. This is how I came to write *The Berlin Sisters*, by understanding that not everything is black and white, that there are often shades of grey in every situation.

One of the most important components to my research for this novel was watching the documentary on Brunhilde Pomsel, who was one of the secretaries working for Joseph Goebbels, in a role similar to that of my character Ava. The documentary is called *A German Life*, and it was a fascinating insight into the mind of someone who had effectively been brainwashed as a young woman. On the one hand, she understands the evil that took place, but on the other she recalls Goebbels to be a very kind, lovely man who treated her well. She is still sad when she thinks about the way he and his family died. That was useful to me in crafting my characters and trying to understand how someone like Ava might have felt, trying to grapple with what she was being told versus what she'd always believed.

The information included in the novel about the Sophie Scholl case is based on fact, as is the assassination attempt on Hitler's life at the Wolf's Lair, including the fact that those involved thought for a few hours that it had been successful. They did return to Berlin and start to make arrests, thinking they were about to overthrow the regime, only to discover that the last-minute change of the location for Hitler's meeting due to the hotter than expected weather, to a room with windows above ground, meant that the assassination attempt was a failure. The pink slips of paper referred to as the daily truths are also factual, with the 'truth' being manipulated constantly by the Nazi propaganda machine.

As always, my primary objective is to show respect to those who lived through these difficult times in history, and to shine light on what happened in the past, so that it is never forgotten. If you want to know more about what was happening in Germany at this time, particularly in regards to resistance, I encourage you to watch *A German Life*, and to look up both Sophie Scholl/The White Rose and the Wolf's Lair assassination attempt on Adolf Hitler.

ACKNOWLEDGEMENTS

Writing a novel is a very solitary process, and for me that involves long hours in my office with my four-legged friends as company. Often my dogs wander in, reminding me that it's time to take a walk, but with this novel I became so immersed in the writing that our daily walks became very short indeed! Needless to say, Ted and Oscar are very pleased this novel is finished!

As usual, I would like to thank the wonderful people who made publishing this book possible. First and foremost, I would like to acknowledge my editor, Victoria Oundjian. Victoria, thank you for everything – for your unwavering support, for believing in me, and for always pushing me to create the very best story that I can. I would also like to acknowledge editor Sophie Wilson, who alongside Victoria forms part of our 'dream team'! I absolutely adore working with you both, and I honestly can't imagine writing one of my historical novels without you!

I'd also like to thank the wider team at Amazon Publishing UK, with a special mention to editorial director Sammia Hamer, who has also always shown huge support for my work (and is still one of my all time favourite editors!). Thank you to my author relations and marketing teams, with special mention to Nicole Wagner, and thanks also to my copy editor Gemma Wain, and proofreader Sadie Mayne. I appreciate you all more than you could ever know.

I'd also like to thank my literary agent, Laura Bradford, who has represented me throughout my entire writing career.

On a personal note, I'd like to acknowledge my amazing writing friends, Yvonne Lindsay, Natalie Anderson and Nicola Marsh. Thank you for the daily encouragement when I was writing this book, I couldn't have done it without you! I also have my wonderful assistant, Lisa Pendle, to thank, who not only helps to keep me sane but also manages so many things behind the scenes for me. My dogs also adore her, which reinforces just how fabulous she is.

Then there is my amazing family. Thank you to Hamish, Mack and Hunter for being so patient when I'm writing a draft or frantically working around the clock to meet a deadline. I'm so lucky to have a wonderful, supportive environment in which to work. Thank you also to my parents, Maureen and Craig, for your constant, ongoing support and love.

And to you, my fabulous readers, I wouldn't be here without you! Thank you for reading my books, for all the reviews and messages, and for allowing me to create the books of my heart. I will forever be grateful for your support. If you've loved this story and want to connect with me, I'd love you to join my reader group to discuss all things books! You can find me at https://www.facebook.com/groups/sorayalanereadergroup.

Soraya x

If you loved *The Berlin Sisters*, then turn the page to discover another gripping historical novel from Soraya M. Lane, *The Secret Midwife*. Out now!

Prologue

Emilia heard the shouts of men as she leaned heavily against the rough wall. Coaxing the baby into the world, she strained to stay upright. She squinted in the dim light, instinctively knowing something wasn't right when the infant didn't cry as she cut the cord then turned him over, feebly patting him on the bottom.

She fought tears, looking down at him, her fingers so frigid from the cold she could barely move them. Smoke clung to the air, the barracks around them still smouldering.

'What's wrong?' the exhausted mother whispered, still lying flat after the exertion of labour.

There was a noise outside, more shouts, but Emilia ignored them even as her legs trembled. The Nazis were gone, but who knew if these men who'd arrived were any better than the guards who'd fled in the night and set so much of the camp alight before they'd left? She refused to be frightened, she'd faced death too many times now to fall to her knees; all she cared about was saving the little life in her hands, because he had a chance to live when so many others had not. He was already a survivor, and she would not let him die, not now. But he was so tiny, his body fraught from lack of nutrients, and his mother likely incapable of feeding him, if she survived at all.

She glanced to her left, as if expecting Lena to be there, waiting to take the baby so she could attend to the mother. *Lena is gone.* She had to tell herself sometimes, remind herself that Lena existed only in her memories now, memories that swirled at times and tricked her, like dust in the air creating illusions that she had to fight against believing were true.

She patted the infant's back more firmly then and carefully scooped her finger into his mouth, gasping in relief when he finally cried, but as she went to lift him to the mother, lying on top of the crude stove, her legs still parted, Emilia realised she was now slumped over and silent.

'No!' Emilia croaked.

Blood coursed from between the woman's legs, a sign in these primitive conditions that she was only minutes from death unless Emilia could act quickly.

The calls outside continued, and Emilia listened as a man spoke loudly in a language she couldn't understand. But then he called in Polish. And as hope lifted inside her, he said the same words in English. He was repeating the same words in different languages.

'We are the Allies. We are not here to hurt you.'

The accent was strong, but the words were clear. Emilia shuffled to the door, her bare feet aching on the snow-covered ground as she stepped out, wishing she could go faster, seeing soldiers wearing thick olive coats, mounted on ponies as they rode through the camp. Some of the remaining prisoners had come to the doors of their huts, those who'd been too sick to leave with the others who'd been marched from the camp, their skeletal bodies hunched as they stared out. If these soldiers killed her, so be it; at least she'd tried.

'Help!' Emilia cried, her throat dry, lips cracked and painful. She still carried the baby, tucked in her arms and barely making a sound. 'Please, help me!'

The alarm on the soldier's face closest to her was obvious, and he yelled something to his men. He was Russian, she recognised the dialect from others she'd met in the camp. When he turned to her, she saw the sadness in his expression, and when she followed his eyes, she could see that he was taking in the naked newborn in her arms and her blood-soaked apron and ragged skirt. Or perhaps it was her stick-like arms and sunken face that alarmed him most.

'I need water, and towels,' she croaked.

'We will get your supplies,' he said, dismounting and passing the reins of his horse to another soldier as he followed her into the barracks. 'Let me help.'

She thrust the baby into his arms and scurried back to the mother, taking her pulse and then reaching for her knife. For so long, it had been the only tool at her disposal, the one thing that no one had taken from her. The bleeding hadn't slowed, and Emilia knew she barely had time to save her; even if the conditions were better it would be difficult. But for the first time since she'd started delivering babies at the camp, this infant had the chance to truly *live*, which meant she wasn't going to let this mother die on the stove, not when mother and son had a chance to survive together, not without doing everything in her power.

'What is your name?' the soldier asked.

From the corner of the room, hidden by shadows, came a raspy reply.

'Her name is Emilia,' Aleksy gasped, as he shuffled forwards on spindly legs barely able to hold him, his cough telling Emilia just how sick he'd become. 'She is the midwife of Auschwitz, and without her, hundreds of babies would have died.'

Tears started to fall down Emilia's cheeks as the hot water arrived, as she sterilised her knife and lifted it. *Because of me, hundreds of babies never had the chance to live.* But bless him, Aleksy only reminded her of the lives she'd saved, not the ones who'd perished because of what she'd been forced to do.

Her legs shook, barely strong enough to hold her as she prepared to save a life. Aleksy wasn't able to help her, so sick he could barely make it across the room, but the soldier beside her cleared his throat.

'Tell me what to do,' he said.

Emilia nodded and gave him instructions, using a towel to stop the bleeding, wishing she had more at her disposal. By the time she was finished, as she completed her final stitch using cotton they'd painstakingly unthreaded from a blanket months earlier in case of emergencies, Emilia was starting to wobble. Strong arms caught her and cushioned her fall as the ground rose to meet her, the first kindness ever shown to her by a soldier at the camp since she'd arrived.

'Rest,' he said, when her eyelids fluttered open. 'I will bring you food.'

He placed a warm jacket over Emilia, *the soldier's own jacket*, and she folded herself into it as a familiar form crawled closer to her. He had a threadbare blanket clutched to his shoulders, his cough rattling as he collapsed beside her.

'We're going to make it,' Emilia whispered, as Aleksy's breath wheezed in and out of his chest. 'Don't give up, you need to stay alive. You can't die on me now, Aleksy, I won't let you.'

She found a strength she didn't know she had and moved the jacket to give him some extra warmth, holding his hand while they shivered beneath it. They were both so small now, so skeletal, that it was easily big enough for them both.

Aleksy didn't say a word, but his fingers tightened around hers. It was all she needed – to know he was still alive. That there was still hope.

Chapter One

EMILIA

LONDON, 27 JANUARY 1995

Emilia would have changed the channel if she could have reached the television remote. As much as she appreciated the efforts of most major networks to pay tribute to the fiftieth anniversary of the liberation of Auschwitz, it was a memory she'd spent most of her adult life trying to suppress. What had happened there, all the lives lost, wasn't something she needed to be reminded of by a documentary.

She was about to call out to her daughter when something flashed across the screen, overlaid across the often-used images of the gates from the notorious concentration camp and the skeletal prisoners who'd survived until the bitter end. Images she usually did her best to avoid.

'Mum, are you ready for—'

'Lucy, turn the volume up please,' she said, leaning forwards in her chair as her daughter walked into the room, the blanket that had been folded over her knees falling to the floor.

'It is rumoured that from late 1943 until the liberation by Russian soldiers in January 1945, a Polish midwife worked with a male prisoner doctor, who himself was also Polish, to save hundreds of babies within the camp. While the fate of Jewish infants was predetermined, many non-Jewish babies were taken and given to Nazi families, after a change in policy in 1943. It has been said that this midwife secretly tattooed the babies immediately after birth, in the hope that they might one day be reunited with their mothers.'

Emilia stared at the screen, her skin clammy as she listened to the reporter, fingernails digging into the arm of the chair. She leaned closer. Sometimes her mind failed her, sometimes lately it had been like trying to think through mud, but the memories that she'd fought so hard to forget never left her. Those had remained crystal clear, despite all the years that had passed.

'Despite our best efforts to find out the identity of this courageous midwife, we have been unable to discover any information about her whereabouts, or whether she even survived. If you have any first-hand knowledge of the prisoner midwives or doctors who worked at any of the Auschwitz concentration camps, we urge you to contact the number on the screen. Any survivors are encouraged to make contact to help us piece together what happened to these children, to share their stories of survival with the world.'

'Lucy,' Emilia said, hastily writing down the phone number on the newspaper beside her, forgetting all about the crossword she'd been doing previously. Her hand was shaking so much, the numbers were barely legible. 'Would you please get me the telephone.'

Her daughter had been watching the television too, standing in the middle of the room, but she glanced back at Emilia now.

'Dinner's ready, Mum. Could you wait until after?'

'Please, I need to make a phone call,' she said. 'It won't take a moment.'

Her daughter gave her an impatient look, but eventually she sighed and nodded, as if she'd been asked to run to the shops instead of step into another room. But Emilia knew she couldn't wait any longer; if she didn't call now, she might never muster the courage.

It's time we told them what we did, Aleksy, before it's too late. We can't keep it a secret forever. What if my memory disappears completely and what happened there, what we survived, is lost forever?

Emilia held out her hand for the phone, not surprised at how much she was trembling. It had been a very long time since she'd said the words she was about to say, and she knew they were going to come as a shock to her daughter. To her, she was just an old woman, a mother in her seventies who needed looking after, an elderly lady who forgot to lock the front door and sometimes got lost on her way back from getting groceries. It was why Lucy had insisted that she come and stay for a while, not liking her mother living on her own after she'd become widowed, convincing her that it would be nice for them to spend more time together. What she really meant was that she didn't trust Emilia to live independently any more. But when it came to what had happened at Auschwitz, to the things she'd done in order to help her fellow prisoners under her care survive, she didn't need help remembering. It wasn't something one could ever forget.

She took a deep breath and gripped the telephone when Lucy returned with it, carefully dialling the numbers she'd written down.

'Mum, who are you calling? Are you sure there's nothing I . . .'

Emilia pressed the receiver to her ear, her heart racing as she waited. It rang six times before a woman answered. Her daughter gave her a tired smile that only reminded Emilia how trying it must be to have her mother living with her, even though it was Lucy who'd insisted she move in.

'Hello?' the woman said. 'Is anyone there?'

She gripped the phone tightly, trying to stop it from shaking.

'My name is Emilia Bauchau. I am the midwife you're looking for.' She paused, glancing up at her daughter. 'I believe it's time for me to tell my story.'

ABOUT THE AUTHOR

Photo © 2022 Jemima Helmore

Soraya M. Lane graduated with a law degree before realising that law wasn't the career for her and that her future was in writing. She is the author of historical and contemporary women's fiction, and her novel *Wives of War* was an Amazon Charts bestseller. Soraya lives on a small farm in her native New Zealand with her husband, their two young sons and a collection of four-legged friends. When she's not writing, she loves to be outside playing make-believe with her children or snuggled up inside reading. For more information about Soraya and her books, visit www.sorayalane.com or www.facebook.com/SorayaLaneAuthor, or follow her on Twitter @Soraya_Lane.

Follow the Author on Amazon

If you enjoyed this book, follow Soraya M. Lane on Amazon to be notified when the author releases a new book!

To do this, please follow these instructions:

Desktop:

1) Search for the author's name on Amazon or in the Amazon App.
2) Click on the author's name to arrive on their Amazon page.
3) Click the 'Follow' button.

Mobile and Tablet:

1) Search for the author's name on Amazon or in the Amazon App.
2) Click on one of the author's books.
3) Click on the author's name to arrive on their Amazon page.
4) Click the 'Follow' button.

Kindle eReader and Kindle App:

If you enjoyed this book on a Kindle eReader or in the Kindle App, you will find the author 'Follow' button after the last page.